Tangled Hearts

TANGLED SERIES

SOPHIE ANDREWS

Digital ISBN 978-1-957580-19-7

Paperback ISBN 978-1-957580-30-2

*Previously published as Flirting with Mr. Serious by Suzanne Baltsar

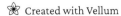 Created with Vellum

Content Note

Tangled Hearts is a steamy and angst-filled open-door romance between a commitment-phobe academic and a Marine vet struggling with a combat injury and PTSD. It also includes some discussions of an eating disorder and divorce.

We played a horrible terrible game in middle school, where we (girls) would message boys (our crushes) on AIM with names of friends to be rated on a scale of 1-10. I was always rated a 5 or 6 while my friends were 9s and 10s. This, along with a few other things, contributed to disordered eating through high school and college, and it took finding the right guy for me to understand what it meant to be confident and feel beautiful.

Kids are stupid and self-esteem is a fickle bitch, but no matter what anyone says, you're a 10.

This book is to remind you, you're a 10, a fucking 10.

CHAPTER ONE

Sam

I could count the number of birthday parties I'd had on my two hands, and even though I was alone in my room, with only my three best friends on Zoom, this one was toward the top.

"Can you turn down the volume of your music? I can barely hear you," Bronte said from the upper right corner of our chat.

"Yes, Miss Hollinger," Gem droned, her chin in her hands in the bottom left.

Laney snorted. "You can take the teacher out of the classroom, but ya can't take the classroom out of the teacher."

I shifted from the floor where I had my laptop on my legs to sit at my hand-me-down desk and chair in the corner of my bedroom before lowering the volume of the Alabama Shakes. "Better?"

Bronte nodded. "How's the cake?"

Dipping my fork into the colorful "unicorn confetti" cake that had been delivered a few hours earlier, I tasted it. When I had arrived home from school to find it, I'd read the card and promptly teared up.

Cheers to 27 years!

XOXO,

Bronte, Gem, and Laney

The four of us hadn't been in the same place together since the fall, when Gem married Jason, her real-life Ken doll and father of their child, almost six months ago. And seeing the gift basket from my friends had my chest filling up with bittersweet melancholy.

"It's good." I swallowed down a bite of the cake. Although it was a tad on the dry side, I'd eat the whole damn thing because this was my birthday party, and cake always tasted better with champagne. I popped the cork of the little bottle, enough for a single serving, and poured it into the coffee mug Gem had gifted me last Christmas that read *Don't Be A* with a picture of a rooster underneath.

"Well, cheers, ladies. Happy birthday, Sammy." Laney raised her own glass of champagne. Gem and Bronte followed with theirs, and I smiled, lifting my mug.

"May it be a good year." Gem clinked what looked like a child's cup against her computer screen.

Bronte fixed her glasses on her nose, grinning in her Zoom box. "Filled with fun and romance!" When I pointedly ignored her, she shrugged. "I'm an eternal optimist."

To which the three of us all said, "We know."

"I have enough romance in my life, thank you very much."

"You still hooking up with Eli?" Gem asked.

I nodded and scraped the overly sweet pink and purple icing off the cake and was met with a chorus of curious hums. Because while they were in committed relationships, I wasn't looking for one of those. Eli was a postdoc in the math department at school, another commitment-phobe who didn't mind the random late-night meetups. It was easy come, easy go, exactly what I liked.

"I'm sorry we can't be together today," Bronte said after a few moments.

I scooped up another piece of cake. "We'll be seeing each other plenty soon."

Laney displayed some kind of countdown app on her cell phone. "Eighty-one more days."

Gem whooped. "Mama's getting drunk!"

"You're drunk right now." Laney let out her signature booming laugh. "Me and you used to close down the bars, and now you're passed out after one drink."

"I know," Gem moaned with a pitiful pout. "Willow stole all my tolerance."

"That's okay. She's cute," I said, referring to her daughter, who was about a year and a half now. The first kid to be born out of our little friend group.

Bronte sipped her champagne from a real glass flute. "Where is the little chicken?"

"She wanted her dad to put her to bed tonight. They've got a whole routine now, where he sings 'Old McDonald,' like, eighteen times. She says *more, more,* and he does more, more."

"She's a daddy's girl," Laney said, and Gem nodded.

"That my Willow?" a masculine voice asked from behind Bronte, and she glanced over her shoulder.

"She's in bed," Bronte told her fiancé before his face came into view.

I waved my icing-covered fork at Chris "CJ" Cunningham, the A-list actor who'd wound up sitting next to Bronte on a flight home after one of our girls weekends together. Even though he'd proposed two weeks ago, they already had plans to get married this summer. Of course. Bronte was the queen of tight organizational schedules.

Although people always talked about the pregnancy and marriage glow, I hadn't ever believed in it. Until I saw it in my friends. First in Gem, when she fell in love with Jason and then had a surprise pregnancy not too long after. Now it was Bronte, whose blue eyes had taken on a new brightness.

"Happy birthday, Sam." Chris smiled.

"Thanks."

"I wanted to send you a stripper, but she vetoed it." Chris tipped his head in Bronte's direction.

I huffed out a laugh. "Party pooper."

"For real." He dodged an elbow from Bronte and pulled her up out of her chair to sit down, towing her to his lap. "What are we talking about?"

"Oh my god, Christopher." Gem laughed. "You're as bad as my husband."

It was still so weird for me to hear *my husband*, but I nodded anyway. Jason and Chris fit right in with the us, even being added to a bigger text thread. Laney named that group chat **Four Chicks and Two Dicks**.

"We're having girl time," Bronte told him, wiggling out of his grasp.

"I thought Jay was going to be on," he said, totally unfazed that Bronte stood next to him, waiting for him to get up and go.

"He's putting Willow to bed."

Chris pouted petulantly. "But I thought she'd be here too. What a dull party."

I nibbled a bit of cake. "Gee, thanks."

"You just wait until we invade your house." Laney pointed her finger, presumably at Chris. "You'll be wishing our party was dull then."

"Yeah," Gem agreed. "I haven't been out *out* since..."

"Since your twenty-fifth birthday," I supplied.

"So, watch out, Christopher, 'cause I'm coming for your entire liquor cabinet and that big whirlpool tub."

"Noted," he said with his famous smile. "All right, I guess

I'll catch up with Jay later." He waved at the screen then kissed Bronte's temple.

"How's the wedding planning going?" Laney asked once he finally left.

"I'm not doing anything." At our shocked gasps, Bronte drained the last of her champagne. "Chris convinced me to let a wedding planner take care of it, and you know what? He was right. It's nice to let go every once in a while."

Gem sang a few bars of a very off-key "Let It Go," and maybe she really was drunk already.

"What about you, Sammy?" Laney asked. "What's happening with everything on your end?"

I took a big swig of champagne and set the mug down on top of a water mark on the desk. I supposed it wasn't even worth bringing the desk when I moved down to Texas. Besides it generally looking like trash, I had to stick a book underneath the one leg to keep it balanced. "When the semester's over, I'm driving back home, and the house is going on the market as soon as we get it cleaned up. But with my dad's surgery and everything, who knows how long that'll take."

"Well," Bronte started, "we're here for you, for whatever you need. You know I'm great at packing. I'll take a trip over, say the word."

"Thanks, but it'll be okay."

The girls all nodded, obviously not believing me.

I tried again, this time lifting my gaze to my computer screen. "It's a lot, but it'll be fine."

"Well, you have a lot to look forward to," Laney said. "You'll be off to Austin soon. You'll love it there, fit right in."

Bronte stuck her finger up in the air. "And don't forget my wedding. We'll swim in the ocean and dance all night."

"And," Gem said with a flare of her hands, "the bachelorette. Guys, I'm so fucking excited, you don't even know."

5

"Oh, we know." I laughed. "The party goblin version of you has been locked up too long."

Her brown eyes went wide and a little wild. "She's been patiently waiting to be freed."

"Eighty-one days," Laney reminded us.

"Until then," Bronte said, "enjoy your time at home, Sammy. Maybe you'll find some old treasures while going through everything."

"And hey, for posterity," Laney said. "Everyone smile!"

We all cheesed at our screens as Laney screenshotted us. "I'll text it to you guys."

The photo came through on our text thread which Gem had named the **4whoresmen of the apocalypse**.

"What's wrong with my eye?" Gem laughed.

"My glasses are crooked," Bronte said.

"Why didn't anyone tell me I had icing on my lip?" I asked.

Laney grinned. "I look great."

CHAPTER TWO

Sam

Two months later, I opened the front door of my childhood home in Akron, Ohio. Not much had changed since the last time I'd been there two Christmases ago.

"Dad?" When he didn't answer, I toed off my sneakers before snaking around piles of boxes and random stacks of books and other items. Upstairs, at the back of the hall, was my bedroom, practically the same since I'd left it almost ten years ago, painted geometric patterns in orange and purple with strings of star lights hung from corner to corner and bits of song lyrics taped up on the walls. I tossed my bags on the floor and flopped back onto the bed. In a matter of months, someone else would be living in this bedroom, staring up at the ceiling. Maybe they'd put their own set of glow-in-the-dark stars up there after I'd taken mine down.

Memories repressed from childhood filtered through my mind, and I wiped at my eyes as if I could wipe away the recollections. But much like the scars buried deep on my heart, those memories wouldn't fade.

"Sammy? Are you home?" My father's voice drifted up from what sounded like the kitchen.

"Yeah. In my room."

A few minutes later, Phil Kohler stood in my doorway, gray mixed in with his dark hair, his face tanned from the sun, his eyes crinkling behind his glasses when he smiled. "Hi, honey."

"Hi, Dad," I said, going into his arms when he opened them for a hug. "Were you gardening?"

"Yep."

He worked as a botanist for the federal government, often traveling to other states to help manage agricultural studies. Gardening was the one thing that kept him focused, and the yard had always been perfectly manicured. The inside of the house, though, that was left to disrepair and disarray after the divorce.

"You look good," he said, inspecting me from top to bottom.

"Thanks. So do you."

His jeans and T-shirt were covered in sweat and dirt, and he smacked his hands along his thighs, a few specks of earth falling to the floor. Both of us dropped their gaze to the carpet, and he let out an exhausted laugh.

"I'll vacuum that later." Although we both knew he wouldn't.

"Gav's at your mom's house, but he'll be here tomorrow...I think."

My little brother was nine years younger than me and graduating high school in June. Even though I didn't talk to my parents a lot, I tried to keep in touch with him as much as the eighteen-year-old, video-game-obsessed kid would let me.

"Do you want me to order pizza for dinner?"

I combed my hand through my hair, pushing some loose strands back into my ponytail. "Yeah, pizza's good."

He offered me a gentle smile before backing away, a slight limp in his step, a reminder of why I needed to come home for the summer. Not only to help him get the house ready to sell, which would be a difficult task on its own because of his hoarding tendencies, but also because of his knee replacement surgery.

"We're having a neighborhood picnic this weekend for Memorial Day and a little celebration for Gavin."

"Oh. Okay." My dad wasn't usually one for parties, but I figured he wanted to do something for Gavin before we left our childhood home.

"I got him a cake for graduation, but your mother's taking him on a trip." He shook his head in that same annoyed way he always did whenever he talked about my mom. I pretended not to see it, like I'd been doing almost all my life, and kept myself busy by unpacking my clothes into drawers, some random socks and shirts still there from the last time I'd been home.

"Okay. Well." He cleared his throat. "I'll let you get settled in. I'm gonna shower, and then I'll call for food."

With my back to him, I nodded.

"Hey, Samantha."

I turned over my shoulder.

"I'm really glad you're home," he said with an unusual catch in his voice. "I missed you."

I smiled at the rare show of emotion. "I've missed you too, Dad."

He touched the arm of his glasses, giving me one more once-over, then headed down the hall to his room.

It wasn't that I didn't like being home; it was that this house and this town hadn't felt like home for a long time. There were very few things I enjoyed about being here, although I could hear one of them coming down the street now. I heaved my bedroom window up as Jimmy pulled into his parents' driveway and cut the engine, along with the music. He stepped out of the rusted yet "classic" Mustang he'd been working on since we were in high school.

9

"Hey!" I leaned my elbows on the windowpane, shouting down to him. "You still listening to that crap?"

Whipping his head to the side, he shielded his eyes as he looked up at me. A smile immediately took over his face. "Mr. Big is a classic!"

I grinned. Everything he loved was a classic.

"You coming down to give me a hug or what?"

In a hurry, I slammed the window shut, splinters of paint falling off in the process—another thing to fix before the house went on the market—and I rushed downstairs and out the back door of the kitchen to leap into the arms of my oldest friend, Jimmy Ewing.

"Been a long time," he said against my ear as he set my feet down on the paved drive.

"I know. Sorry." I squeezed his shoulder. "You've been working out or what?"

When he stepped away from me, I finally noticed his sneakers, blue athletic shorts, and Nike T-shirt. "Actually, yeah. With Mike. That's why I'm here."

"Here?" I self-consciously tugged at my tank top.

"Yeah." Jimmy twirled the lanyard with his keys around his fingers. "Didn't I tell you he was living here?"

I shook my head, running my hand over my hair. We kept in touch pretty regularly over text messages, but he most definitely left out that tidbit of information.

"You all right?" He laughed, and it grated my nerves that he could see I was very clearly not all right.

Gem, Bronte, and Laney were my best friends, but I'd known Jimmy basically my whole life. He knew me as well as they did, maybe even better since he'd been around to witness...everything.

"Yeah, I'm fine." I waved him off. "Tired from the drive."

"When did you get in?"

"'Bout half an hour ago."

He held his arms out. "Then I got here right on time, huh? You wanna come in? See Mom and Dad, Mike?"

Just like I had known Jimmy my whole life, I knew his family too. I was eager to see them again, but it was the suggestion of seeing Mike that had my heart fluttering in a funny way.

Growing up in this neighborhood full of kids, I had been the lone girl. There were Ben and Brody, Kyle, Louie, and of course, my neighbors, Jimmy, Mikey, and Adam. I had no choice but to ace video games and learn to throw a spiral. Jimmy and I were the same age and connected at the hip for a long time, which meant I spent a lot of time next door.

The eldest Ewing kid, Adam, was seven years older than me and Jimmy, so he hadn't been around them much. He was always watching *Star Wars* and reading science fiction books but treated me like a little sister, and I appreciated that.

Jimmy was the neighborhood menace. He had often convinced me to join him TPing houses or re-setting Christmas decorations in erotic poses, which usually left us both grounded. Everyone had always assumed we'd end up together, but ever since I punched him in the stomach for wanting to play doctor in the third grade, our relationship was clearly defined. Jimmy had eventually found other girls to play doctor with.

It was the middle brother, quiet and mysterious Mikey, who had caught my eye. He was three years older and, back then, barely glanced my way. I hadn't seen him since he left for boot camp almost—

"Sam?"

"Hmm?" I flicked my attention to Jimmy, forgetting about the math of when I'd last seen Mikey, almost twelve years ago, and pasted on a smile.

"Do you want to come in?"

"Oh, no. No, that's okay. You go do your thing. I've got to unpack all my stuff. My dad's ordering pizza for dinner, and I should probably shower since I've been in the car all day."

With a crimped brow, Jimmy snorted a laugh. "Okay?"

"Yeah, yeah." I threw him one last wave as I jogged back to my house. "We'll talk later!"

"Later, weirdo!"

I would talk to Jimmy later. We had all summer to catch up.

All summer to get my childhood home packed up and sold.

All summer next to the boy I had been in love with as a kid.

CHAPTER THREE

Sunshine with a high of seventy-five painted a picture-perfect day. Motown soared through speakers. Little kids ran through sprinklers, burgers sizzled on the grill, neighbors laughed, gossiped, and played games. The yearly Memorial Day block party was always the big kick-off to the summer, but for me, it wasn't so relaxing.

A lot of people wanted to shake my hand, thank me for my service, and then I did that thing that always made people wince by reminding them Memorial Day was to remember those who died while in service, not to celebrate veterans. But enjoy your hot dog!

I swiped my palm down my jeans and took a swig of my now-warm Bud Light before placing the bottle on a nearby picnic table. I plastered on a semblance of a smile for the two octogenarians in front of me. Too bad I couldn't remember their names.

"Did I ever tell you about my service in Korea?" the old man asked.

"No, sir. I don't believe you have."

"I was an ensign in the Navy, and my—"

"Excuse me."

I blew out a relieved breath, grateful for my brother's interruption.

Jimmy exchanged a few pleasantries with the older couple then said, "You mind if I borrow my brother for a while?"

"Of course not." The woman smiled. "You go have fun."

"Here." Jimmy passed a cold beer to me. "Thought you could use this." He led me to a round table in the shade of an umbrella, where our older brother was seated, cradling a beer in one hand and his four-month-old daughter in the other.

"Double-fisting?" Jimmy quipped.

"Multitasking." Adam sipped his beer and tilted his chin to me. "How you holding up?"

I shrugged. "Good."

"Good." He nodded, not bothering to push for more.

Unlike Jimmy, who slumped back in his chair, flapping his hand out to the party. "You're practically the prom king of this shindig, and you're not enjoying it? Not even a little bit?"

Jimmy was the definition of the baby of the family, a spoiled rotten attention-seeker.

I ignored him and pointed to Emma, in my brother's arm, her tiny head covered in wisps of curly hair. "Mind if I...?"

Adam didn't hesitate to pass her off. The baby whimpered and crinkled her little nose, kicking her legs before nestling back into the crook of my elbow, but she never even opened her eyes. I found myself wishing she would. I loved those big brown eyes of hers.

I hadn't been around when Amelia was born, but I was there to hold Emma in the hospital. When everything in my life felt like it had crumbled to ash around me, she was one bright spot. She was so tiny and delicate, I'd been afraid to hold her, but with some practice, I had come to love cuddling her. Good thing too, since Adam and his wife, Lauren, named me her godfather and the baptism was a few weeks away.

"Where's your other half?" I asked, looking around.

Adam nodded over my shoulder, and I turned to spy Lauren and Amelia, my energetic four-year-old niece, playing with a border collie. "Whose dog is that?"

"That's the Kohlers' dog," Jimmy said, waving at someone.

I followed my brother's line of vision to a woman standing opposite Amelia and Lauren, and I squinted. She looked familiar, in denim shorts, the kind with the pockets hanging out of the bottoms as if she'd cut them herself, with golden tanned legs and brightly colored hair. I couldn't remember anyone in the neighborhood who—

"Is that...?"

"Sam," Jimmy supplied.

I sat up to get a better look. "Sam? As in Samantha Kohler?"

The woman in question clapped and laughed then crouched to pet the dog. She wrestled a tennis ball from its mouth and tossed it. The dog jogged after it, but I couldn't tear my gaze away from Samantha as she stood up.

"You want to wipe that drool off your face there, Mikey." Jimmy nudged me with an elbow, and I immediately slanted my eyes away from her, ignoring my brother's laughter. Last I remembered of Samantha Kohler, she was a young girl with braces, running around with Jimmy. Now, she was a woman.

I had been away for so long, I'd missed so much. I had changed, those around me had changed, and even though I'd adjusted to my life over the last year, it was still jarring to find new pieces to fit into the puzzle.

"Look at my boys! All together again!"

I jerked attention to my mother and amateur photographer.

"Stay like that! Exactly like that!"

She pulled out her DSLR and snapped away. She was forever taking pictures. We had dozens of photo albums filled with documentation of every important and inane thing that happened in our lives, but since I had come home, it was as if she was on special assignment to make up for every birthday, Christmas, and Thursday she didn't get to capture with me.

"Come on, Mom." Adam waved her off. "We're trying to relax here."

"And it's perfect. A candid moment." When she finally put it down, she walked around the table, ruffling Jimmy's hair, then reached for Emma. "The food's ready. Mikey, are you hungry? I can make you a plate."

"No, thanks," I said. Even after all this time, she still coddled me. People often treated me on opposite ends of a spectrum. They either stayed completely away from the subject of my injury in the most awkward way possible, or they overcompensated and wanted to do everything for me.

But I guessed my mother would baby me no matter what. She was happiest when she could dote on all three of us. Jimmy lapped it up. "I'll take a plate."

I knocked my brother upside the head then made my way to the table covered in platters of food. Samantha was already there, grabbing a few carrot sticks. I picked up a paper plate and helped myself to some chips and macaroni salad and greeted her. "Hey."

She lifted her eyes as if only just now noticing me even though she'd definitely watched me approaching the table. She'd be a terrible spy. "Hey, Michael." She cringed and scratched at the side of her nose with the tip of one finger, where a silver ring crisscrossed up to her knuckle, and cleared her throat. "H-how are you?"

I couldn't help but smile, genuinely smile, at her obvious apprehension. Although why she was so nervous, I didn't know. "Good. How 'bout you?"

"Okay," she said and then shook her head, briefly shutting

her eyes before opening them again and trying on a smile. She had a really cute smile, wide and all teeth. "I'm fantastic, I mean."

I stared at her for a beat, completing a quick catalogue of her features: her dark arched eyebrows, light-brown eyes with the slightest ring of honeyed green on the edge, her hair faded from dark brunette to purple at the bottom. And I licked my lips, a reflexive curl on them. "Fantastic."

"Are you, um..." She waved a carrot stick in the air. "What do you think?"

It was kind of cute how nervous she was. "Of what?"

"The picnic."

"It's great." I grabbed a cheeseburger from one of the platters while she scrubbed the side of her fist against her forehead.

"Dear Jesus," she murmured. "The soundtrack of this conversation is like an anvil falling from the sky."

I stuttered on my breath as I laughed. I didn't laugh often, but when her shoulders sagged in relief—or maybe embarrassment, I wasn't sure which—and she gave in to her own laugh, I couldn't help myself.

I squirted ketchup on my burger before placing it back down next to the other condiments. "Are you the coyote or roadrunner in this scenario?"

"I'm not sure." Her cheeks flushed, and I found myself smiling again.

When she bit into the carrot stick, my attention snapped down to her mouth as she chewed and swallowed. And for one moment, one long and heavy moment, everything seemed to still, the light breeze, the birds, the music, it all quieted around us. Or maybe I imagined it because once our eyes met again, it all went back to normal, sounds and feelings and anvils crashing around me.

And I had to get away.

"It's good to see you," I said then cut across the yard, back to my table, where Jimmy smirked at me. "What?"

The little shit shook his head, snagging a potato chip from my plate.

"*What?*"

He lifted one shoulder. "What was that with Sam? You trying to flirt with her or something?"

"Leave it alone, Jim," Adam scolded, propping Emma up on his shoulder.

"I don't flirt." I curled my shoulders over my plate, sticking my fork into the macaroni salad.

"No?" Jimmy stole one of my pickles. "Of course you don't. You don't do anything fun. One hundred percent serious, one hundred percent of the time."

I shoved a forkful of food into his mouth. "Fuck off."

He patted my shoulder as he stood up. "Didn't quite catch that grunt, but I heard bears like to eat alone."

"Fuck off," I said louder and clearer this time, to the horror of our mother at a nearby table.

"Michael!"

Jimmy slid his arm around her shoulders, innocent as always, while Adam stifled a laugh. Then I really did let out a grunt and tucked back into my food.

Little shit.

A little while later, Mom was calling out for pictures.

"Let's get Sam and Jimmy together. Come on, you two!"

Determined to document everyone at the picnic, she had Samantha and Jimmy stand together by the dessert table. They wrapped their arms around each other, totally at ease.

"Smile!"

I took advantage of the moment to study Samantha. When I'd left her last, she usually wore her dark hair in two braids down her back. Now, it was loose, barely touching her shoulders, which were bare save for the skinny straps of her tank top. She was still on the shorter side but no longer all elbows and knees. She was sure of herself, confident in the way she threw her hand on her hip and cocked it out to the side.

Mom snapped a few pictures with the two standing straight, smiling nicely, then Jimmy leaned down and blew a raspberry on Samantha's neck. She screeched, tilting her head back in laughter, batting him away. And for the first time, maybe ever, I felt a small pang of jealousy toward my little brother.

"Mikey, why don't you get in there?" Mom suggested, poking my shoulder, but I was reluctant to move.

"Go ahead," some woman said. I think her name was Nancy. "On the other side of Sam." She smiled encouragingly, although with the way she eyed me up and down, I guessed maybe she wanted in on the photo op too.

I couldn't say no without looking like a jerk, so I made my way over, and Jimmy threw his arm out to me. "There he is. Get in here, you beautiful thing, you."

Samantha smiled shyly at me when I took my place next to her. "Hi again."

"Hi."

"Move over, Mikey," Mom instructed from behind her lens.

I did, brushing up against Samantha's arm. "Sorry."

"It's okay," she whispered, eyes on her Vans.

"Come on, Michael." Mom jabbed her finger to the left. "At least pretend you're having fun."

Jimmy piped up too. "Yeah, Mikey. Come on."

I flipped my brother the bird low, so only we could see, then slung my arm around Samantha's shoulders, forcing myself to loosen up. She peered up at me, a sweet smile crawling across her features, reaching all the way up to her eyes. I turned back to my mom as I felt an arm reach around my waist a moment before she rested her head against my shoulder.

"Smile, everyone!"

With Samantha leaning against me, I grinned.

"Aw!" the woman with roaming eyes cooed, breaking the spell, and my mom put her camera down.

"Where's Gavin?"

Samantha picked up her head, taking the scent of her shampoo with her. "Hiding in his room."

"Ah shoot. I wanted a few pictures with the two of you."

Samantha flicked her fingers in the air. "Don't worry about him. But I do want some of his cake."

My mom stepped forward and offered Samantha, Jimmy, and me each a kiss on the cheek before picking up a knife to cut up the cake with Gavin's name on it, even though he was nowhere to be found. Samantha and I both grabbed a piece and accidentally bumped into each other. Then came the half-laugh, half-apology thing. It was awkward.

But also kind of nice.

Because, damn, she was cute when she bit into her lip like that.

When we eventually escaped her orbit, I made my way back over to the table where Adam and Lauren sat with their kids, leaving Jimmy to talk with Samantha.

I knew the two had been best friends as kids and still seemed to be. I shouldn't have cared about how close they stood, how easily she touched his arm as she laughed, and yet I couldn't stop watching them together. Couldn't stop trying to figure out why I had a hard time keeping my eyes off her.

Jimmy eventually dropped into the seat next to me, and Amelia crawled into my lap. "Are you gonna eat your cake?"

"Why? You want it?"

She nodded, her toothy grin splitting her face.

"All right. Who can say no to that smile?"

"Not you," Jimmy mumbled. As if he wasn't a pushover for her either.

"You got all the icing! Uncle Mike, you're my favorite!"

Jimmy snorted. "Sure, bribe the kid with dessert."

Amelia finished the cake in record time and used the back of her hand to wipe pastel-colored icing off her mouth, proceeding to smear it more. "Uncle Mike, can I see your transformer?"

"Of course." I scooted her back on my lap so I could lift my left pant leg, revealing my prosthetic, which always delighted my robot-loving niece.

She held up her arms, buzzing and beeping before tilting her head up, and I knew what she wanted before she even asked.

"Transformers roll out," I bellowed, picking her up by the waist to fly her above me as we both made zooming sounds until she lost it in a fit of giggles.

She patted my cheek after I settled her back on my lap. "You're the coolest."

I locked my hands behind my head and arched my brow at my brothers. "Out of the mouth of a babe. I am the coolest."

"That's not fair." Jimmy nodded to my leg. "You have an advantage."

Adam sucked in a breath, glaring at him like he had three heads, but I laughed it off. "Well, at least it's good for something."

CHAPTER FOUR

Sam

Finding a seat at a table next to Nancy, a neighbor from down the street, I plopped on the chair as my brother pleaded his case to our father.

"I told Ava I'd be there."

Dad leaned one elbow on the table, his other hand reaching out toward Eddie, sniffing around the grass for crumbs. "So?"

"*So?*" Gavin repeated on a whine, swiping his shaggy hair out of his eyes.

"So, you can stay here," Dad said. "This is your graduation party."

"This isn't my graduation party. This is a party that happens to be a few weeks before my graduation, but my girl-friend is having an actual party with my real friends that I want to go to."

"You have friends here."

Gavin banged his forehead on the table. "Oh. My. God."

Dad searched the block to find anyone Gavin's age—there were none—and I snickered. "You're killing the poor kid, Dad. Might as well let him go."

At my assistance, Gavin picked up his head, eyes wide as saucers, waiting for Dad's reply.

"But I got you a cake."

Gavin sighed. "I don't want cake."

I shrugged. "He doesn't want cake."

When our dad didn't budge, Gavin trudged over to the table with the desserts piled up on it and unceremoniously cut into *his* cake, decorated with little graduation caps. He splatted a piece on a plate and grabbed a fork to shovel it into his mouth on the way back over to our table.

"Really good," he mumbled, and I had to slap a hand over my mouth to cover my hoot of laughter.

"Fine." Dad gestured toward the street. "Go. Be careful driving, and text me when you get there."

My brother hissed out a celebratory "Yes," tossed the remains of the cake onto the table, and grabbed his car keys.

I nudged my shoulder against Dad's, snagging his attention from where he'd been watching Gavin get in the car. "That was the right choice."

With his usual suspicion of his own parenting skills, he raised his brows. "Yeah?"

I nodded. He hadn't been emotionally or physically present much during our childhood, mostly due to his travel and work schedule, and some because of his scatterbrain. But since everything had gone down between my parents, he'd started trying. The problem was, by then, it was a little too late.

I thought back to my adolescence. The years my parents spent fighting over how my dad was never home, and when he was home, how he hadn't paid attention to my mom. All the time my mother's coworker, Lina, spent at the house or how close they sat. I pretended not to notice how happy she looked with Lina and how unhappy she seemed with my dad. Instead of facing the truth in my home, I spent all those years next door.

When my gaze drifted up, I took in the three brothers at the table under the shade of the umbrella in the Ewings' yard. Adam with his two daughters, Jimmy telling some story with his hands gesturing widely, and Mikey, leaned back in his chair, elbow propped up on the side, nodding every once in a while at whatever Jimmy said. Never smiling, though.

That's what knocked me back when we'd spoken. He smiled at me.

Mikey was always so serious. Even as a kid, it was hard to earn one of his smiles. It wasn't very often a person got the full effect. But that was what I liked about him. He never gave in to whim. He was thoughtful and sure of himself. If you had his attention, you had his full attention. If you got one of his smiles, you'd never forget it.

I had suffered from low self-esteem as a teenager. I'd given in to all the negative self-talk—my frame was too boxy, my legs too short, my bottom teeth too crooked—but after lots of therapy, I'd thought I'd grown out of that. Especially around guys. I was always cool, always level-headed, and oftentimes aloof. I'd been called a "frigid bitch" by some randoms at a bar a time or two, but I prided myself on being in control at all times.

Yet, I fell all over myself with Mikey.

He had always been tall and well-built, but now, he was even bigger, with broad shoulders and tattoos covering almost all of his left arm. Gone was the finger-length wavy hair, replaced by a short and tidy style, although it was still as dark as I remembered, and his scruffy beard contrasted against light skin. His jungle-green T-shirt clung to his muscled chest, like a tree I wanted to climb.

As if he could hear my thoughts, he glanced over, and our

eyes met. For the briefest of moments, my heartbeat pulsed thick against my wrist and neck. I hoped maybe he felt it too, the heat of attraction, but then he brought his beer to his mouth, his attention flitting away again, and I couldn't help but feel a tiny stab of disappointment. I was still invisible to him.

"Who's that?" asked Nancy, startling me out of my daydream.

"That's Michael Ewing. He's Brandon and Lucille's son," my dad explained, seeing as she was relatively new to the neighborhood. "The one who was in the Marines."

But he stopped there. Nobody ever wanted to finish the story.

"Oh." She understood, nodding. "Well, he's rather handsome. Isn't he? He keeps looking over here," she said in a whisper, fixing her tank top so it showed a little more cleavage.

I tried not to frown. "I doubt it."

By the time the sun had set and most of the party had died down with it, I grabbed my favorite threadbare Pitt sweatshirt and headed toward the Ewings' backyard, where I knew the last ones standing would be.

The beer pong table was out, and Jimmy stopped me from having a seat with my dad and Mr. Ewing. "Play with us. We need one more."

"No. You know I'm a lightweight."

He waved a dismissive hand. "You don't have to drink."

"What do you mean, I don't *have* to drink? That's the game."

"Come on. Mike needs a teammate." He tugged on my wrist, and when I didn't move, he tried a different tack, smoothing his hand around my waist, sweetly pulling me next to him.

"Where's Adam?" I asked, pushing him off.

"They all went home. Girls' bedtime." Jimmy held up his hand, counting off the people with his fingers. "That leaves Mr. Zukowski, who's reliving his glory days with our dads, you, or Nancy."

"Nancy?"

Jimmy jerked his chin to where Mike stood with one hand in his pocket and the other around a red cup, while Nancy nearly humped his leg.

"I knew I didn't like her."

"She put away an entire bottle of Chardonnay already," Jimmy told me out of the corner of his mouth.

"All right. Fine. I'll play."

"Nice." He pivoted around, pumping his fist in the air. "Sam's in. Let's go, Albie. Line 'em up!"

Mike yanked his arm out of Nancy's grasp. She frowned but took the hint and headed in the direction of her house.

"You're quite popular today," I said, and Mike let out a tiny huff into his cup before he took a drink.

"Yeah. Thanks for saving me."

"Anytime." Our gazes met then darted away like we were at a middle school dance. This was silly. I had to get a hold of myself. I was a confident, grown woman, not a prepubescent kid.

Albie, the guy from two houses down, clapped his hands once, explaining the rules of the game. As if we didn't already know.

Jimmy and I stepped up for the first throw, keeping eye contact the whole time. Of course, I missed. He made it.

And with that, the reign of Jimmy and Albie began.

Mike and I were down by four cups when I dared to touch his elbow. "Sorry I'm no good at this."

He leaned down, saying, "But shouldn't you be?" Between the heat of his breath and the softness of his voice, I shivered involuntarily. The kind of shiver that started with a flip of the stomach and ended with a flutter between my legs. "You've been in college for how many years now?"

I tried not to preen at the fact that he knew I was still in school. "I'm in my last year. But I didn't major in partying like that one over there," I said, motioning to Jimmy with my ball as he made crude gestures to throw me off my game. It didn't take much. My ball hopped in and out of the corner cup. "It's amazing he molds the minds of future generations."

"I know. It's unbelievable that underneath all that..."

"Absurdity. Idiocy. Immaturity," I supplied, and Mike sniffed an amused sound.

"Yeah. Underneath *all* that is a pretty good brain." He said something else, but at the other end of the table, Albie sank one, and I picked up the cup.

"What?" He had spoken so softly, I couldn't quite hear over Jimmy's and Albie's cheering.

"You're getting a doctorate, right?" he asked. When I nodded, he added, "In what?"

"Psychology with a concentration on health and nutrition." I finally looked up to find him staring at me. It was distracting. So much so that neither one of us noticed when Jimmy missed and the ball landed at my feet.

"Hey, you two." Albie snapped his fingers a couple of times. "Your turn."

I picked up the ball and miraculously made it.

"Nice." Mike took his turn, but he missed, hitting the rim of a corner cup.

Feeling brave, I grabbed his bicep. "Don't worry. I'll carry this team."

He glanced down at my hand on his arm then back at my face. I noted a tiny scar above his top lip and one bisecting his right eyebrow. The few freckles on the bridge of his nose, the

27

one thing left over from childhood. And finally, when my eyes rounded back up to his, a sea of endless dark brown that I thought I could get lost in, I lowered my voice. "No man gets left behind."

He smiled, a big whopper of a grin, and I went hot all over. "*Semper fi.*"

"Oorah!" Jimmy shouted from the other end of the table. Mike repeated it, and just like that, a wall came down, his smiles coming easier as the game went on, offering high fives to me whenever one of us made it in.

It wasn't long before Jimmy sank the last cup, ending the game.

I placed my last empty cup on the table. "All right, I think that's it for me."

Jimmy booed me, refilling the cups on their end, but I swung my arm around to the now-empty backyard. "Everyone else went to bed."

Albie dismissed the thought. "It's Darwinism. Only the strong survive."

"Yeah, you want to be the one to regress the evolution of humankind, Samantha Kohler?" Jimmy added.

I rolled my eyes then turned to Mike, who offered me a boyish smile with the lift of his shoulder. "One more game?"

He could have asked me to jump through flaming hoops, and I still would've said, "Okay."

———

One buzz after another, my cell phone wouldn't stop, and I blindly reached for it without opening my eyes. I'd learned early in my undergraduate college career that I wasn't a good drinker, and after a night of partying, it was best to sleep with one leg off the bed. Last night was no exception.

Finally feeling my phone wedged under my pillow, I swiped at my eyes and rolled over. I'd missed lots of messages from the **4whoresmen**. I replied to them without reading.

> I'm hungover. Do I need to read all these? Give me the summary.

BRONTE

> You're hungover??

LANEY

> Who'd you drink with?

GEM

> No blurry selfies or drunk messages to us? I'm mad about it.

I checked the time on my phone. It was almost eleven.

> Neighborhood picnic. Jimmy talked me into it.

BRONTE

> Jimmy as in your childhood bff?

LANEY

> Jimmy as in the guy Gem hooked up with whenever he came to visit you at Pitt?

GEM

> Is he still cute?

> Is no one going to summarize the previous texts for me?

I groaned and sat up, my head ringing like a bell struck with a sledgehammer. That was when the FaceTime call request came through from Bronte. "It's easier to recap this way," she said once we were all on.

"Man, you did drink a lot last night," Gem said, ever the truth-teller.

I brushed my hair away from my face. "Thanks. So, what's happening?"

"Wait, before we start in on my life, let's catch up with Sammy," Laney said.

I downed the glass of water I'd set on the nightstand before I fell into bed last night. "There's nothing to catch up. I'm home. Gavin barely looks at me because he's always texting his girlfriend. My dad is struggling to walk with his knee. I haven't seen my mom yet. And, yes, Jimmy is still cute."

Gem leaned into her screen. "Are you going to spend some time with cute Jimmy this summer?"

"Number one, no, because he's like a brother to me, and number two, there are not enough degrees of separation between you and me."

Gem wrinkled her nose at that.

"Is there someone else you're going to be spending your time with?" Bronte asked, the usual hopeful tone in her voice.

"No."

"Liar!" Laney laughed. "You touched your ear."

I reflexively touched my earlobe. "I did not."

"You did," Bronte said, and Gem nodded in agreement.

Laney smiled. "Who is it?"

"What does he do?" Bronte asked.

Laney folded her hands under her chin, more than interested. "What's he look like?"

"How old is he?" Gem added.

I narrowed my eyes. "I hate you guys."

"Yes. We know," Gem said. "Please continue."

"He's thirty, he's got dark hair and eyes and gives Bronte a run for her money with how pale he is. I'm not sure what he does now, but he was in the military. He was a Marine."

"Ah, shit," Laney mumbled. "Here she goes."

"You're serious?" Gem scoffed. "The American military?"

Before I could say anything, my best friend got out her metaphorical soapbox. "You know why we aren't doing anything to combat global warming? Because we supposedly have no money, nobody cares. But you know how much congressional spending on the military is up to?"

Bronte butted in with, "Is he nice?"

"Is he nice? He's part of the industrial military complex. Why would someone *want* to join a government agency that routinely occupies other countries and—"

"He's really nice," I said. "A little shy, though. He's always been quiet and sort of keeps to himself. He's still that way."

Gem snorted. "I read an article the other day about sexual assault in the military and—"

"You can't paint everybody with a broad brush," Bronte said. "There're bad people in every profession. There's a teacher at this one high school here who was on a field trip and got drunk. Who does that?" She shook her head, as if her point was proven.

"Sorry, Sammy," Gem mumbled after a few seconds. "I'm sure your Marine is fine."

"He's not my Marine, and now that it's settled, can we move on, for the love of all that's holy. What's going on, Laney?"

She tucked her hair behind her ear and blew out a breath. "It's Bobby."

Laney had been with her boyfriend for a few years now and even accepted a position to work for him and his burgeoning restaurant conglomerate. Bobby Magnate was like the Australian Gordon Ramsey, guest judging on different cooking shows, a little rude but in a funny way.

"I thought everything was going well," I said. "Living the high life."

She swiped one finger under her nose. "I've been at the

restaurant a lot, getting behind-the-scenes stuff for his socials, and there's this new sous chef. She's gorgeous and cool and French."

Gem thumped her fist on the table. "I hate her already."

"The other day, I was there to get some videos of the line while they prepped the kitchen, and I noticed Suzette wasn't there. When I went out to go to the bathroom, she was in the hall with Bobby, and they were whispering and leaning into each other. They noticed me and backed away really quick, like they were caught, you know? I brought it up to him, and he said it wasn't anything. He said she's always really flirtatious with everyone, and I know, I've seen it, but I got a weird vibe seeing them together."

I nodded. I knew that feeling. I'd gotten that same suspicion about my mother and Lina so many years ago. "So, what happened?"

Laney rolled her eyes to the ceiling, shaking her head slowly. "Nothing. He told me he loved me, talked about eventually getting married."

Bronte leaned her chin in her hand. "What are you going to do?"

"Nothing." Laney dropped her attention back to her screen. "There's nothing for me to do. I love him."

"But you gotta trust your gut," Gem said.

I agreed. "And what's your gut telling you?"

Laney sighed. "She's burned out from too much dairy and gluten."

"Hot girl problems," I said, and they all laughed.

"Well, hey." Gem raised her hand. "How long until we take over LA?"

That got a grin out of Laney. She held up her phone, displaying the countdown. "Thirty-seven days!"

"Thirty-seven days! I can't wait to see your faces in person," Gem said.

Bronte danced in her seat. "I'm already packed."

"Of course you are." Gem rolled her eyes. "How many pairs of underwear?"

"Well, not everyone goes commando like you."

"So, thirteen pairs?" I guessed.

"Thirty," Bronte corrected, and Laney's laughter boomed. "But I'm going to be staying there for the summer! I need a lot."

I smiled. "I love you. I love you all, but I need to go. I smell like a frat party."

"Say hi to Jimmy for me," Gem said with a flirtatious wave.

"Say hi to your husband for me," I shot back, and she got those cartoon hearts in her eyes again.

"He's right here." She moved her screen so we could all see Jason laid out along the couch, fast asleep with Willow in his arms.

Bronte and Laney aww'd appropriately, but I was too hungover to show the proper amount of love for the wholesome family. "I gotta go."

"Take a picture of this Marine for us."

"Preferably full length, please and thank you."

"How about of all three brothers? To compare?"

"You guys are the worst. I'm leaving now." And then I hung up on my giggling friends to brush the taste of beer out of my mouth.

CHAPTER FIVE

After peeling my face off my mattress, I assessed how I felt. From my head to my toes, it was like I'd been left in the washer, waterlogged and clumped together. Swiping my hands down my face and bare chest, I shifted back in my bed and blinked around. I had been blessed with amazing parents, who helped me get back on my metaphorical feet. What used to be a place where my brothers and I would sneak beers and watch late-night television, with wood paneling on the walls and dusty paintings of ducks, was now my little apartment.

It was great, truly, but it didn't feel like home. Or, at least, I didn't *want* it to feel like home. Even though I appreciated my parents and all that they did for me, I didn't relish living under my parents' roof as a thirty-year-old man.

That stifling feeling clutched at my chest again, and I took a few deep breaths before moving to the edge of the bed to put on my prosthesis. After brushing my teeth and splashing water on my face, I headed outside and settled on the front stoop, my elbows on my knees as I tilted my face up to the sky.

"Hey, whoa, wait. Wait, wait, wait."

I snapped my head over to the right, where the night-roughed voice was coming from. My lips quirked to the side at the sight of Samantha tussling with her dog, the leash wrapped around one ankle.

"Morning."

When she turned toward me, I lifted my hand from where I'd been shielding my eyes to see her and waved. She froze for a long moment, and that was when I realized I was still in the shorts I'd slept in and no shirt. But she didn't stare that long. In fact, she dropped her head, letting out a loud laugh with a stiff shake of her head. "My friends are such assholes."

I liked that she always seemed to blurt out whatever was going through her mind at the moment, and I found myself standing up to take a few steps closer to her, wanting to know what she was smiling about. "You all right?"

She squinted one eye at me. "Yeah. It's... I was talking to my friends, and...it's nothing. I'm a little hungover from last night."

"Me too. Sorry about that. I was the one who asked you to keep playing."

With the leash and dog under control, she met me halfway between our yards. "We got better as the night went on, though, huh?"

"If by better, you mean drunker."

She looked everywhere but at my chest, making it so obvious that I had to cover my growing grin with the palm of my hand. "I better go," she said. "This guy will choke himself with the leash if we don't get walking soon."

I didn't know why I asked, maybe the need to clear my head with fresh air. Or maybe the way she looked up at me. Either way, the words were out before I thought better of it. "You mind if I come with you?"

Her eyebrows rose ever so slightly. "Uh, yeah. Yeah, of course."

I held up my finger, saying, "Give me one minute," before

going inside for a quick change into track pants, a Marines T-shirt, and a baseball cap.

"That was more than a minute," she teased when I met her back out front. "I thought you military guys were supposed to be on time."

I clucked my tongue. "Not anymore."

"I'm sorry." She grimaced. "I didn't mean—"

"Don't worry about it. Lead the way."

After walking a while, she sighed. "It's not fair. You look fresh as a daisy, and I'm like death warmed over."

My gaze swept over her. "Nah."

"Don't patronize me." She laughed and pushed her sunglasses farther up her nose. I stayed quiet. I didn't know if she was fishing for a compliment or not, but I didn't think she'd believe me even if I confessed I thought she was beautiful. So, I didn't say anything.

It wasn't until we walked another two blocks that I finally said, "The last time I saw you, you had braces."

She spared me a quick glance. "I was going through an awkward phase."

"Sure you're not still in it?"

On a gasp, she turned to me, her lips twisting up from a reluctant smile to a growing grin as she pushed at my shoulder. "Rude."

When she faced forward again, murmuring something to her dog about walking in a straight line, I took the opportunity to study her. My attention drifted from her ear, where she had three piercings in her cartilage, to her nose and the tiny stud in it, then her lips, wide and a tempting pink, and finally to her hair.

"What's with the purple?"

"It's called ombre."

"Ombre?"

"Yeah. Last month, it was red." She combed her fingers through it, the slight breeze lifting a few strands so they settled across her cheek.

Using the tip of my finger, I pushed them back behind her ear. "It's nice."

Color rose in her cheeks, and she cleared her throat. "Want to go to the park?" She tilted her head in that direction, and I nodded. But on hearing the word "park," the dog charged ahead, pulling on the leash. "Slow down, Eddie!"

I tossed her an amused look. "You named your dog Eddie?"

She tipped her chin up, nose in the air. "His full name is Edward Anthony Masen. I went through a big *Twilight* phase in high school, when we got him."

I stared at her blankly. I had no idea what *Twilight* was.

"They're a series of books and movies that came out about this vampire named Edward, who fell in love with a human, and she was—you know what? Never mind. You just have to watch them."

I shrugged. "If you say so."

"I do."

"Okay. It's a date."

I didn't mean it like *that*, but she froze like I did. I hadn't dated since the Bianca debacle, and I certainly wasn't looking to get back into another relationship anytime soon. Although with the way she offered me a gentle, vulnerable smile, I almost wished I were.

At the park, Samantha and I sat on a pair of swings with Eddie tied up to a pole so he could sniff around the grass. For an older dog, he still had a lot of spunk, and I appreciated that since sometimes I physically felt like an old dog trying to learn new tricks. After a scratch on the dog's head, I leaned back on my swing as a breeze kicked up again. Samantha gathered up all of her hair to push it to one side, exposing her neck with skin tanned from the sun and a small shooting star tattoo behind her ear.

She looked so good with a little bit of a rock-star vibe, the colored hair, and piercings. I wanted to tell her how pretty I thought she was, but the words stuck in my throat. Instead, I closed my eyes and tipped my face toward the sun for a few breaths.

"Are you trying to float away or something?"

I swiveled my focus to her. "Hmm?"

"You've got this look on your face, it's like you're trying to float away or something."

"Or something," I said and rocked on my heels to move the swing back and forth.

"What are you thinking about?" She lodged her bottom lip between her teeth like she didn't mean to speak those words, and I was tempted to reach over and tug it out, but I kept my hands firmly planted on the metal chain-link holding the swing up. She pushed her sunglasses onto the top of her head. "You don't have to answer that. I'm sorry, that was really nosy of me."

I shook my head. "I was thinking how nice it was to be out here with you."

"Yeah?" She smiled. "You like being home?"

"I don't know. It's weird."

She tilted her head to the side. "Why?"

It was a long story, and I didn't know how much she knew or if she even wanted to hear it.

I'd had a rough road, physically and mentally, these last two years. After I was injured, I'd spent a lot of time in the hospital, rehab, at doctor's appointments, but I'd worked hard to recover. I was well on the way to a new life, or so I thought. Until Bianca left me and everything I thought I knew was gone. For the second time. I had to start over. Again.

Stuck in a never-ending cycle.

"How can I move forward if I'm going backward?"

"Because you're living with your parents?" she guessed, and I nodded. "But something like twenty percent of people aged twenty-five to thirty have lived or are still living with their parents."

"Great. Exactly what I want to be, a statistic." My voice was sharper than I intended, and I stood up, my hands on my hips. "I'm sorry. I didn't mean for it to come out like that."

"No. It's okay. It's fine."

"It's not fine. I shouldn't have snapped at you like that." I swallowed down my guilt. Samantha was here, listening to me, and she didn't deserve that. "I apologize. It's..." I took a breath. "My life hasn't turned out like I thought it would."

She was quiet for a few moments, her gaze thoughtful. "I don't want to pry, but you feeling this way... Does it have anything to do with someone named Bianca?"

I rolled my eyes to the tops of the trees on the outskirts of the park and crossed my arms. It was more than Bianca, but she was the reason my life was in its current state of affairs.

"How'd you know?" Although, I already knew the answer.

"I don't know the specifics, but Jimmy called me a few months ago, asking if I wanted to take a road trip to egg Bianca's house. He didn't explain who she was but said something happened between you and her, and that he needed a driver."

If I weren't so frustrated over the situation, I would've laughed at my brother's stupid but heart-in-the-right-place antics. I paced a few steps toward the jungle gym then came back to stand in front of Samantha on the swing again. "She was my girlfriend."

"Was?"

"We were together for a while before I went on my last tour." I skipped over most of the details, not wanting to rehash it all. "She'd come and visit me in the hospital, and even found us a place to live in together, but..." I shook out my fingers from where they had involuntarily balled into fists at my sides. "All the rehab and appointments got to be too much for her. When I decided I wanted to amputate my leg, I guess that was the last straw for her. She said she couldn't handle it."

"Couldn't handle it?" Samantha repeated, her voice slow and tinged with anger. "Goddammit. I wish I'd taken Jimmy up on that offer. This girl sucks." She waved her hand, reaching for her cell phone. "No. You know what? I'm texting him right now to get a carton of eggs."

My bad mood abated, and I placed my hand over hers. "Everybody thinks Jimmy's the troublemaker, but clearly, you're not as innocent as everyone believes."

She pursed her lips as she slipped her phone into her back pocket. "I take offense to that, sir. I'm always good."

"Sure you are."

"I am, I swear," she said with a laugh, leaning back to tip her swing forward. "But this Bianca chick deserves a lot more than a few eggs on her car and house."

"What? You gonna beat her up for me?"

Samantha angled her head, huffing as if I affronted her. "I would, at the very least, change out all her spices. Put cinnamon in the chili powder. Exchange cumin for the garlic powder. Coffee grounds in the pepper shaker."

I bit back a smile. "You devious woman."

She lifted one shoulder, accepting the title. "Push me?"

I stepped behind her, gently pressing my palms to the middle of her back, and she kicked her feet out and back in time with my pushes, gradually swinging higher and higher.

"Okay, okay." She squealed. "Too high!"

I stopped pushing her and leaned against the pole as she

slowed down, brushing her sneakers along the dirt with every pass until she slowly rocked back and forth.

"You have big plans for the summer?" she asked.

"Not really. Just working."

"What do you do now?"

"I recently got certified to be a personal trainer."

She pitched her lips to the side. "Since Bianca's out of the picture, do you have a girlfriend right now?"

I found it curious that her voice hitched up, and I moved closer to her, my sneaker a few inches from hers. "No. How about you? What are you doing home?"

"My dad wants to put the house up for sale by the end of the summer because my brother and I will both be gone. Plus, he's scheduled for a knee replacement in July. I came home to help him out." She toggled her head side to side. "Although, I have a feeling I'll be doing most of the work. But I do have a weekend trip to Los Angeles for my friend's bachelorette party at the end of June. That'll be fun."

I reached my hand out to hold on to the metal chains, my pinkie barely brushing her knuckle. "Why Los Angeles?"

"She spends her summers there. Her fiancé is—"

When Samantha clamped her lips shut, I leaned down. "What?"

She only shook her head.

"You let out any little thought that crosses your mind, and *now* you're going to keep a secret?"

She puffed her cheeks out as she exhaled audibly. "So, you picked up on that brain vomit, huh? I'm not normally so loose-lipped. I..." She shook her head again. "I don't know."

I suspected that maybe she felt the same way I did, thrown off. No matter. I was interested in getting inside her head now. "You going to finish your sentence? Her fiancé is..."

"No. I don't know if I'm allowed to tell you."

"*Allowed* to tell me?"

"Yeah. My best friends, we all met freshman year at Pitt, but we live all over the place now. So when we get together, we normally have to drive awhile or fly. Bronte met her fiancé on one of those flights. He lives in LA."

I tilted my head. "And you weren't supposed to tell me that?"

She opened her mouth then closed it again.

"I'm guessing there's more?"

"Why are you trying to get all my secrets?"

I bent at the waist, so we were eye to eye. "Because I'm a good secret-keeper." I tapped my temple. "Steel trap."

"It's not your memory I'm worried about, it's who you'll tell."

I stood up straight again. "Who I'd tell? I don't have anyone to tell."

"Jimmy."

"Jimmy?" That set me back. Whatever this secret was, she hadn't told my brother, her supposed best friend. Yet here she was, playing at this game with *me*. "I won't tell him I don't tell that kid anything. I don't tell anyone anything."

"Yeah." Her gaze roamed over my face. "I got that. A real lone wolf."

Again, she wasn't wrong.

"Tell me, and you can be part of my pack." I didn't really care about whatever it was she was holding back from telling me, but I liked the fact that she wanted to tell me something so important she didn't even divulge to Jimmy.

"Bronte is marrying CJ Cunningham."

"Am I supposed to know who that is?"

She raised her palms up, like *obviously*. "CJ Cunningham's an actor. A pretty famous one."

"Really? What's he been in?"

"Um. Last year, he was in that one about the boxer and the heiress, *Gilded Cage*? He was nominated for an Oscar."

"Doesn't ring a bell."

"He got famous because he was in that James Dean biopic a few years ago."

"Nope."

"Okay, here..."

She pulled out her cell phone and Googled the guy to show me a picture. "Oh yeah, okay. I know him. He was in *The Interviewer*. It's really good. What's he like?"

She tucked her phone away. "He's actually really sweet—and over-the-top, disgustingly in love with Bronte. It's going to be a small wedding on this private island in the British Virgin Islands in August."

I rubbed at my jaw. A private island wedding was some real celebrity shit. "What about you? Getting hitched anytime soon?"

She flicked her hand. "No. I've got more important things to do, millennial stuff."

I took my hat off to run my hand over my head before putting it back on. "Millennial stuff?"

"Yeah, we're ruining the average for marriages and children. You didn't know?" She rattled off information about age groups, the middle class, and how it all intersected with new wave feminism. "I wrote about it as part of my master's thesis: *Confidence of Millennials*."

"So that's how you knew I was a statistic?"

"We're all statistics." She batted at me, and I caught her hand midair. "You're not that special," she said, her teasing trailing off as I wrapped my fingers around the back of her hand, pressing my palm to hers.

My chest tightened in a way I hadn't felt in a long time.

And from the way she sucked in a breath through parted lips, I assumed maybe she hadn't either.

"You ready to head back?" I asked, rubbing my thumb along her skin to see how she would react. "I could use some coffee."

She avoided eye contact as she hopped off the swing and dropped my hand. Her eyes briefly strayed to my fingers before darting up to my face then off toward Eddie. She bent down, untying his leash from around the end of the monkey bars, and wrapped it around her fist.

"Thanks for coming with me," she said as we started back in the direction of our neighborhood.

"Thanks for letting me crash your walk."

With a hopeful lilt in her voice, she asked, "Maybe we could do it again?"

But I was like a bull in a china shop. "What's up with you and Jimmy?"

"Me and Jimmy?"

"Yeah."

She looked at me like I'd sprouted horns and really did become a bull. "Nothing."

I took a few more steps, remembering how easy she and Jimmy were together. Cozy. "Really? It didn't look like nothing."

"What are you talking about?"

"You guys were always together. All the time. I know you slept in his bed once or twice." I recalled all the days and nights they'd spent together. They were two peas in a pod. If she and Jimmy were such good pals, odds were something was going on between them.

"We were kids, and we're still good friends."

"That could be more, though, right?" I didn't think the idea was unreasonable, but she outright laughed at me.

"I don't know if you know this, but your brother is kind of a slut. He's been that way since forever. Sure, we're good friends but strictly platonic. I puked in his lap in fifth grade, and he showed me a weird rash on his balls that he thought was an STI in high school."

I didn't know whether I should be appalled, disappointed, or all of the above.

"It's never been that way between us."

A beat passed, and she turned to me, stopping both of us in our tracks. She lifted her sunglasses and seemed to mull something over before finally saying, "He's never been the brother I was interested in."

It took a while for her words to sink in, and when they finally did, my heart rate spiked. But I needed to make sure I understood correctly. "What are you trying to say?"

"I figured since we're both home now, maybe..." She bit into her lip, shook her head, then started again. "I've got a lot going on, I'm sure you do too, but, you know, I'm open to something."

I didn't need a map to see what direction she was going in when she said *something*. And I was ready to pack my bags and camp out there.

"I'm leaving for Texas at the end of August, but—"

I stepped back, setting my mental bags back down. "You're leaving?"

"Yeah. My internship's in Austin."

I wanted to say yes to her. I wanted more of her laughter and mischievous eyes and flirting, but I had never been impulsive. I was well planned and meticulous. My career in the military required it, and that carried over into my everyday life. I didn't go on random dates with women. There were no casual hookups or flings. When I cared for a woman, I knew immediately, and I didn't think I could agree to merely a summer.

"I, um…" I rubbed my hand along the back of my neck. I had only ever been in committed, long-term relationships, and I didn't know how to give her what she was asking for. "I don't know, I—"

"Oh, it's cool." She shoved her sunglasses on. "Forget it."

"It's not that I don't wa—"

"Really," she said, lightly pressing her hand against my forearm to silence me. "Please don't think I'm all heartbroken or whatever. It's fine. Completely." Then she took off at a quick clip, and I had to jog to catch up.

"Hey, Samantha, hey. Hold on. I'm not as great at running as I used to be." I meant it as a joke, but her mouth turned down in a frown. They had taken my leg off below the knee, and I needed to put on a different prosthetic for a lot of physical activity. "Let me explain," I said, "I've never…"

"You've never what?" She took her sunglasses back off, surprise coloring her face. "Are you a virgin?"

I rolled my head to the side, tamping down a laugh. "No, Samantha, I am not a virgin."

"What?" She tossed her hands out. "There'd be nothing wrong with that."

I dragged my hands down my cheeks, scratching at my beard. "I've only ever had serious girlfriends. I was with Kaylie Magee in high school."

"I remember." She crossed her arms, and was that a bit of jealousy I heard?

"We were together for three years."

"I know. Why are you telling me this?"

"So you can understand." I wrapped my hands around her upper arms until she loosened them to her sides. Then I reached for her hand not holding the leash. "We broke up because she was tired of waiting for me to come home, and she said she wanted the normal college experience." Now that I'd started, the words were tumbling out. I didn't know why I felt like I needed to tell her, yet I couldn't stop. "I met Madison when I was stationed in Arizona. We were together for a while but broke up before I went overseas for the first time. And you know about Bianca."

"Okay," she said, her voice lilting in question.

"There has never been anyone else. No one-night stands or anything."

"Oh." She stared down at where our fingers had somehow become interlocked together. "So, you've only slept with three women?"

"Yeah." I wasn't embarrassed, but I'd lost some of my confidence since Bianca had left me.

"I..." She blinked up at me. "I figured girls would have been throwing themselves at you."

"Well," I said, slanting a brow. "That's what I'm trying to tell you. I don't do casual. I don't know how."

"In full transparency, my number is much higher," she said, completely measured and unapologetic. "The last guy I was with was a postdoc I knew from school, and we'd see each other whenever it was convenient for both of us. I don't do relationships."

"Okay." I flicked the bill of my hat back a little. "Where does that leave us?"

She swiveled her head right and left. "In the middle of Abington Street."

"Smartass." I playfully rolled my eyes at her. "When do you have to be in Texas?"

"My internship starts September first," she said, and I did the mental math. That was three months away.

"So, until then?"

"Until then..." She deliberately eyed our joined hands.

47

"Maybe if I slow down a bit and you speed up, we can meet in the middle."

I wasn't sure what I wanted the answer to be and couldn't quite pinpoint if I was excited or unhappy about her suggestion. Probably both. But I brought my other hand up to her chin, sweeping my thumb across her lower lip. "Can we start with a kiss?"

When she nodded, I bent down, pressing my lips to hers once, twice, and a third time before parting them with my tongue. It was slow and sweet, and over far too soon since she was the first one to pull away, bringing her hand to her collarbone as if she needed to catch her breath. "So...I usually go for walks every day. Will you be joining me?"

I fitted my hat back on my head and turned to continue on our path. "All summer."

CHAPTER SIX

Mike

I slowly inhaled, lowered the bar toward my chest then exhaled, pushing it back away.

"Six," Jimmy said.

One more rep.

"Seven."

Another rep.

"Eigh—"

"You don't have to keep counting. I think I can handle one through ten." I forced the bar away from me again.

My brother smirked, upside down from my vantage. "Never know with you."

I finished my reps and racked the bar before wiping my face with a towel and throwing it at him. "Fuck off."

He laughed and switched places, lying on the bench.

"Think you can handle 280, little brother?"

He snorted. "Yeah."

"If you say so." Even though we'd been working out together pretty regularly the last few weeks, I knew Jimmy couldn't bench-press 280 pounds. Not with his scrawny arms.

I helped him position the bar over his chest then let go, leaving all of the weight in his hands. He breathed deeply through his nose, then lowered the bar a few inches before shaking. Another few inches down lower, and he yelped, dropping the bar to his chest. I immediately pulled it off, eyeing him.

He sat up, brows narrowed. "Shut up."

I quietly chuckled as I removed a few plates from the bar and set them on the floor then gestured to the lower weights. "Here you go, Hulk. Try this."

My brother settled back on the bench, wrapping his hands around the bar, managing to press it away from his chest with much more ease.

"It's weird that you don't listen to music while you work out," he said as he finished his set. "It's too quiet."

I shrugged. I never really noticed. My mind blanked when I exercised.

With my paid clients, I worked out of a gym, but exercise equipment had taken over almost half of the basement for my own use. I had a multifunctional cage with Olympic bars, two different benches, a freestanding pull-up bar, kettlebells, anything and everything I would need for my daily workouts.

"I like the quiet."

"I think it's weird, man. I can't get motivated." Jimmy tapped his phone a few times, and a Run-D.M.C. song blared out from its tiny speaker before he put it down behind us. "Mom said you've been going out every day." He lay back down on the bench and started his second set.

I stepped up next to him to spot, ignoring the unasked question.

"Nothing? You're not going to give me anything?"

I still didn't answer.

"Not even about Sam?"

I held on to the bar, stopping my prying brother from another rep.

"Mom said she sees you two together, leaving for a walk. Where is it you two are going?"

"Are you going to join Mom's book club too, so you can drink wine and gossip?"

He racked the bar and sat up. "Thought about it."

I grabbed my water, chugging some of it.

"So?" Jimmy asked, raising his hands. "What's going on with you two?"

"Nothing." There was no way I was going to tell anyone, especially my loudmouth brother, about what I had going on with Samantha.

"Where do you go?"

"Nowhere."

"Seriously? She's been my friend since we were in first grade, and you're not going to tell me if you're fucking her?"

We'd only walked to the park and back every day. Eddie had a lot of energy, and Sam mentioned that it was her normal routine to go swimming at the local Y or for walks when the weather was good. She'd told me she usually walked for a few miles, and I suspected that if it weren't for the pit stop we made at the tree on the far end of the park, where I would back her up against the trunk for a few minutes while Eddie ran himself in circles around the swing set, she'd be doing her usual miles. Except she couldn't, not with the time we spent kissing. Although, it wasn't *that* big of a deal.

Only her gasped breaths when I held her waist, plying her mouth open with mine. Only her fingers fisting my shirt. Only her smile against my throat as I told her how sweet her lips tasted.

Especially since we were both currently residing in our parents' homes, and it made anything else difficult.

I avoided my brother's question with my own. "If you're such good friends, why don't you ask her about it?"

"Because she won't tell me. I asked her already."

This piqued my curiosity, but I turned my back on Jimmy and reached up to hang on to the pull-up bar. With a deep exhale, I hoisted myself up with my back and arms, head rising above the bar. "What *did* she say?"

"That you guys are friends."

I completed another pull-up.

"Is it true?"

I did eight more reps before standing and blowing out a breath, tired from the physical exertion and this conversation. "That we're friends? Yes. Why're you so interested?"

"Because I see the way she looks at you, has looked at you since we were kids, and she's—"

He stopped, and I hated to admit I wished this was one time my brother didn't. I wanted to know everything about Samantha. I wanted to fill in the blanks.

"She's been through a lot," he finally said. "You have too. But..." He raised his eyes to meet my stare. "If you're looking to work out whatever you have going on in your head, don't do it with her, okay?"

For all his clowning, my brother did have a heart of gold, and I brushed off his assumptions. Jimmy was looking out for his friend. If only he knew that he had it backward. Samantha was the one who propositioned me.

Then again, was that what I was trying to do? Work out or work off all the things that still haunted me? I didn't think so, yet now that Jimmy brought it up, I couldn't help but doubt if I was as "over it" as I thought.

I thrust my hand over my head and neck, wicking away the sweat there. "She's cool to hang out with."

My brother studied me for a few moments before he stood up and clapped me on the shoulder. "She's like a sister to me. To all of us."

Not at all, actually.

I didn't feel brotherly toward her in the slightest, but I didn't say anything else as Jimmy grabbed his stuff and made his way upstairs to leave.

Samantha wasn't like a sister to me. She was a beautiful woman who made me laugh and kept me company. She wasn't like a sister when she pulled me in for a kiss, or as she stared at me when she thought I wasn't paying attention. But I always paid attention to her.

I paid attention to the way her lips rounded on certain words, like *you* and *for* and *really*. I noticed how she never had fewer than three braided bracelets on her wrist at a time. And I certainly didn't miss how her ass looked in the tiny shorts she wore yesterday.

Nothing about the feelings I had for her were familial.

But she was only here for the summer, and our time was rapidly slipping away.

CHAPTER SEVEN

Sam

Dad and I had devised a plan. Get as much of the big stuff done as possible before his surgery, while he could still get around. Then while he recuperated, he could sort through the piles of junk he'd acquired the last few years. He didn't need to move much to box things up, as long as Gavin and I did most of the heavy lifting. That's why I was currently covering up the bright colors of my bedroom walls. I'd taken a picture of the *before* and sent it to the girls with a sad face, then started in on the beige.

Bending to dip my roller in the paint again, I caught my reflection in the standing mirror, next to the twin bed and bureau I'd pushed toward the center of the room. My hair had fallen out of its messy bun, and I took a moment to redo it before taking account of my body, covered in paint-splattered mesh shorts and a T-shirt.

Therapy had taught me to understand that my body was my vehicle, and I needed to take care of it to keep moving. I didn't study it in the mirror, wishing it could be different anymore. Now when I stared at myself, I saw strength and determination. I saw shoulders and arms that powered through the water, legs that went for miles-long walks.

I was no longer ruled by the number of apple slices I ate. I didn't write down everything I consumed, and I definitely didn't count calories anymore. Instead, I focused on my energy and used food for fuel to live a healthy life. And most importantly, I was on my way to becoming a counselor for other people who suffered with eating disorders.

With a smile at myself, I grabbed the roller once again. My family life might not have been perfect, my road to happiness and health was rocky, but I'd made it. Although it was sad to cover up all the memories—both good and bad—I'd made in this bedroom, it was only up from here.

"This sucks!" Gavin yelled from his room, next to mine, where he was supposed to be cleaning up. "Why are we even doing this? Why does Dad have to move?"

"Why shouldn't he?" I shouted back, extending the roller up toward the ceiling. This time, it barely dripped on the sheet I'd spread out on the floor. I was getting better as I went on. Practically HGTV material.

"Because packing sucks."

"Well, you need to do it for school anyway. Might as well get a head start." Before continuing my next pass, I set the roller down and walked the few feet to my brother's bedroom. His top half was buried in his small closet that looked like a bomb had gone off inside. "You should make piles. One to take to school, one of stuff to keep at Dad's new place, and a throw-away pile."

"Yeah, yeah," he said, scuttling backward out of the closet with three pairs of shoes in his hands. "You sound like Mom."

I raised one shoulder. I did inherit more from our mother than her physical attributes.

"She keeps talking about you coming over." He tossed the shoes toward a corner of the room with a mound of random stuff. "She's so annoying about it. Why don't you just go over?"

Because of our age difference, Gavin had different memories of our parents and the divorce. Gavin was pretty well-adjusted. Me, not so much. I'd been old enough to remember and understand their fights. Our parents had worked out a shared custody agreement, but by then, I had grown up in this house, and I wasn't particularly fond of being shuffled back and forth between what then became our dad's house and our mother's new house with her "friend," Lina. A year later, Mom had broken the news that she and Lina were engaged.

I loved my mother and was happy for her, but I'd never been able to get back to a really good relationship with her, with either of my parents. It was...okay.

"I will," I told Gavin. "She's planning some big dinner for you before your graduation ceremony."

"I know." He ducked back into his closet for a duffel bag. He began to shove everything in the corner of his room into it. "She invited Ava's parents. That's so awkward."

"Why is it awkward?"

"Because," he said, zipping up the bag and tossing it at my feet, saying, "School pile."

"I think you'll need to take more than one bag of clothes, Gav."

"That's what you think." He combed his hair back from his face for it to fall right back down. "Like, I don't even know if me and Ava are gonna stay together," he said, going back to our last point. "Why would Mom invite them over and then me and Ava break up after?"

"Are you planning on breaking up with her?"

"I don't know what school's gonna be like. It's..." He let out a breath and turned his back on me, going back to his closet, this time with a garbage bag. "It's whatever."

I knew that *whatever*. All my relationships with men were

whatever, but before I could think too much about it, my phone buzzed with a text, startling me from my thoughts.

MIKE
I need help.

My stomach dropped.

What's wrong?

MIKE
I have a suit that doesn't fit.

I blew out a breath, glad it wasn't an actual problem.

I thought something was really wrong.

MIKE
Something is really wrong. Did you read what I wrote?

MIKE
My suit doesn't fit.

I bit into my bottom lip, stifling a laugh.

What do you even need it for?

MIKE
Emma's baptism.

MIKE
I bought a random one online, but it's too long. So can you help? I heard it through the grapevine that you could.

That's a small grapevine.

MIKE
That a yes or no?

Yes.

"Why are you smiling like that?" Gavin said to me. "You look creepy."

"Shut up."

———

I knocked on the Ewings' door, holding my sewing kit under my arm, and smiled when it opened. "Hey, Mr. Ewing."

"You know you can call me Brandon."

"I know, but it feels weird."

He squeezed my shoulder in a paternal way as I stepped into the house. "How are ya?"

"Good, thanks. Is Mike around?"

"Downstairs. You let us know if you need anything, okay?"

I nodded my thanks, and I could imagine why Mike felt like he was moving backward. The Ewings were great people, but it must have been tough for him not to have his own space, especially after years of living on different bases. Then, of course, Bianca. He had wanted to make a life with her, and that asshole told him no. *No.*

The girl wasn't merely selfish but stupid too.

I clomped down the carpeted steps to the basement, calling out for Mike, and when there was no answer, I turned in a small circle in the middle of the room. I hadn't been down here in a long time, and it had been totally refurbished. The wood paneling had been taken down and replaced by sandy-brown paint. A bed was pushed against the wall on the right side, its light green sheets tucked in at the corners, perfectly made. There was also a little fridge, a TV, a dresser, and a mirror. The other side was basically a small gym with a big freestanding metal rectangle, a few bars across it, and weights racked on multiple stands.

"Hey."

I jumped in surprise at Mike's voice behind me. I spun around, finding him in a white T-shirt thin enough to show the outline of his tattoos which extended up his left arm, to his shoulder and collarbone, and down over some of his chest. He raised that arm to run his hand over his head, and the movement wrenched me from my thoughts of tracing the inked shapes with my fingers and tongue.

"Didn't mean to scare you," he said, taking two steps in my direction.

I inhaled deeply. He smelled like mint, forest, and clean cotton.

"I was in the bathroom."

"I know," I said then immediately went hot. Way to play it cool.

"Yeah? How long have you been here?"

"Barely a minute. I smelled—never mind." I was not about to tell him I smelled his soap and guessed he'd been taking a shower.

He smiled, one of those rare, honest-to-goodness smiles. "What?"

"Nothing. So, should we get started? Where's the suit?"

Instead of taking the hint, he crowded my space and brushed his thumb down my cheek before kissing the corner of my mouth. I both hated and loved those innocent little kisses. No one had ever kissed me like that before, like I was something to be cherished and enjoyed slowly.

Or maybe that was by my choice.

Either way, I couldn't help but sink into him.

"You're cute when you're embarrassed."

His compliment made the blushing even worse. If I could

move, I'd try to cover my face with my hair or at least try to step away from him, but I was frozen in place as he cupped my jaw with his palm. I slowly brought up my hand to cover his, my fingertips smoothing over the rough skin of his knuckles and the soft hair on his wrist.

His hands were callused from work, yet soothing and tender when he touched me. He stared down at me, his unreadable eyes moving over my face to settle on my mouth. Then he leaned down and drew his tongue across my lower lip before pulling me in so that I could feel his hard planes against all my soft ones. He was both gentle and commanding, leaving me weak in the knees, but he kept his hands on me until I was steady.

Although, this time, we weren't in public, there were no children running around or Eddie tangling himself up in his leash. Now Mike kissed me like he had all the time in the world, and I wrapped my arms around his neck, angling my hips against him, meeting his tongue with long, languid strokes until my nipples pebbled.

"Do you guys want any snacks?"

Mike and I flew apart at Mrs. Ewing's voice calling down to the basement. I swiped at my mouth, caught red-handed, yet she didn't appear on the steps. Mike slapped his palm to his forehead. "No, Mom!"

"Are you sure? I was at the grocery store. I got those chips you like."

He let out a breath through his nose, and I covered my laugh. It was truly like we were kids.

"We're good, Mrs. Ewing. I'm pinning Mike's pants. I wouldn't want to get them dirty with crumbs."

"Oh, good point!"

After a few moments of quiet, when we were sure she had walked away, Mike dropped his chin toward his chest. "That's embarrassing."

"It's funny."

He lifted his focus to me, his pupils so large his eyes looked entirely black. "It's torture."

I flicked my hand in the air, pretending it didn't bother me when I said, "We have all summer."

Or, more precisely, eleven and a half weeks. That was all we had left.

As if he could read my mind, he dragged his thumb across my cheekbone and tucked a loose strand of hair behind my ear. Even as my brain screamed at me to tear my gaze away from Mike, to save myself, I couldn't.

It might have been a few seconds or a few millennia, I couldn't tell after the years we'd spent staring into each other's eyes like that. Odd how an innocent gesture could be so much more intimate than anything else, but I wouldn't and couldn't follow my emotions down the rabbit hole. I finally freed myself enough to pivot away from him, not interested in complicating this thing with *feelings*.

I pointed to the garment bag, where it hung on a closet doorframe, and I opened up my kit. "Go ahead and put it on," I told him. "I'll get it all pinned up so I can work on it tomorrow. It shouldn't take long."

He turned down the hall to the bathroom, giving me time to find my center once again.

But because life never went as planned, Mike appeared a few minutes later in a navy suit, the White Rabbit leading me to Wonderland.

My eyes drifted from the tips of his shined shoes to the slim-cut pants that fit his muscular thighs like they were made for him, then up to the jacket left open, showing off his expansive chest in a white shirt.

"Wow," I said after who-knew-how-long of ogling him.

He tugged on the sleeves. "Yeah?"

I laughed at the suspicious question. "Yeah, Mike. I don't know how many girls fell over themselves to get to you in your Marine uniform, but if this suit is any indication, it must have been in the double digits any time you went out."

He lifted his head to the side, checking himself out in the mirror. "Eh. Maybe triple." When I backhanded his shoulder, he picked up his solid fuchsia tie. "But seriously, what do you think? They showed this with it, so I bought it all."

I took the tie from his fingers and settled it against his torso, a chance to sneak a quick pat of the solid wall of muscle. "Real men wear pink."

He buttoned the jacket and shook out his arms. I stood back a few feet from him and turned on a critical eye, taking in the parts that needed to be tailored. I knelt down and folded up the bottom of his left pant leg, catching sight of the metal that made up the bottom of the prosthetic, and pinned the material. Then I moved over to his right leg. When I finished with the hems, I skimmed my hands down over his knees and tugged on the pant legs, making sure they weren't too tight.

On Mike's audible intake of breath, I shifted back, looking up at him from my position on the floor, finding color high on his cheeks. With parted lips, he stared at me for a few moments longer, and my body responded to him automatically with goose bumps and flushed skin. When his fingers twitched next to his right thigh, I found my voice. "Are you okay?"

He nodded and cleared his throat. "Yeah, sorry."

I blinked to clear my mind then stood up. Back to business.

I ran my hands over his shoulders, down his arms to the wrists, tugging on them. "The jacket fits well. How does it feel?"

He flapped his arms up and down a few times. "Good."

I checked the fit of his pants. "What about here? Do they sit okay?"

He didn't answer, his attention directed at my fingers, tucked into the waist of the slacks. With a mere two or three inches of space between us and my hands much too close to the noticeable bulge between his legs, he shook his head. "I need to figure something out. Because..." He glanced around the basement then back at me. "This ain't cutting it."

I lifted one shoulder. It was awkward, but what else could we do? "I don't know. Do you think your mom would make us some pizza rolls?"

He growled and grabbed my ass, squeezing it hard enough that I let out a surprised squeak. "You think this is funny? This little situation of ours?"

"Yeah," I breathed. "A little."

He bent to drag his lips down my throat, pressing an open-mouthed kiss over my jackhammering pulse. "I'm glad you find my misery so comical."

I had trouble swallowing as he kissed across my jaw and pushed against my lower back, his length solid against my stomach. Heat coursed over me, and I thrust my hands into his hair, dragging his lips to mine so I could make my pleas into his mouth for more.

He stepped me backward against the nearest wall and grasped both of my wrists in one hand to hold them above my head. My back arched into the wandering touch of his other palm, up my side and over my breast. When his thumb whispered over my nipple, I whimpered, and he gave me one last quick kiss before lifting his head, waiting until I opened my eyes to him.

He lifted his brow. "See? It's not so funny when you're interrupted, now is it?" He dropped my wrists. "You want to get ice cream?"

My brain was too scrambled to comprehend anything. "Huh?"

With two steps back from me, he started taking off his suit jacket. "Ice cream. You want some?"

"After..." I licked my lips, still tasting him there. "But what about...?"

"Yeah." He had a glint in his eye as he turned away from me. "Sucks to be interrupted, doesn't it? But if you're so interested in pizza rolls, I guess you could work something out with my mom."

I threw my hands on my hips. "You tease!"

He clucked his tongue. "Just wait."

Then he grabbed a hanger and hung up the jacket and unbuttoned his shirt. Good god, I couldn't wait.

CHAPTER EIGHT

Mike

I browsed list of flavors above me. The whirring sounds of the freezers and machines oddly comforting. Ice cream on a hot day was exactly what I needed. Especially after the torturous twenty minutes I spent alone in the basement with Samantha. I had trouble focusing on anything other than the shape of her ass in her little flowered number, but when she got down on her knees in front of me...sweet baby Jesus, my mind went wild.

And I hated that I couldn't give her more. My own place. It was so humiliating to bring her to my parents' basement, and even though she said she didn't care, *I* did. It was one thing to swallow my pride and move in with my mother and father, but I didn't know how much more I could take of my mom asking me about snacks while all I wanted to do was strip Samantha naked and tie her to my bed.

And when I finally had her pliant and moaning under my hands and mouth, I pulled away, all for the sake of what? Proving a point? Torturing her, like I was being tortured?

Now I had to walk around with the worst case of blue balls known to man.

"What are you thinking?" Samantha asked next to me, verbalizing the exact question knocking around in my head.

I shot my gaze down to her. "Hm?"

"What are you going to get?"

"Oh, uh..." I let my hand skim up and down her back, these little touches becoming more and more natural with every passing day. I wasn't even aware I'd done it until she leaned her shoulder against me. "I think I'm going strawberry. With rainbow sprinkles."

"Really? You don't seem like a strawberry and sprinkles kind of guy."

"Real men eat strawberry," I said, echoing her words from earlier, my fingers indenting her waist. Because why not pile innuendo onto my dumbass delayed gratification strategy?

With one thin eyebrow raised, a playful curl spread on her lips. "Did that sound as dirty to you as it did to me?"

"What can I say, I really love eating strawberries." I threw my arm around her shoulders, towing her into me, her cheek against my chest. I kissed the top of her head then dropped my mouth to her ear, whispering, "Don't you love it when guys eat strawberries?"

"Oh yeah." She tipped her head back, her tongue slipping over her lips to wet them. "Especially in the morning before I'm even really awake and the sheets are warm. A special treat to start the day."

And now all I could think about was Samantha first thing in the morning, wrapped up in the sheets, her hair all wild, and —according to my imagination—wearing nothing but one of my T-shirts.

"Hi, what can I get for you?"

I blinked over to the young girl behind the counter. "Uh, yeah. Sam?"

66

"I'd like a scoop of peach and a scoop of chocolate in a cup, please."

The girl grabbed an ice cream scoop to fill her order, and I grimaced. "Peach and chocolate? That sounds disgusting."

"Sounds gross, but it's so good."

The girl handed Samantha her ice cream then looked to me. I ordered my strawberry with sprinkles in a cone and paid before we hunted for a table. A middle-aged couple was not quite finished with their ice cream, but the man eyed my leg and promptly got up from the table. "Do you need a seat?"

I waved. "No, we're good. Thanks, though." Then I led the way outside to find a seat on a bench. "This okay?"

Samantha nodded, and we both sat. After a minute of eating in silence, she asked, "Was that weird for you?"

"I'm used to it. I've gotten used to the stares or assumptions, the questions. I'm in an online group for amputees, and the posts are..." I shook my head. "It's amazing what some people think is appropriate to say. But, for me, it's the fawning I can't stand more than anything else."

I turned to face her and her interested gaze, like I was a puzzle she was trying to put together. She asked questions because she was interested in me. As opposed to some morbid curiosity other people sometimes had in war stories.

"I got hurt doing my job. It really sucks, but I don't want to be treated any differently than a construction guy who hurt himself while roofing or something."

She tapped her spoon on her bottom lip, and I focused there as she spoke. "Makes sense, but you were also hurt doing something that most people won't or can't do. If Superman fell from the sky with a broken arm, I certainly wouldn't know what to do or say."

I stretched my arm along the back of the bench. "I'm not Superman."

"No." The corner of her lips twisted up into one of her snarky smiles. "Just a cog in the industrialized military complex. So says one of my friends."

"Too right." I joined the Marines because I was a kid who didn't want to go to college, and the recruiter was a smooth talker. The guy promised a life of travel and brotherhood and security, a life the military would provide for me. So, I signed up, and they sent me off. Like most of the guys I served with, I was simply trying to make a living.

I gestured with my cone to her cup to move on to a different topic. "How's your ice cream?"

"I'm telling you, it's delicious. Here, try it."

She spooned up a bit of peach and chocolate and held it out to me. I paused only momentarily before leaning forward to have a taste. Our eyes met as I wrapped my mouth around the spoon, the two different flavors mixing on my tongue. It was delicious, and the glint in her eyes showed she knew it.

"You're right. It's good." I licked my lips, and she mimicked the motion with her own.

"I told you."

I held out my ice cream cone, offering it to her, and without words, her pink tongue peeked out of her mouth to lick across the top scoop of strawberry, taking some colored sprinkles with it. Instead of tasting the ice cream on her tongue, like I wanted, I changed the subject to the least erotic thing I could think of.

"Are you coming to Emma's baptism?"

"I wasn't planning on it." Her spoon scraped the bottom of her Styrofoam cup. "Isn't that more of a family thing?"

"Yeah, but you're basically family."

She tossed her empty cup and spoon in the garbage before returning to me. "You want me at your niece's baptism?"

"Yeah. Why not?"

"I don't know, that's kind of—"

"It would make me feel less of a fool standing up there if I knew you were there." I had never been good with stuff like this, having to socialize with people I didn't know. I was anxious about standing up at the altar in front of a bunch of strangers.

"You're not a fool. You're Emma's godfather." She lowered her voice to a raspy growl, pinching her thumb with her index and middle fingers. "I hope your first child is a masculine child."

"*The Godfather*, really?" I laughed, choking on my bite of waffle cone, and she patted my back as I coughed. "That's a terrible impression."

"Can't all be perfect."

When I polished off my ice cream, I swiped my hands along my shorts. "So, you're going to come on Sunday?"

"Yeah," she said, reaching for my hand when I extended it. "I'll be there."

———

The clang of the plates, whir of cardio machines, and steady rotation of Ariana Grande and Megan Thee Stallion were often background noise while I worked, but today I couldn't stand it as I tried to surreptitiously listen to a voice mail from Samantha. I leaned against the counter, hiding behind the computer at check-in so I could lower my ear toward my phone, trying to discern what song she was singing that was occasionally interrupted by random grunts. She'd apparently butt-dialed me while clearing out her dad's garage.

I had to work early this morning, so we didn't get our walk in, and I hadn't seen her since our ice cream rendezvous yesterday. I wondered how much of an idiot it made me that I couldn't stop thinking about her. It was pathetic, really.

This was just a summer fling, and yet there had been no flinging to speak of. But there was a lot of really great conversation, which was exactly the opposite of what we were supposed to be doing. We should have been fucking like rabbits. I should have taken her to a hotel or—

"Hey!"

I whipped my head up and tossed my phone down. "Emily, hey. How's it going?"

"Great." She held her aluminum water bottle up in a cheers. "This morning, I found a box of Girl Scout cookies I hid in the back of the freezer, so it's a good day."

"That's a great day." I pushed all thoughts of Samantha out of my head and held my fist up for a bump as I rounded the counter. "How're you feeling besides that?"

Emily nodded, her short black hair bobbing around her face. "Pretty good. Unless you're planning on making me do burpees, and in that case, I think I pulled a calf muscle."

I gave in to a laugh and waved her over to a space by the free weights. Emily worked with Adam, which was how she'd found me, and even though she was almost two decades older than I was, we had a great relationship. Emily, though she jokingly complained, worked hard and always showed up on time.

"Let's get you warm with some step-ups," I said, nodding to a bench, and Emily got right to it, immediately reviewing her work week with me. This was our routine—I'd give her directions, and she'd follow as she got out all of her stress. That was one of my favorite things about my job. I was able to witness a person come into the gym anxious and leave feeling better. That was second only to watching them become stronger physically and mentally.

"You ready for some fifteens?" I asked, holding the weights out to Emily. "For squats."

She took them from me, pretending like they were fifties weighing her down, until I got behind her, meeting her gaze in the mirror. "We're going for twelve with a couple pulses on the last one."

She rolled her shoulders back, standing up tall, dumbbells at her sides. "I like how you always say *we're* when I'm the one doing them. You just stand there."

"Oh yeah?"

"Yeah."

I inclined my head to her in acknowledgment and grabbed a pair of weights. "*We're* going for twelve with five pulses on the last one. Ready?"

She grinned, and so did I. "Let's go."

Together, we knocked out three sets, much to her delight. "Great job." I set my weights back down. "How's your hip feeling?"

She drank a few gulps of water, absently patting her right hip. According to the intake I completed with every new client, she'd wanted to start training because she'd never had much interest in exercise, besides some occasional yoga that she could "do in my bedroom in my pajamas," and now that she'd been having some aches and pains as she aged, she had decided she needed to seek out some help.

"Okay, we're going to try static holds but add in movement. So you'll still strengthen your foundation but hit on some range of motion too." I demonstrated how I wanted her to hold a lunge then carefully lift her knee up toward the ceiling before lowering back down to the lunge. "We'll start with five seconds for five reps. What do you think?"

As she eased back into a lunge, she frowned.

"Hey, it's only five seconds. You can do anything for five

seconds, come on." I kept my fingertips on her elbow to make sure she was steady and balanced as she completed her reps.

"You know, you're really good at this," she grunted on the last one.

"I'd hope so. Could be really dangerous if I didn't know what I was doing."

"No." She switched feet, settling into her lunge. "I mean your disposition. I've always been afraid to come into a gym, and if you weren't Adam's brother, I probably wouldn't have reached out. But," she said on an exhale as she picked up her back leg, almost tipping over until I righted her and got her back into a lunge, "you're really good at this, very calming and encouraging."

"Thank you. But you're not getting out of your last three reps."

She grinned and finished up before sitting down on a nearby bench. "I've never told you about my nephew. He's in seventh grade, and my sister told me that he wants to start working out but isn't really sure where to start. He was born with a lower limb difference."

I swiped my hand over my mouth and beard, scratching at my chin as I listened.

"You know boys at that age, he wants to get a girlfriend, he wants to look good," she said with a tired smile. I knew she was a mother of two children, one daughter in high school and one son in college. "But I guess he's struggling to find exercises that he can do." She leaned back on her hands, tilting her head to the side. "Have you ever thought of that? Providing an adaptive program for people?"

I had thought of it, but only for myself. I had needed to figure out how to get back into my normal exercise routine after my amputation by trial and error. Through that experience, I'd realized I could help other people in their fitness journeys, but it had never occurred to me to make that my focus.

"Who better to provide that service than you?" Emily said with a smile as she stood up. "Something to think about."

I would think about it. I'd think a lot about it.

CHAPTER NINE

I checked my watch for the tenth time in the last ten minutes. Samantha still wasn't here. I didn't think she'd blow me off, but...it's not like we were together. I couldn't expect her to show up to things for me. She didn't do relationships. She explicitly said so.

It was my own fault for getting in my head about all this, and I ignored the punch of disappointment as Adam shuffled over to me with the gray-haired minister to let me know we were about to start. I nodded, casting my gaze through the church for one more search.

And there she was.

Tugging down the hemline of her dress as she tiptoed into one of the last rows. She fluttered her fingers when she caught sight of me, and I don't know what it was about this girl that made me feel like I was Superman. Like I could do anything, be anything. She was an addiction I didn't know how to kick. Or if I even wanted to.

Which was a problem in itself when she'd be gone in weeks.

I'd be going cold turkey if I didn't settle down.

Lauren's sister, Emma's godmother, stood opposite me as

the ceremony started with a couple of readings by the minister, and as time went on, the more uncomfortable I felt. I couldn't stop shifting my weight, hot under the lights, and fidgeting with my tie that wanted to strangle me. It wasn't until Samantha craned her neck up as if she knew I couldn't calm down, and offered me a little flirtatious smile. Like a dart straight to my heart.

A moment later, Lauren handed me Emma, positioning us by a podium with a bowl of water to pour some over her head. Then the minister closed the ceremony with a blessing and welcomed everyone to greet the family.

I beelined it right for Samantha, but my brother beat me there.

"What're you doing here?" Jimmy asked.

"Mike invited me."

"Really?"

She jerked her head back. "What?"

"Nothing."

Her brow crimped in what seemed like annoyance at Jimmy before I interrupted. "Hey, thanks for coming."

"You looked great up there," she said. "Very dapper."

I brushed off my suit jacket. "All because of you."

Jimmy bounced his attention back and forth between us before finally facing me. "I'm heading out. You riding with me?"

"Uh..." I turned to Samantha. "You coming to eat?"

"I don't want to intrude on your family thing."

"You're not intruding."

"Still, I—"

"Samantha." Mom appeared out of nowhere. "So nice of you to come today. Are you going to come to eat with us?"

I crossed my arms in an I-told-you-so kind of move.

"It's our treat," Mom continued. "Lauren's family is coming

75

as well. A little get-together. About ten people. So, we'll see you there?" She patted Samantha's shoulder, answering for her. "Good."

Jimmy snorted once our mother was out of hearing range. "Endless soup, salad, and breadsticks it is, then?"

"Guess so." She huffed out a laugh.

With my hands in my pockets, I rocked back on my heels. "Mind if I ride with you?"

"Of course not," she said, ignoring Jimmy's raised eyebrow. She waved him off, and I followed her outside to the car, where she blasted the AC.

"Hot as the devil's asshole," I grumbled, getting myself situated in the passenger seat.

"Eloquent."

"Oh, you're not impressed?" I pressed my hand to my heart, playing at hurt, before tugging my jacket over my shoulders. She openly gaped as I removed my tie and threw it in the back with my jacket. "I think normally people tip for a strip show."

She snorted. "You haven't taken off enough clothes."

I undid the top two buttons of my shirt. "Sorry."

"You've got a nice collarbone," she blurted, and I huffed a laugh.

"Yeah?" I rolled up my sleeves, revealing the tattoos on my left forearm where the grayscale forest scene started. "Nice collarbone?"

"It's an underappreciated body part," she said after a while.

Once her eyes rose up to meet mine, I cocked my head to the side, and her face turned an adorably embarrassed red. "I'll take your word for it."

She spun her gaze out of the windshield. "I like your art."

"I like yours too." I dragged my finger down to the top of

her shoulder blade, where the rainbow-colored phoenix was tattooed. "The symbol of rebirth?"

She turned the ignition and drove out onto the street, and we were both quiet for a few minutes. It was my turn to stare at her. Not that I ever really stopped. It was my most difficult task, doing anything other than gazing at her.

Especially when I could tell something was on her mind. She might not have wanted to admit it, but she could confide in me. Every secret or insignificant detail of her life, I wanted them.

"Will you tell me about it sometime?" I asked, settling my palm over her tattoo.

She glanced over to me at a stop sign, her hazel eyes warring with some emotion I couldn't read. After a few seconds, she nodded. "Yeah, one day."

And I smiled, dropping my hand to squeeze her thigh.

At the restaurant, we followed the hostess to the long table in the back. Jimmy was there already, and Samantha sat down across from him, leaving me to take the chair next to Mr. Ballman, Lauren's dad.

He was a portly man with a full head of white hair. He stretched out his arm, booming, "Michael, have a seat, my boy."

Samantha, like the sweetheart she was, leaned across me to introduce herself to Mr. and Mrs. Ballman, allowing me a good glimpse down her dress. If I weren't already fixated on her, it would be impossible to ignore the way the soft lavender cotton accentuated the shape of her shoulders and breasts. Or how she was practically in my lap.

Not the worst way to eat dinner.

Adam and Lauren showed up a few minutes later with their kids and my parents in tow, and everyone settled into quiet conversation once our entrees were ordered.

Mr. Ballman spooned out a large portion of the salad onto his plate along with two breadsticks before passing them on, as if they weren't both refillable. It was Olive Garden, for Christ's sake.

I took the bowl and considered the few scraps of lettuce that were left before turning to Samantha. "You want the rest?"

"Sure." She took it with a smile and scooped the pathetic salad onto her plate.

I watched her pop an olive into her mouth, her lips pursing as she bit into it. Lips I was desperate to kiss. Right there in front of everyone. But even I, a new student of the casual game, knew that was a big no-no.

"So, Michael, what are you up to these days?" Mr. Ballman asked, drawing my attention away from the woman next to me.

"I'm working at a gym."

"Working at a gym?" he repeated before shoveling more food into his mouth.

"As a personal trainer."

Mr. Ballman took his time wiping his mouth. "Surely a man such as yourself has better prospects than working at a gym."

My jaw worked back and forth. I didn't appreciate the judgmental comment or the fact that Ballman spoke like a steel kingpin from the 1900s.

"I can't imagine you're making much money," he went on, needling me on the very thing that was a thorn in my side. "You need to go into business for yourself to make the big bucks. Don't work for the gym. Own the gym," he said, brandishing his fork with a flourish.

I stared hard at the painting on the wall. I was trying to expand, find more clients, and after my chat with Emily the other day, it was the only thing that could take my mind of Samantha. I was trying, but Ballman was definitely one of those pull yourself up by the bootstraps types, who had no real idea what it meant to struggle. Although, I wasn't about to get into an argument. I had officially become a godfather today. I couldn't fuck up on setting a good example already.

"What about you, missy?" Ballman asked, tilting his head around me to Samantha.

She put her fork down and rested her hand on my leg underneath the table, as if she knew I needed it. "What about me, Mr. Ballman?"

"What do you do?"

"Well, I'm home for a few weeks before I go to Texas," she said, pausing to take a sip of her peach iced tea. "I'll be finishing up my doctorate there."

"A doctor? Of what?"

"Psychology, specializing in counseling people who suffer with eating disorders."

His brow rose, sufficiently impressed, as he leaned back in his chair, his gaze shifting back and forth between us. I felt more and more inadequate by the second. I was a thirty-year-old man living in his parents' basement, struggling to make a decent living. Not great "prospects."

"Hey," Samantha whispered quietly, her breath hot on my neck. "You okay?"

I blinked, clearing my thoughts, and leaned in closer to her. "You know what we should do?"

She twitched ever so slightly when I briefly nuzzled my nose along her shoulder. "What?"

"Watch that horror movie you talked about. That one you named Eddie after."

She bit her lower lip, obviously trying not to laugh. "*Twilight*'s not a horror film."

"You said it was about vampires."

She narrowed her eyes, still alight with humor. "It's a romance."

"I'm not really into romance," I said, but if it was her favorite, I'd watch it.

I disregarded my brother's curious gaze as she put her hand on my arm, saying, "You'll love it. Like peach and chocolate ice cream. Trust me."

Two words were never easier to accept. "I do."

CHAPTER TEN

Sam

I shoved another pizza roll into my mouth as I scooched back up the bed. "It's starting."

From inside the bathroom, the light flicked off, and Mike came into view a moment later in black cutoff sweats, hitting right above his knees. He'd worked late, until seven, but still insisted we watch *Eclipse*. "Did I miss anything important? Did he sparkle again? Finally get in her pants?"

"Just the credits." When I chucked a pizza roll at him, he caught it and tossed it into his mouth, before raising an *is that all you got?* brow.

"That's your last one. Your mom specifically said she made these for me."

"Who do you think asked her to get them?" He stretched out on what had become his side of the bed—the left—and handed me a peach iced tea. Once he found out it was my favorite, he'd stocked up on a bunch. And now, asking his mom to get me pizza rolls?

"You're sweet. You know that?"

He snagged another one of the tiny snacks, deliberately biting into it. "I've been called lots of things, but never sweet."

"You're sweet to me."

"Just watch the movie, spider monkey," he said all gruff and tumble, but I only smiled in return. Underneath all the tough guy exterior and the muscles that made him look like he could snap a tree in half, Mike was a marshmallow. Especially when it came to his family.

Although I was pretty positive I didn't want children, seeing him hold Emma at her baptism last week had tugged at something deep inside me. Watching how his face had lit up as he smiled down at her, so tiny in his big hands, I nearly cried. And here he was pretending he didn't use his powers for evil with the stronghold he had around my heart.

I pressed two fingers against my sternum as if I could rub the feeling away. But it wouldn't budge. I hoped I could ignore it if I tried hard enough.

Although, that strategy hadn't been working out well for me so far.

When Mike had suggested watching the entire *Twilight* series, I assumed it was an excuse to get me in his bed, yet to my amazement, he actually *watched* them. Aside from a few quick pecks, he hadn't even attempted to make a move.

We were more than two weeks into whatever this was, and we still hadn't had sex or gotten anywhere close. The crazy thing was, I didn't care. I enjoyed hanging out with him, getting to know each other. Normally, "movie nights" were code for "take your pants off." I didn't avoid spending time outside of bed with Eli or any other guy who was my hook-up of the week or month, but I didn't seek it out either. And I certainly wouldn't have ever let them know about my *Twilight* fandom.

But I allowed Mike to witness my giddy nerd come out as I compared and contrasted the books and movies, and he laughed along as I did some impressions, which were—in opposition to what he said—spot-on. After we had watched the first movie, I explained to him how I'd found the books in high school when I was going through a tough time. They had made me happy, and I'd glommed on to them and then the movies. Instead of judging me, like some "academics" tended to do when they found out I enjoyed them, he'd simply said, "Good for you."

"I still don't get the sparkling," Mike said after a while. "Vampires are supposed to be scary. What's so scary about looking like a disco ball?"

"Didn't you listen to Edward's whole spiel in the first movie?" I elbowed him. "They can be very scary, but they're beautiful to attract their prey."

"But why sparkle?" He fluttered his fingers as if his own skin were glittering. "They haven't addressed it. Since they don't show it to humans, it's not about hunting, so there's no purpose. I'd think it'd be a dangerous disadvantage. They're giving away their position."

"Careful. Your military is showing."

He turned, a barely there curl to his lips, but I had become somewhat of an expert in his smiles. This was the reluctant one. The one that hid a secret. "I would make an excellent vampire army."

"Really?" I tucked into his side. "I thought you'd play for the wolves."

"Oh yeah, one hundred percent." He waved his hand toward the television, where the wolves were currently running. "But I think I could make a better leader for the vamps than Jasper. I mean... Does everybody ignore the fact that he fought for the Confederacy?"

I sucked air through my teeth. "Yeah, but look, this part's important, so pay attention."

"Okay." He shifted his arm behind my head, and all I could smell was his forest-scented soap. All I could see was the rise and fall of his chest when he breathed. All I could feel was the warmth of his skin.

So much for paying attention.

"Oh, come on," he said, dragging me out of my haze. "You don't think it's gross that he's one hundred years old and is trying to get in her pants?"

I blinked up at him, a bit confused since I'd been off in space with Mike's fingertips lazily tracing my upper arm. "I, um...technically, she's the one who's trying to get in his pants."

"None of this makes any sense to me." For someone who was supposedly *putting up with these movies*, he certainly had a lot to say about them. "He's old, he's controlling, he's creepy and stares at her while she sleeps. Why's she so attracted to him?"

"It's not creepy," I argued weakly. When he slanted his eyes to me, I gave in with a laugh. "Okay, so maybe this doesn't hold up well, but still... He wants to protect her."

He angled his head on the pillow so we could see each other eye to eye, combing his fingers through my hair, brushing my scalp. "That's what you think is hot? Protection?"

I dropped my gaze to his left arm draped across his torso. He was completely solid, pure muscle from head to toe, but nowhere did it seem more obvious than his arms, from his huge bicep to the veins and tendons running thick along his forearm. The tattoos made it all the more impressive. But my favorite part of all of him was his hands.

Hands that could protect me. Fingertips rough and palms callused, his hands were used to hard work. And nothing made me feel safer than having them on me.

I raised my attention from his worn T-shirt to his shoulder, which I often resisted laying my head on, and up his neck to his face, rugged and worn from experiences I knew still haunted him. He looked older than his thirty years, but when he grinned at me, it was with pure, boyish enthusiasm.

"Tell me," he said. "I want to know what turns you on."

"Tattoos," I said, and he rotated his arm back and forth, casually inspecting it before resting it back down.

"What else?" He licked his lips, and I didn't have to think of my next answer.

"Kisses. On my throat."

"Yeah?" He twisted to his side, one arm still behind my head, the other settling on the mattress next to me, caging me in. "Here?" He opened his mouth over my pulse, first dragging his tongue and then his teeth there until I shivered.

"Ye-yes."

"How about here?" He kissed across my throat to the other side of my jaw, where he sucked at the skin under my ear, and I writhed next to him, imagining him sucking on other places.

I had trouble swallowing as he moved down, nipping at my collarbone. "Here too?"

"Yes," I whispered.

"It's an underappreciated body part," he said with a smile against my skin, and I moaned my agreement into a kiss before he backed away. "What else?"

"Your hands."

He let out a sound that was awfully close to a satisfied groan as his hand wandered over me. Starting at my neck, he dragged his fingers across my shoulder, down my arm to my waist, where he slid his thumb along the small expanse of skin exposed between my T-shirt and shorts to the button above my fly. He toyed with it for a moment when I honestly thought I might expire if he didn't take them off, and I practically panted the words, "You owe me."

"Can you be quiet?" he whispered, and I nodded, silently.

His only response was a flash of a wicked smile before he

buried his face in my neck and undid the button and zipper. He slid his hand under the waistband, teasing his long fingers over me until I lifted off the bed, silently begging for more. The tip of his middle finger slid between my flesh, ghosting over my clit, and I curled my fingernails into his shoulder until he relented, giving in to my needs. With his teeth and tongue on my neck, and his fingers working me over, he murmured a rough, "Tell me what you need," in my ear before biting my earlobe. "I want to make you come."

I gripped his forearm, steadying myself as I circled my hips, chasing a thrill that had been building over these last few weeks. Finally, I'd get my release. "More. I need more."

He rasped a curse and shifted over me to get a better angle, adding another long finger inside me. "Fuck, you're so warm, so wet."

I whimpered at his words, and he breathed more over my skin. Telling me how gorgeous I looked, how hot I felt, how he was desperate to see me come, he found the rhythm I needed, softly petting the spot inside me to pull pleading sounds from the back of my throat.

"Shh," he reminded me. "I don't want anyone else in this house to hear your fuck hot little noises."

I looped my arm around his neck, pulling him toward me. If I couldn't make a sound, he'd have to help stifle them. He pressed the heel of his palm against my clit and swallowed my cries with his kisses, pushing me higher and higher until my skin pebbled with a rush of pleasure and light burst behind closed eyelids.

My childhood crush had just given me an orgasm. This was the fulfillment of a fantasy. He was wonderful, patient, and tender, wanting to learn my needs, and yet something about this didn't feel right. *More.* I needed *more.*

He left little kisses along my jaw and the corner of my

mouth until I opened my eyes. Then he skimmed his hand down my leg, curling his fingers around my knee possessively. "Good girl, staying so quiet."

I ignored the flutter in my belly at his praise and licked my dry lips, wiggling my fingers to bring some feeling back into them after holding on to him so tight. I prayed he didn't notice the tiny hole he pierced in my chest.

"Next time I want to hear you," he said, leaning back, but I caught his T-shirt to keep him from moving away from me.

"What about you? I want to find out if you make any noises," I said, needing an equal exchange to get back on even footing. Back to what I was used to. Pleasure for everyone to go home happy. When I stretched toward his tented sweats, he shifted out of reach, and I furrowed my brow. "I thought..."

"Not yet." He fixed the pillow behind his head before slipping his arm around me as if nothing had happened.

"Not yet?" I forced out a laugh and lifted my leg to straddle him, but he caught my thigh and gently pushed it until I lay back down in the cradle of his arm.

"Hey." At first, I ignored his prodding, but then he drew the tip of his finger up my arm and over my collarbone. "You've introduced me to my new favorite body part." When I rolled my eyes to him, I couldn't hide my smile at his outrageously proud face, and he squeezed his arm around me until I curled against him.

All those years of daydreaming about Mike had nothing on what it was really like to touch him. What it was really like to hear his heart beating in his chest, feel the heat from his body.

"I want this," he started, dragging the elastic band out of my hair and sliding it on to his wrist before running his hand over my head. "I want you. I..."

"What?" I threw my arm around his torso, aiming to get

my fingers under his shorts, though he stopped me again. He drew my hand up so he could kiss my palm.

More.

"I want to take you out tomorrow," he said after a thousand years of second-guessing myself and this arrangement. How could I want more when I couldn't have it? I was leaving. More was not an option.

I tilted my head back to meet his gaze. "Really?"

"Yeah. Why are you so surprised?"

"I don't know." I ducked my head so he wouldn't see me lie. "I didn't know we were doing that."

"I didn't know there were rules to this." I felt rather than heard his curious rumble as he tugged on my hair until I lifted my head. "So, what are the rules?"

I didn't know what the rules were because I'd never had to make them before. There had always been an understanding between me and whomever I was sleeping with. Get in and get out. *Those* were the rules.

"I guess the first one is don't get attached. There is a firm end date to this. Obviously." Although at this point, I said it out loud more for my own benefit than his.

"Obviously," he repeated, his face blank. "Number two, there is no one else."

I jerked back. "My number might be high, but I've never cheated."

He dragged his nose along the inside of my wrist then kissed it. "I didn't mean to imply anything. I'm reiterating facts. Like your firm end date."

Nodding, I let my gaze wander around the basement, to the framed family photo on the dresser, to the sneakers haphazardly left by the wall, a pair of socks sitting outside of the laundry basket because when he'd come home, he hurriedly showered and changed while I cued up the movie. How very domesticated.

"Can I take you out tomorrow? Is that okay?" he asked, luring my attention back to him when he squeezed my side.

With the way his eyes searched mine, maybe he could feel me giving in to traitorous emotion. And maybe he understood that I didn't want to feel anything more than physical attraction, but he was still asking to take me on a date, to let go of what was holding me back. Although to soften the blow to my well-fortified wall, he added, "I want to make you come so many times, you're screaming my name."

"Oh." I laughed. "Well, then."

"Tomorrow?" he suggested.

"I can't tomorrow. I'm going to my mom's for dinner."

"Day after?"

I shook my head. "Gavin's graduation.

He heaved out an impatiently playful sigh. "The day after that?"

"Free as a bird."

———

I knocked twice on the front door of my mom's ranch home before entering. Classical music played quietly in the background as voices filtered in from the dining room. "Hello?"

"Sweet pea!" Mom attacked me with a hug and kisses. "I'm so happy to see you."

"You too," I said, kissing her cheek as Lina appeared.

"Hi, Sammy."

I hugged my stepmother. "Hey. Nice to see you."

"Good to have you home."

Lina was great and she made my mom happy, but this

house was never my home. I hadn't had a home since the divorce, and it was hard to keep up the one big family act, which was why I chose not to visit either of my parents very often.

"You look wonderful, sweetie," Mom said, squeezing my hand. With a long, flowing dress and a slouchy cardigan sweater, she appeared every bit the kindergarten teacher she was.

"Thanks. How's school? You've got a couple days left, right?"

She folded her hands together in front of her chest. "We finish next week, but of course, Lina has some more work to do."

Her wife lifted one shoulder, her long gray hair brushing it. She and Mom had met when they taught at the same school, but Lina had since moved on to become principal at another elementary school. Ironically, Jimmy took Lina's old job, teaching second graders.

"And then you're going to Colorado?" I asked.

Mom and Lina both nodded. Lina's parents lived out there, and they were taking Gavin for a month.

"Should be fun."

"You know our offer still stands," Lina said, referring to their invitation for me to tag along.

"I know, but Dad needs help."

Mom dropped her hands to her sides with a huff. "I told him to hire movers to get it over with. You don't need to be stressed out about going through all that junk."

"It's fine. I don't mind. Plus, the surgery…"

"Yeah, I know." She slid her arm around my shoulders. She was two inches shorter than me and stood on her toes to kiss my head. "You're a good person. Much better than I." She flicked her fingers up by her temple. "That man tries the patience of a saint."

Lina tugged Mom toward her. "Are you trying to say you're a saint?"

They both laughed as Gavin poked his head out, his hair much neater than usual. "Ava and her parents should be here soon."

"You nervous?" Lina asked, fixing his button-down shirt so it looked less wrinkled. "You seem nervous."

He snorted. "I'm fine."

My mom and I caught each other's gaze, exchanging knowing smiles at his lie, and for a moment, we were like one happy family.

"All right, then." Mom clapped her hands. "Gav, you finish setting the table. Sam, can you grab some drinks from the refrigerator? Honey, you stay beautiful." She kissed Lina, and Gavin gagged. "Hey. Don't think I didn't see you making out with Ava in your car last weekend. Didn't hear me making a peep about it, didya?"

Gavin's cheeks flamed red as he turned his back, fulfilling his duty to set out the plates and utensils.

Ava and her parents showed up a few minutes later, and dinner was fine, if not a little awkward. Her parents appeared to be a little too happy with Mom and Lina being together. They tried to prove how cool they were with it by telling everyone they smoked pot in college. Real liberal flagbearers, they were.

But at least I got a good laugh out of it. Anything to take my mind off Mike.

Which wasn't the easiest thing to do.

I spent the entire next day trying not to think of the boy next door. We'd gone for our usual walk in the morning, and aside from some sly smiles, it wasn't much different. But all afternoon as I cleaned out the kitchen cabinets of anything unnecessary, he sent me texts. Online quizzes of what *Twilight* character I was or theories about how some people thought Bella was part wolf or that she was really a reincarnation of Edward's soul.

Then during the stuffy graduation ceremony, I recalled our time together in his bed. His mouth on me, his hand in my underwear, his fingers bringing me to orgasm. I didn't know if I was sweating from the memories or because there was no air conditioning. Either way, my bra was soaked with perspiration by the time I got home, but the cold shower didn't help.

I had a mere two months left here, and then I was gone. I needed as much of Mike as I could get in as little time as possible. Even as I knew it wouldn't be enough.

Not when I needed more.

CHAPTER ELEVEN

I dressed in jeans and a pale blue polo shirt before grabbing my keys. I didn't have an exact plan for tonight, only that I wanted to get Samantha alone and not in the basement of my parents' house.

Days ago, I had her pliant and soft, breathing hard with pink skin, begging for more, and still, I held back. I couldn't determine exactly why I kept stopping myself—no, fuck. I knew why. This summer fling had a time limit, but I wanted to make it last for as long as I could.

I'd always been patient and understood that good things took time, even as a kid. Improving my swing in baseball, it took time. My mother's homemade chocolate chip cookies that were so delicious but piping hot out of the oven, I waited, unlike Jimmy, who stuffed them in his mouth, inevitably burning his tongue. Getting back on my feet after my amputation, that was weeks, and to get back to what I could physically do before took even longer. But I put in the hard work. Now, I was attempting to slow time down, wring out every last moment I had with Samantha. Just because this was summer fun didn't mean I wanted it to be forgettable.

Walking upstairs, I was greeted by my mother. "Hey, where are you headed?"

"Out." I jingled my car keys, and when I didn't say any more, she smiled.

"Okay. You think you'll be late?"

"I'm not sure," I said, desperate to get away, though she hadn't budged. In fact, with the way her eyes swept over me, I didn't think I'd get out of the house in the next minute, so I set my feet for her oncoming conversation.

"You know your father and I love having you here. It's been so nice being able to see you every day, I feel spoiled."

I forced a smile, waiting for her point.

"I want you to know you can stay here as long as you'd like."

I skimmed my hand over my beard. "That's nice, Mom, but I'm really not planning on it being long."

"Oh, well..." She shrugged. "I just thought I'd remind you." She squeezed my elbow. "It's been over a year, and I know you weren't planning on it being that long, but that's okay."

I ground my jaw, trying not to climb out of my skin at my mother's sweet sentiment, reminding me once again that my best-laid plans had yet to come to fruition.

"Don't feel like you can't live your life," she continued, completely unaware of how I was sinking in quick sand. "You're an adult, I get it. I was only asking where you're going and if you'll be late out of habit, you know? It's hard to stop being a mother hen when one of her chicks has come home to roost." She laughed at her joke and stretched to kiss my cheek. "I love you so much, honey. Here for whatever you need."

"Yeah, thanks, Mom," I said and clawed my way out of the front door.

I should have appreciated her little pep talk, but it only

proved my failings. Another hit to my ego. The last thing I needed before my date with Samantha.

Outside, I inhaled a cleansing breath and pushed my anxiety about my seemingly unattainable future away before crossing through my yard to next door. I took note of the utility van parked in the driveway and opened the front door. I rang the doorbell, and when I heard hammering from somewhere, I poked my head in. "Sam?"

"Yeah. Come on in!"

I stepped inside and leaned toward the racket coming from upstairs, but a moment later, two guys dragged a rolled-up carpet down the staircase. I moved aside so they could carry it out the front door, Samantha trailing behind them.

"Hi," she said, smiling in a flouncy white skirt and the same peach-colored top she'd worn to the Memorial Day picnic. Between her love of the color, ice cream, and tea, I picked up an obsession.

Funny, because I'd become obsessed with her.

"We're getting new carpet upstairs," she explained, pointing to the two men now loading the carpet into the van.

"So, the house is almost ready, then?"

"Upstairs is, yeah. This floor and the basement still mostly need to be sorted and cleaned."

I glanced down the short hall, leading to the kitchen. It was stacked with boxes. "Do you need help with any of it?"

She squeezed my bicep. "If I do, I'll let you know."

"So, you ready?"

She turned over her shoulder, shouting back toward the stairs, "Dad! I'm leaving!" When her father didn't answer, she flapped her hand absently. "He forgot they were coming even though I reminded him twice, so he's all frazzled up there."

And then, as if they'd heard her, the carpet guys opened the storm door. The first man, probably in his forties or fifties with tattoos up and down both arms, said, "We're finishing up. Planning to be out of here in the next ten minutes or so."

She nodded. "All right. Thanks."

He headed back upstairs, but the second one, who looked to be early twenties, hesitated as he swept his gaze over her. "If you ever need any other work done around the house, you could give me a call." He handed her a scrap of paper with a phone number on it. "I'm pretty handy...with almost everything." Then he winked at her.

I scoffed and reached for her hand. "Ready, Peaches?"

She angled her head up at me, eyes shining with humor. "Yeah."

I kissed her temple and laced our fingers together as we walked to the door, leaving the carpet guy to his daydreams.

Once we reached the sidewalk, she lifted our linked hands. "So, we're here now?"

I unlocked my car with the key fob. "Here?"

"Holding hands, kissing in front of other people?"

I tugged her in front of me, my hands moving to her waist. "I wouldn't call that a real kiss."

"A real kiss?" The sunset behind her highlighted the violet in her hair, and I brushed a few strays away before combing my fingers into it, resting my palm against her cheek. "As opposed to a fake one?"

"Real, like this," I said, curling my hand around the back of her neck, using slight pressure to pull her even closer and tilt her head to the side. After a teasing lick to her lower lip, she opened up for my tongue. She tasted like mint and smelled faintly of chlorine.

"Did you go to the pool today?" I asked against her lips, and she nodded, holding on to my forearms.

"Why?"

In answer, I pinned her against the car, easing my mouth

down her throat, eliciting a soft sound. I knew she loved to swim, and that for a while, she was on the swim team in high school—some peripheral memory informed me of that—but I wanted to swim with her. I wanted to experience as many of the things that she loved while I could.

With one last kiss, I pulled away from her. "Any place special you want to go tonight?"

She fixed her hair, piling it up on the top of her head. "Yeah, but we have to stop at the store first."

Twenty minutes later, I followed Samantha around with a blue basket in my hand. She had picked out organic grapes, a bag of fancy-looking chocolate-covered blueberries, and a sleeve of multicolored plastic cups. Now, she browsed the small wine selection, but I was too busy studying her legs to pay attention to anything else.

Her innocent white skirt landed a few inches above her knees, so that when she bent over, I came close to learning what color underwear she wore. Good goddamn.

"What about this one?"

The question drew my gaze up from Samantha's thighs to her eyes, brows raised.

"It's a little dry. Do you like dry reds?"

I didn't know anything about wine and usually preferred a Budweiser if I had a choice, but whatever she wanted, I'd drink. "Sure."

She placed the wine in the basket and sashayed off toward the cashier. "And if you're going to check someone out, you might want to work on making it a little less obvious, Marine."

"I'll work on it." I placed the basket on the small counter next to the register and emptied the contents for the attendant to scan then went back to gawking.

"You're doing it again. Staring."

"I like to look at beautiful things."

She blinked, seemingly unaware the cashier informed us of the amount owed, and I looped my arm around her to slide my card into the machine, paying for our groceries. I grabbed the receipt and the bag before guiding her to exit through the sliding doors and to my car. Once we were both settled, I reversed out of the parking space with my hand on the back of her seat and left it there as I drove out of the parking lot.

At the stoplight, I turned to her. "You're shy all of a sudden."

"I can't help it. You're really..." She met my eyes. "Intense."

I couldn't argue with that assessment. I was always direct and honest, and when it came to Samantha, I couldn't hide my attraction to her. "Are compliments against the rules?"

She dropped her gaze to her lap for a few seconds. "I guess not."

"You actually have to think about it? Why?"

"Because." She pushed her head back against the headrest and threw her attention out of her window as I drove on. "I've never had to have a conversation about it before."

"And that makes you uncomfortable." It was a statement not a question, because I already knew the answer.

But I wasn't the only perceptive one. "For someone who doesn't speak a whole lot, you say a lot of things."

"I find that you learn a lot more from listening, and usually, people who feel the need to fill the silence don't ever say anything of substance."

She shot me a faux sober look that broke into a giggle. "Always so serious."

I shrugged and took hold of her hand, threading our fingers together. "So, where are we going?"

"The soccer fields off Lincoln Avenue."

I knew the fields she named and made a left. The sun had dipped almost completely behind the horizon, the sky darkening into navy by the time I parked the car. A few birds flew overhead, calling out to one another, and cars passed on the road behind us, but we were alone. Samantha grabbed the bag of food and wine and started out to the slight hill off to the side.

I trailed after her, down to the sloped ground, with nothing but a few empty nets off on the field in front of us and the glow of the half-moon above. The grass was soft beneath the spread Samantha laid out. She opened the bags of grapes and chocolates before unscrewing the cap of the wine. She poured some into two cups and handed one to me. "Cheers."

I tapped my cup against hers and drank the red wine, holding back a wince at the taste.

"Do you like it?" she asked, licking a drop of the dark-colored liquid off the corner of her mouth.

I sucked down another terrible gulp, and she popped a few of the tiny chocolates into her mouth, satisfied in my non-verbal response. "So, how'd you find this spot?"

"A couple years ago, I was driving around and decided to randomly park here," she said after a sip of wine. "I like to come here to think. It's quiet at night."

I caught one of the last fireflies flitting about and held my fist out to her, opening my fingers to show her the glowing bug. It flew up and landed on her shoulder.

"I used to catch fireflies." She watched the insect, its neon glow disappearing for a moment before returning. "Kept them in jars with some grass like a little aquarium or something."

"I know. I remember," I said, thinking about a young Samantha playing in the yard next door while I threw a football through an old tire.

She brushed the firefly away, the loose fit of her sleeve swaying with the movement.

"I like that shirt on you."

She tugged on the bottom of it, stretching the thin, gauzy material over her breasts. "Thanks. I made it."

I wasn't surprised since she'd tailored my suit so well. "Lady of many talents." I plucked a handful of grapes from the vine and offered her one. "Where did you learn how to sew?"

She nibbled on a grape, and it was a long time before she answered. "In high school, I went away to a camp. Sewing was one of the things I learned there."

"I don't remember you going away."

"It was after you enlisted."

When she didn't say anything else, I lounged back on my elbow, admiring her in the moonlight. Her skin shined, wisps of hair that had fallen from her bun waving in the slight breeze. "Was it a summer camp?"

She downed the rest of her wine before refilling it, and I considered saying something about how fast she drank that last cup, but her nervous demeanor held me back.

"It was a residential facility for treatment of eating disorders," she said quietly.

I sat up immediately. "I didn't know. Are you okay?"

"I'm fine now, completely healthy."

I wrapped my hand around her upper arm, double-checking—just to be sure—before stroking up and down her spine. It took me a few seconds until I found the courage to push her on the subject. "What happened?"

She glanced over her shoulder, meeting my eyes for a moment then returned her gaze out in front of her to the night sky. "The usual teenage girl stuff, plus divorced parents."

I shook my head in confusion. Even though her parents had divorced before I'd left for basic, I didn't know what that was like, nor what it meant to be a teenage girl.

"You know my parents argued all the time, right?"

I inched even closer to her until my shoulder brushed hers.

"My dad was never home, and my mom wasn't happy. I suspect they thought having my brother would somehow make everything better. I think my mom assumed my dad would start coming home in time for dinner if there were two kids, like he would start pulling his weight or something." She offered me a small, sad smile. "Lina was always over. My mom said they were best friends, and I think, at first, they were, but it was easy to see it was more than that, even for a fourteen-year-old. And I think my dad suspected something was going on as well, because they started arguing over her too. The divorce wasn't messy. They didn't fight over the house or money or me and Gav... In that regard, it was easy, but..."

I barely held myself back from kissing her pulse point in her throat and settled for placing my hand over hers.

"They didn't speak for about a year after they divorced. They spoke through me, like it was fifth grade, and it was so immature of them. I resented them, hated the whole situation, and I felt a little out of control. Add in the social pressures of high school, and I was ripe for all kinds of mental health issues."

"I'm so sorry," I said because I didn't know what else to say.

"My coping strategy was to control the one thing I could." She looked straight into my eyes then. "I got down to ninety pounds."

I wrapped my arm around her waist, this time not for physical evidence but for reassurance that my Samantha was perfectly well. She was strong and healthy. I couldn't imagine her any other way. I didn't want to.

"Ironically, it's what made my parents realize what they were doing wasn't right. They were both really supportive of me and found an in-patient treatment facility in Cincinnati. That's where I picked up sewing. It was a good way to relate to what my body looked like in reality when I had to make clothes for myself."

"I can't believe that happened." I shook my head, at an absolute loss for words. "And you had to go through all of that by yourself in another city."

This time when she smiled, it was genuine. "I wasn't by myself. I was with other people dealing with the same issues. And the counselors were amazing. They changed my life. It's what I want to do. Help other people in the same way."

I kissed her forehead, dragging my thumb down the side of her face from temple to jaw. I couldn't help what happened to her, but I could certainly understand her battle and what it took to come back to the person she was. In the moonlight, I could see how she blinked back unshed tears. And if I could, I'd take on the entire world, to make sure she never cried again.

CHAPTER TWELVE

Sam

I blotted my fingertip under my eyes. I'd stopped crying over my situation a long time ago, but hearing the sincere emotion in Mike's voice was a little too much to keep inside.

I pressed my head into his neck, breathing in his scent, allowing his arms to completely encompass me, warm and protected. Like nothing could hurt me. His fingers skimmed down my neck before returning to the back of my head, stroking the same path over and over. Every once in a while, he'd kiss my temple, offering me comfort I didn't know I needed.

With one last breath, I pushed away from him. "Your turn. I told my secret. You tell yours."

"Mine isn't a secret."

"I don't know what happened." I understood why he wouldn't want to talk about it, but it seemed there was no line we weren't crossing tonight. "Tell me?"

He relayed his story clinically with a calm voice, as if he had told it so many times before. "We were outside of Mosul, supporting Kurdish troops. We were doing a routine patrol when a car bomb went off, and a skirmish broke out. I got blown back a couple yards and knocked unconscious. I took some shrapnel in my side and got a good chunk of my leg taken out. I was in a coma for a couple of days, I'm told it was touch and go for a while because of the infection in my kidney."

"How long were you in the hospital for?" I asked, remembering when Jimmy had called me to tell me his brother had been hurt. Jimmy had tried to play it off like he wasn't worried, but his jokes hadn't hidden the tremble in his voice, and I'd held it together for him until we hung up. Then I'd cried for the boy I knew and loved growing up, and actually prayed to whatever god would listen to bring him back.

He did eventually come back. Now, here we were, sitting together.

Mike pulled a few blades of grass from between his legs and raised them up, letting them fall to the ground, tiny wisps whirling in the breeze. "A couple weeks, then I flew back out to California with Bianca."

I held back my physical reaction and stayed quiet.

"It was okay for a while, with me and her, I mean. But I'd had a lot of trouble with my leg. I had a lot of therapy appointments, counseling, but I think I'm lucky. I'm better off than a lot of others, which is sick, right? I got off easy. I even went to the White House to receive my medals. And then there are guys who go home physically fine, but mentally—"

He broke off, shaking his head. He didn't have to finish that statement; I had studied post-traumatic stress disorder and knew the statistics. Twenty-two veterans died by suicide every day. It was horrifying that those young men and women couldn't get the help they deserved, but I was beyond thankful Mike did get help and was doing so well.

"Are you okay, though?" I asked, insinuating the question about his mental health.

A long time passed, and he plucked more clumps of grass, releasing them like rain.

"For the most part. I don't remember anything from that day or much after. The problem was my leg. I was in so much pain." He leaned back on his hands. "It was debilitating. I couldn't do anything, I couldn't enjoy anything, and, I admit, I took it out on Bianca. She did try to help."

This time, I didn't stay quiet. "Until she didn't. If she really loved you, there should have been no expiration date."

After a few moments, during which I thought maybe I stepped over some imaginary line, he nodded. "When I decided to get the amputation, my parents offered for me to come back home. I knew I would need a lot of support, so I took them up on it."

"I'm sorry that happened to you, but my offer still stands. I will make her kitchen life hell. Is she one of those girls who likes to bake bread? I bet she is. You seem like the type to be into that."

He huffed a laugh but didn't deny it. I had no interest in baking, bread or otherwise. Although that was of no consequence. We were on a time limit. And I wouldn't be learning how to bake him bread any time soon.

"I'll switch out her baking soda and flour."

"No, that's okay." He dragged one hand over the side of his face, scraping his fingers along his beard. "I'm good."

"What's wrong?"

He dropped his hand. "Hm?"

"You sounded funny when you said that. 'I'm good.'"

"I don't know. I, uh... I don't want you to think I'm struggling with any of this. The PTSD, Bianca, my leg. I'm good."

"You don't have to convince me, but it would be okay if you weren't."

He found my eyes even in the ever-darkening sky. "I was depressed for a while and had a couple of bad months, but I'm in a good place now. I'm not some kicked puppy who needs to be coddled."

"Nobody thinks that."

He let out a skeptical grunt. "Sure they do. With their sad eyes. They act like I can't do anything for myself. Or they don't say anything at all, which is sometimes worse because I know they'll talk about me later." He let out a derisive sniff. "I'm a sad story people tell."

I crawled into his lap, taking his face between both of my hands, my palms against his tense jaw. "Hey, hey. Look at me."

It was a long couple of seconds before he picked his head up.

"You are not a sad story." I smoothed out the lines between his eyes with my thumbs then moved down to his mouth. I traced his top then lower lip, slightly reddened from the wine that he pretended to like for my sake.

If only he could see himself the way I saw him. Strong, patient, and selfless.

"We all have scars," I whispered, closing the space between us. "Some are just more visible than others." Then I softly pressed my lips to his.

A few seconds passed where he let me be gentle with him, but eventually, I wrapped his arms around my waist, forcing me right up against him, and all the sadness I had been feeling vanished, replaced by the contours of his chest against my breasts and his thick thighs under my legs. He was so big he engulfed me, once again taking control of our kisses, our bodies like magnets, our mouths the meeting place. Even when I broke away to let my hands roam over him or when he trailed kisses down to my throat, we always came back to our lips and tongues and whispered pleas.

With his hands holding my waist, he pulled my hips forward to meet his, urging his hard length against me with every roll, and I dragged my fingers through his hair, tugging at the roots.

"More?" he rasped.

"Always."

With a low growl, he rolled me to my back as he hovered over me on his side. The grass was cool beneath me, some patches still slightly wet from the morning rain, and I knew my white skirt would have green stains on it, but with Mike's muscled body over me, I didn't care. I pawed at his shirt, lifting it up enough to find the warm skin of his back, and dragged my hands up and down his spine. I wished I'd paid attention in biology class so I could properly name and worship each of the muscles there.

He nipped at my jaw then soothed it with his tongue. This man was everything, gentle and hard, sweet and domineering. When his touch became too much, his fingers just this side of bruising on my hip, he loosened his grip and stroked up my side to my rib cage, teasing the skin under my bra which had been revealed when my shirt somehow inched up.

"What do you like?" I dipped my fingers inside the waistband of his jeans to skim over the elastic of his underwear. "What turns you on?"

"You turn me on."

"What exactly?" I nudged him until he was on his back, and when he attempted to pull me on top of him, I held on to his wrists. "I'm going to undo your pants, okay?"

He murmured a soft agreement, I unbuttoned his jeans, and together we shimmied them down his thighs, revealing the top of the liner of his prosthesis.

"Is this okay?"

"I'm not made of glass." His voice snapped through the quiet. "Touch me, Samantha."

That was all the direction I needed. Pulling his boxer briefs down, I took him in hand. "How do you like it?" I put one hand on his thigh as I licked up his length of his thick cock, and his muscles shuddered underneath my palm. "Tell me what you want."

"I want you. Whatever you do is—" His words cut off with a moan when I licked over the soft head before taking him in my mouth as far as I could. He combed his fingers into my hair until he hit the elastic. With a quick motion, he yanked it out and dragged his hands through my hair over and over, caressing and authoritative, showing me the depth and speed he wanted. "Like that. Fuck, Peaches, just like that."

I had never liked pet names, but I liked him calling me that in his hoarse voice as he wrapped my hair around his hand.

"Jesus," he hissed. "Sam, I'm— Your mouth is amazing. I'm gonna come."

With one last swirl of my tongue, I twisted my hand up and down his shaft until his back arched, and he finished with a groan, spilling into my palm.

"Fuck," he said again, his breath heavy as he shifted away from me. "I'm sorry, Sam. I don't—"

"Why are you apologizing?" I grabbed a napkin to clean off my hand.

He sat up and scrubbed his hands over his face. "It's been a long time since I was with a woman, and I didn't expect to go that fast."

"I liked it. You're this beast of a man, and I made you come in, like, three minutes. I mean, I'm basically a goddess."

He dropped his chin toward his chest, eyeing me under heavy lids. "If you're trying to make me feel better, you're not."

"Okay." I settled back into his lap. "Then make it up to me, if you feel so bad."

He let out one of his delicious grunts as he squeezed my

sides, fitting me more firmly on his lap as he started to lie back down.

"You *are* a goddess," he said, "and you're mine."

I barely had time to process those words before headlights shone in our direction, and he let out a curse, swiftly moving me behind him. Still dazed, I couldn't quite comprehend what was happening. We were mostly hidden behind the slant of the hill, but he still kept his arm out, shielding me.

The car parked, and he tensed, a panther ready to pounce. I kept my head tucked against his shoulder blade as a couple of car doors opened and closed, followed by some voices. It seemed like whoever they were hadn't noticed us in the grass.

"It's a bunch of kids," Mike said quietly.

In the silence of the summer evening, their raucous laughter was easy enough to decipher, especially when the scent of weed wafted our way.

"Think they're here for medicinal healing," Mike said with a laugh in his voice. He finally moved, dropping his arm, and we both put ourselves back together, righting our clothes, and fixing our hair. He offered me his hand to help me stand so he could swipe at some grass on my butt, and I tossed him a look over my shoulder. He lifted his hands, all innocence and virtue. Then we grabbed our leftovers and garbage, packing it all back up in the bag.

He wrapped his hand around my neck. "You okay?"

"I'm great."

He rubbed the pad of his thumb in a circle below my ear, and even that tiny touch was a little too teasing and certainly not enough after our roll in the soccer field, and I sighed. He must've known why because he said, "Yeah, me too," and then held my hand to lead me back to his car.

"Hey, man. Didn't see you there," one of the kids said as he tried to hide the joint.

Mike waved him off. "Don't worry about it."

The kid nodded and kept the pot out of sight as Mike and I walked past them. It didn't escape my notice that he put himself between me and the group of teenagers. A small detail, but one that lent itself to the type of man he was. Always shielding, even if it was against a handful of kids about to get the munchies.

Once we were seated in his car, he looped his arm around the back of my seat. "One of these days, I'll get you completely alone."

I laughed. I wasn't sure that ever would happen. But damn if I wasn't up for trying.

CHAPTER THIRTEEN

I slapped a tired hand on the table. After yet another Google search on "easy ways to build a website," I swore under my breath. I'd been trying to work on growing my client base, and all signs pointed to better marketing. I needed more of a—or really, any—social media presence, but that was one thing I didn't have patience for. I'd been an officer in the Marines, deployed twice as a specialist, but ask me to introduce myself in a ten-second video clip?

Couldn't do it.

I was confident in my abilities—as Emily said, I was good at my job—but I didn't know how to begin to talk about myself or set up a website that was more than a photo and a few lines of a biography. Although waiting for clients to come to me at the gym wasn't cutting it, and I was never going to get out of my parents' basement at my current rate.

Needing to take a break and stretch my legs, I unfolded up from my cushioned seat and checked my phone one more time. Samantha and I had been texting back and forth all day. She said she needed to help her dad repaint the living room and then run some errands, but when I told her I didn't have any clients today and needed to get out of my house, she suggested

Starbucks. She agreed to meet me. Over an hour ago. The last text was about fifteen minutes ago.

PEACHES

I'm on my way. I swear.

I put my phone back into my pocket and got in line, reading over all the choices for coffee. I wasn't much for these froufrou drinks but did have a hankering for a pastry. As I was about to order, Samantha snuck up next to me.

"Hey."

I stepped back, taking in her flushed appearance. "Where were you? Running a marathon?"

"Something like that." She laughed and turned to the barista. "Can I have a tall vanilla sweet cream cold brew?"

I didn't have any idea what that was, but the young barista with a name tag of Millie tapped it into the register before looking to me. "I'll take one of those blueberry muffins and a medium coffee, please."

"Grande," the girl said.

"Yeah, grande. Whatever."

Samantha snorted beside me as I paid, and I raised my brow at her.

"You're cute when you're huffy."

We moved to the other end of the counter to grab our drinks before heading to the table in the corner for cream and sugar.

"I am not cute. Cute's for rabbits and puppies." I tossed my garbage away and turned to find her fighting to keep a straight face.

"Cute can be for anything or anybody." She sat down at my table. "I think you're cute. You don't think I'm cute?"

Fuck no, she wasn't cute. She was gorgeous.

She was every color of the rainbow.

She was sweet and hot and peaches and chocolate.

"Yeah, you're cute," I said as she wrapped her lips around the straw in her iced coffee, and images from last night poured into my mind. The way she licked and sucked me had been an out-of-body experience. I was a boiling frog. I hadn't even known my orgasm was even building until it consumed me.

But she'd merely smiled and lifted her shoulder, all proud of herself. And damn if I didn't find *that* cute.

Too bad those kids showed up before I could repay her.

I let out a big exhale and slumped back, putting some much needed space between us to clear my head. I sipped my coffee and nudged my muffin toward her. "So, where were you that took so long?"

She broke off a piece. "I saw there was a sale at Ulta, and I ended up getting a makeover."

"Ulta?"

"It's a makeup store. I don't normally wear so much, obviously," she said, gesturing to her Black Keys T-shirt and cutoffs, like she wasn't up to snuff.

"You look pretty." The makeup around her eyes was a dark purple-gray color with long, curling lashes, and her lipstick was a tempting dark berry. "But you always do."

She smiled shyly as she swallowed her bite of muffin. "Thanks. I wanted to get something special for my trip."

"Trip?"

"To Los Angeles."

I'd forgotten about the bachelorette trip. "Oh yeah. When do you leave?"

"Thursday."

Thursday? As in the day after tomorrow. There went my hopes for the weekend. "What does this big bachelorette bash consist of?"

She dropped her chin in her hand, mindlessly stirring her

drink. "The usual, I guess. Short dresses, strong drinks, and big dicks."

I choked on my muffin and coughed a few times. She leaned across the table and patted my back. "You all right?"

I nodded and coughed again, following it with a few gulps of coffee. "Say that again?"

She sat back in her seat, grinning like she didn't knock me sideways. "Which part? The dresses, drinks, or dicks?"

I eyed her, unsure of how to play this. Clearly, she was out to have all the fun she could, and it wasn't as if I could stop her. But I couldn't help that I didn't like the idea of her going away, all made-up with the long eyelashes and the pouty lips, to find some "strong drinks and big dicks." Sure, it was all bachelorette fun, and yet...

"Is somebody jealous?" she teased.

"No."

She tilted her head back and forth flirtatiously. "Sounds like you are."

I hated that I was and that she could tell.

"I'm not." I pushed away my half-eaten muffin, appetite gone. "I don't care what you do. It's not like we're together or anything."

The smile fell from her lips, her eyes dipping down to where her index finger scratched at a dent in the table, and I was such an asshole. I'd been in a foul mood all day because of my business stuff, and the LA thing put me over the edge. "I'm sorry, Sam. I didn't—"

"It's fine." She took a breath and lifted her head, meeting my eyes straight on, and she was so much braver than I was. Putting herself out there again and again. And I acted like a dick in return.

"You're right. We're not together, so... You're right." She pushed away from the table. "I gotta go. Laundry's calling."

I mumbled a few words of apology as she grabbed her things. She didn't look at me as she looped her purse over her arm, and for once, I was happy for her to go. I needed some time to myself and let her walk away.

No use dragging her down with me.

CHAPTER FOURTEEN

Sam

I hung up my new purchase next to my trusty old black cocktail dress. The sparkly gold number wasn't something I'd normally choose, but when the girls had texted pictures of what they were packing, I had decided to step up my fashion game. Looking at it now, though, I second-guessed myself. It was loose-fitting with geometric patterned sequins, yet even the 1980s genesis of Cher would find the hemline risqué.

Then again, we were going out in LA. It wouldn't be *that* scandalous.

With a shake of my head, I put both dresses in my suitcase. "You can decide later," I said to myself, kneeling on the floor to fold up a few tops and jeans and approximately a dozen pair of underwear. "It's three days, you maniac. You're morphing into Bronte—"

"Do you have an imaginary friend I don't know about?"

A gasp leaped from my throat as I dropped back on my butt in fright, spying my intruder. "Mike." I sagged in relief. "I didn't hear you make a sound."

He didn't move from his stance, leaning against the door-frame. "Good to know I'm still as stealthy with half a robot leg."

I refused to smile at his attempt at a joke and moved back to my position at my suitcase, double-checking my toiletries. I wasn't purposely ignoring him—I couldn't, not with his large presence—but I didn't want to give him any more attention. Not after yesterday.

I hadn't meant to go and catch feelings for him, but I couldn't pretend this was my usual habit. Mike was unlike any other guy I'd ever been with, and the time we spent together wasn't purely physical. We had opened up to each other and took turns showing off the broken and jagged bits of our hearts before sewing ourselves back together with kisses and caresses. Despite how hard I'd tried, I had let my guard down and he'd practically waltzed inside, so for him to be so flippant was hurtful.

Even if I didn't want it to be. Even if I knew that this tiny pain now would be a whole lot worse in a few weeks.

"How'd you get in here?" I asked, keeping my attention on my suitcase.

"Your dad."

Ugh, the traitor.

"Can I come in?"

"Sure." I still refused to look at him, fearful of giving myself away. I already gave too much, thinking I could kiss him and keep my feelings separate. But that was idiotic. To me, Mike hung the moon and stars, he always had and maybe he always would, but he could also wound me. Yesterday proved it.

"Here." He dropped a plastic bag at my feet as he sat down across from me. "I thought you might need it for your trip."

I held up the small bottle. "Sunscreen?"

"Heard it's pretty sunny over there."

"Thank you." I tucked it away and reluctantly met his eyes. Eyes that were so much softer today than yesterday.

"I came to apologize."

I tried to glance away, find solace somewhere else, but something in his gaze held me, called to me. "For what? There's nothing to apologize for." The words didn't feel right on my tongue, but I didn't want to lose any more of myself to him. To this. And when he appeared ready to dispute me, I stopped him. "You said it, and you're right. We're not together. There's nothing to apologize for."

"No?" He raised an incredulous brow, his body shifting toward me almost—*almost*—imperceptibly. His reserved, nice-guy persona was gone, replaced by the sizzling tension flowing from his body to mine. A familiar crackle between us. "There is something I need to apologize for."

"Oh? Hmm."

"I lied to you when I said I wasn't jealous. I was. I am."

Good god. What was it I was supposed to do? Be strong? Ignore him?

Every fiber in my being felt on edge, my skin already on fire, and he hadn't even touched me yet. "That's not—there's nothing...no. There's nothing for you to be jealous of. Right?"

With his hands on the floor, Mike moved forward a few inches, crowding my space. I swallowed, a helpless fawn hunted by a wolf.

He curved one palm around my ankle. "I am under no illusions here, Peaches. I know you are much better at this than I am."

I swallowed, shaking my head infinitesimally. Because, no, I was not better at this than he was.

"But I can't help it. I am jealous of every guy who will get to dance with you, flirt with you, see you in those dresses. I'm jealous of every person who gets more minutes with you than I do."

I breathed out slowly, afraid if I made any sudden moves,

he'd stop. And I didn't want him to stop. I needed his rasped words to be true. To be real.

With his hands smoothing around my knees, up my outer thighs, he dropped his voice even lower. "I want you to go and have fun on your trip. I want you to dance and flirt, and while you're drinking the drinks guys will buy you, I want you to remember what my hands feel like on you. How you squirm with my mouth on your neck."

His fingers played with the soft cotton of my lounge shorts, his touch and words winding through my chest, bubbling up too many feelings. And I barely held back from confessing that I could never forget, that I never wanted to, despite what he may think.

Taking control, I slipped into his lap, no longer the prey. He gripped my hips with a rough squeeze, and I took that as an invitation to push him down to the floor, crushing my mouth to his. He tasted like cinnamon, and his lips felt like heaven, sucking and prodding. Under my fingers, his muscles tightened and released as he tugged at my clothes.

"I'm sorry, Peaches." He kissed across the shoulder he revealed when he pulled over the collar of my T-shirt. "I don't know what I'm doing, and I can't stand the thought that I made you upset."

"I'm not upset." I held myself over him, absorbed with his flushed cheeks and the spark of heat in his dark eyes.

"I was in a bad mood yesterday," he explained. "I shouldn't have taken it out on you."

"What happened?" I asked, but when he seemed like he wanted to skim over it, I stopped his hand from inching up to the clasp of my bra. "Tell me."

He grunted a noise of disagreement, but whatever it was he saw on my face—maybe the fact that I wasn't going to drop it —made him give up. He guided me to lie on the floor next to him, tucking me up against his side, and ran his hand over his face a few times before dropping his hand on his sternum. I covered it with my own hand.

"I wasn't going to college," he started after a while. "I wasn't good at school. I didn't like it, so I knew I didn't want to be an academic, but I didn't know what else I wanted to do. Or what I could do. You know? I was an athlete. When the recruiter came, the Marines seemed like a good deal. I could have a career in the military, that's what I planned for. The long haul, maybe...I don't know, a position in the government or something. I'm a team player by make." He turned to look at me, a faint curl to his lips that I traced with my index finger.

"I know," I said.

He moved his attention back to the ceiling, and my finger slipped to his jaw and beard. I instinctively rounded into him, offering silent support when his throat bobbed a few times, like the next words were difficult. "I was a good service member, which feels weird to say. I was taking and giving orders. I was good in combat..."

I hid my grimace against his neck. He didn't need to finish that sentence. I wasn't sure if I could truly hear him say it.

"It was my job," he said, his words a little sturdier. "And most days had nothing to do with fighting or war or shuffling us around like we were playing chess. But the days when I did... my job...they were hard."

His voice broke on the last word, and I laid my head on his chest, his heart *thump thump thumping* under my ear. He brushed a big hand through my hair a few times, and I could hear and feel how his pulse settled down.

"We helped people. That was what I focused on. We were training Kurds to be able to defend themselves. We weren't always on the offense. We gave them supplies. I was helping people," he said as if to remind himself.

"I know." I kissed his chest.

"When people find out I served, sometimes they want to shake my hand and thank me, and I never know what to say. I did my job. You know? People don't shake the hand of the guy working at the gas station or the woman serving our coffee. Everybody is doing their job. I was doing my job. I don't need a handshake."

When he didn't say anything else, I lifted up onto my elbow. "That's why you were in a bad mood yesterday?"

"After my first contract was up, I knew there was nothing else for me, so I reenlisted. I didn't have any other skills besides what they taught me, and I thought I'd retire from service. But now..."

I palmed his jaw, forcing him to finally meet my gaze.

"I'm trying to make a living the best way I know how, and I'm failing at it. I could lead a United States Marine battalion, but I can't figure out how to get people to like my Facebook page. I pulled people out of the rubble of a building, but I can't even get enough clients to fill my week."

His eyes bounced between mine. So dark, so intense, so hardened, and he didn't want or need meaningless words of praise. He wasn't a *You can do it!* kind of guy. So instead, I did the thing I was good at. "How can I help?"

"I don't know." He let out an exhausted breath. "You know how to code a website?"

"I don't, but my friend Laney is a marketing guru. She might have some tips or know someone who can do it for cheap. Do you want me to talk to her?"

I could physically see him swallowing his pride after a minute. "Yeah." He sat up. "I guess." But before I could respond, he went on, "What time do you leave tomorrow?"

"Flight's at eleven."

He stood up, pulling me with him. "Me and my brothers

are going out for dinner tonight, but do you have a ride to the airport tomorrow?"

"I was going to get a Lyft."

"I'll take you."

"Okay." I smiled, and he kissed my cheek.

"I'll let you finish up. I just wanted to come by to apologize. I didn't mean to..." He gestured to the floor as if his guts were spilled there.

"I'm glad you did."

He offered me one more kiss on my lips, infinitely sweet but much too short, before backing away. "Text me later. Let me know what time you want to leave."

———

The next day, I met Mike out on the sidewalk.

"Lemme grab that," he said, reaching for the small suitcase. "All set?"

I smiled my thanks and got into his car, buckling my seat belt. Behind the wheel, Mike paused the small movement of putting the key in the ignition. "Is that my shirt?"

I plucked at the white V neck, practically a dress with the sleeves reaching down to my elbows. I'd knotted it at my waist. "Uh, yeah." When he cocked his head to the side, that single eyebrow with the slash through it raised, I tucked my sunglasses on my head, pretending my whole body wasn't going up in flames. "Remember, like, two weeks ago, when your mom made ribs, and Jimmy and I came over? I got barbecue sauce on my shirt, and you gave me this to put on."

He took me by surprise when he leaned over, tugging my chin between his fingers to press his mouth to mine. His lips were always so soft, the softest part of his body, and I didn't hesitate to wrap my hands around his neck, pulling him to me.

He was so big yet so gentle, and with a stroke of his tongue to my lower lip, he pulled back, resting his forehead against mine.

"Hi."

I breathed out a laugh. "Hi."

He shifted back another two inches and cleared his throat. "I don't know what that was about. Some kind of Cro-Magnon gene still hanging around inside me that really, *really* likes you wearing my T-shirt."

I lifted a shoulder. "I like wearing your T-shirt too."

After one more kiss, he turned the ignition over. "What're your plans while you're over there? Besides all the drinks and dicks."

"That's pretty much it, I think."

He tossed me a heated look, one that made promises as well as threats, both of them delicious.

"The dancing will be totally PG, and I'm not planning on bringing anyone back to the house."

He grabbed hold of my hand, twining his fingers with mine.

"Bronte said Chris hired us a personal chef for the weekend, so I'm going to eat my face off."

He kissed the back of my hand.

"And maybe we'll watch some horrible movies."

"No *Twilight*," he said sternly. "You can't watch the last one without me."

I bit back a smile. "I won't. I promise."

We may not have had a lot of time, but we had this. These moments together when he kissed the back of my hand, when he returned a smile, when everything didn't seem so hard.

At the airport, he got out and grabbed my suitcase from the back seat. "Have a safe flight."

"Thanks."

He wrapped one arm around my waist and bent down,

kissing my jaw. "And when you get there, don't do anything I wouldn't do."

"Well," I said, giving his biceps a squeeze, "you haven't done all that much, so..."

He guffawed and swatted at my butt when I turned away from him. "Have fun, Peaches."

"See you when I get back." I offered him a wave over my head, excitement fluttering deep in my belly at the way he watched me, yet I forced myself to face forward. I had my best friends to get to.

Eight hours and one layover later, we were all together again. Screeching and hugging and dancing. Gem arrived with her new pixie cut, Laney brought a bag of *Golden Girls* tumblers, and Bronte had a penis tiara.

Chris and Bronte's house in Studio City was gorgeous, relatively small for the outrageous real estate but with a perfect outdoor space. Twinkle lights hung from the trees over a stone patio that was big enough for a matching set of table and chairs, and the pool, of course, was heated, so at nine o'clock at night, we took full advantage.

Chris had taken care of everything. He had hired private transportation and a chef for the entire weekend, gave each of us a hug before he kissed Bronte and headed out the door for a quick movie shoot upstate.

"Only three weeks," Bronte informed us as she refilled her Rose tumbler. "It's a small arthouse film, at least that's what Chris said. I still don't understand what arthouse means."

"French?" Laney suggested from her perch atop a unicorn floaty, holding the pink cup with Dorothy's face on it.

"I was going to guess a movie that's not big budget," I said, munching on a chocolate-covered strawberry, my Blanche cup in the holder of my inflatable lounger.

Gem laughed. "So, not good?"

Bronte flicked her with water. "Hey!"

Gem covered the top of her Sophia tumbler so as not to get water in it as she slipped off her inner tube to head over to the side of the pool, to the plate of vegan treats made especially for her. "Your fiancé really does spoil me."

"He spoils everybody," Bronte said, all dreamy.

Laney raised her glass. "And we love him for it."

"You haven't changed your mind about bringing Willow to the wedding?" Bronte asked Gem, who shook her head. "You know he spoils her the most. He was hoping you'd bring her. He wanted to get her a little flower girl dress."

I polished off the last of the chocolate-covered strawberries. "But you guys aren't even having groomsmen or bridesmaids."

Bronte pointed at me. "Exactly."

Gem snorted. "How 'bout I put her in a box and ship her to you guys for a few weeks so me and Jason can catch up on sleep and sex?"

"Chris would love that."

Gem slammed an imaginary gavel. "Done!" Then she tipped her chin to Laney. "How about Bobby? Is he coming?"

Laney kicked her feet, riding her unicorn toward the snacks. "He would never miss a party."

"So, everything's good?" I asked.

"Yeah, he's been extra affectionate lately. Spending more time at home than at the restaurant. We're good. How about you?" She aimed her cake pop at me. "How's your Marine?"

"He's not *my* Marine."

"No?"

"Why have we not gotten any pictures of him yet?"

"About that," I started. "He's a personal trainer, and he's struggling to build his business. I told him you might be able to help him out?"

Laney nodded absently as she grabbed her phone from the edge of the pool. "What's his last name?"

"For what?" I asked.

Laney kept her attention on her screen, thumbs tapping away. "Stalking."

"Obviously," Gem added.

I chucked an ice cube at Laney and missed by a mile. "He's not on social media a lot."

"Good for him," Bronte said, her vowels becoming a little longer, her head tipped back up to the night sky.

"That's why he needs help," I finished.

With her gaze still down, Laney asked, "What's his last name?"

"Oh!" Gem lifted her fist in triumph. "I know. It's...something animal-sounding, right?" She snapped three times. "Jimmy did tell me back then. It's... What's the name of a baby cow?"

I rolled my eyes. "Calf?"

"No, that's not it." She waved like she was scrubbing down a whiteboard. Clearly, the alcohol was getting to everybody.

"Veal?" Bronte suggested.

Gem slapped her hand down on the water. "I meant calf isn't his last name."

"Dear Jesus." I poured myself more champagne.

"Found him!" Laney held up her phone, beaming. "It's Ewing!"

"Ewing!" Gem hissed like she thought of it. "Record time. Excellent work," she said, giving up her Sophia tumbler and drinking straight from the bottle.

With her attention still down, Laney asked, "But Ewing, what animal is that?"

"A ewe is a female sheep," I told them.

She shrugged. "Whatever. He's got an Instagram."

126

"He does?" Besides our short conversation the day before, Mike and I had never discussed social media or traded handles. Better to have as few attachments as possible.

"Mike Ewing, 259 followers," Laney said. "Well, now sixty."

"What? No! Don't follow him." In my haste, I fell off my raft with a splash in the water, and by the time I came back up, Laney had already passed off her phone.

"He's cute, Sammy."

"Aww, look at the one with his brothers. They all kind of look alike except for their hair. That one's Jimmy, right?"

"Yeah, he was very sweet. Remember he was going to school to be an elementary school teacher?" Gem said to Bronte, and then to me, "I assume all three brothers are good people, huh?"

"Yeah." I attempted to grab the phone from Gem's hand, but Laney got it instead.

"Ha, look. He followed me back."

"Oh my god." I covered my face with my hands. "He's going to know we were talking about him."

"So?" Bronte reached for my abandoned float. "You did ask Laney for help. Of course we're talking about him."

"Yeah, but not, like... That's... It's not... I don't..."

Laney pushed her index finger to the center of my forehead. "Power reset."

I slapped at her, and Laney's laughter echoed around us.

"You know, it's okay to admit you have feelings for the guy," Bronte told me.

Gem had her phone out too. "Followed."

"I don't have feelings for him," I said.

"Sure you do." Gem saluted me with the champagne. "Coming from a fellow commitment-phobe, I get it. And it's okay. It's scary, but the first step is admitting your feelings."

I stole the bottle from her. "Har har."

Bronte gasped in delight, folding her hands together. "You should invite him to the wedding."

"Absolutely not."

"Why not?" Laney stepped out of the pool and went into the house through the sliding door, leaving it open so she could yell, "A few days on a private island to have your wicked way with him, why wouldn't you?"

"I haven't had my wicked way with him yet."

"You haven't?" Gem asked, holding out her phone screen so we could see the photo on it. It must have been from a few years ago. Mike wore fatigues, his muscles on display with his tight green shirt.

Laney returned with what looked suspiciously like my phone. "That's not like you, Miss Hit It and Quit It."

"We've done other stuff, though," I rushed out, covering my tracks. "And don't you dare, Delaney."

"Too late." She grinned and tossed the phone to me, my Instagram up to Mike's profile. I was now following him. "Ah, shit." I downed some champagne as an alert came in that @mewing417 followed me back.

"Well, come on. Let's give him something to look at. Smile, Sammy." Laney held her own phone up, positioning it for a selfie of the four of us.

Gem with the champagne bottle high in the air.

Bronte in the midst of hiding the light-up penis tiara.

Me shaking my head.

And Laney grinning.

CHAPTER FIFTEEN

I lounged in my bed, staring at the ceiling. Samantha was scheduled to be home tomorrow, but my impatience made it impossible to sleep. Especially after I repeatedly flipped through her social media posts. In an unexpected turn of events, as I was watching TV late Thursday night, my phone had gone off with multiple notifications. I had new followers on Instagram, someone named Delaney Hargrove, who had thousands of followers and looked like a movie star, another named Gemma Mitchell, who mostly posted information about a yoga studio and vegan meals, and finally, Samantha. Obviously, they were her friends, and as much as I enjoyed that her friends were now sort of my acquaintances, their photos were cruel.

I couldn't stop staring at them, at Samantha's smile. There were the pictures of the group hugging at the airport, of them laughing as they popped champagne, another of them all lounging around a pool at night, and one of Samantha in an aggressively short gold dress with her brightly colored hair curled and lips painted red. I'd gone back to that one again and again.

I tried to avoid the videos of her taking shots and dancing

with random guys, but some masochistic tendency had me studying her posture to see how comfortable she was. I visualized other men with their hands on her hips, her legs, her ass, and heat pooled in my chest. It was absurd to feel like I had some kind of claim on her. But there it was.

Totally absurd.

My phone buzzed with a text, and I picked it up, shocked someone was contacting me so late. And even more shocked that it was my Samantha.

> **PEACHES**
> Still up?

> Yeah.

> **PEACHES**
> Isn't it 3 am there?

> Yeah.

> **PEACHES**
> Man of many words.

> Why aren't you out partying?

> **PEACHES**
> We were but somebody figured out who Bronte was AKA CJ Cunningham's fiancée and Gem got a little loud with them so we decided to come back. Bronte's asleep, Gem and Laney are eating tacos, but I'm pretty sure they're both going to puke them back up.

I liked that she talked to me as if I had any idea who Bronte, Gem, and Laney were. Like she was inviting me into her life.

> You're not drunk?

> **PEACHES**
> A little. I wanted popcorn and my PJs.

What are you doing now?

PEACHES

Texting you.

Smartass.

PEACHES

I'm in my pajamas and eating popcorn. Obvs.

I've been looking at your pictures.

Are your pajamas as hot as that gold dress?

A minute passed before her reply came through.

PEACHES

I guess. If you think a shirt with a weird yellow stain on the front and old Pitt sweatpants are hot.

God, she was perfect, and I sunk farther back into my pillows.

You paint a good picture.

She sent a photo of her legs clad in said sweatpants with her bare feet on top of the comforter.

Is your hair up or down?

PEACHES

Down.

Bra or no bra?

After a minute in which my imagination ran absolutely wild, she finally responded.

PEACHES

ARE YOU SEXTING ME RIGHT NOW?

I laughed.

You were the one who said I haven't done much. You tell me.

PEACHES

I've never done this before. I'm not sure what I'm supposed to do.

All you have to do is tell me bra or no bra.

She finally responded after an eternity.

PEACHES

No bra. Or underwear either.

It was easy to picture the flush of Samantha's skin, probably a little bit nervous, maybe a lot excited.

PEACHES

What do you wear to bed?

Nothing.

PEACHES

Poor thing. You must be cold at night.

Guess she wasn't so nervous after all.

You could keep me warm.

PEACHES

I could.

You'd have to take your clothes off too

For body heat

Even in the dark with the air conditioning blowing, my body automatically warmed from our exchange, and I dragged one hand over my face and throat, resting it on my chest.

PEACHES
OK. Mine are off.

Your clothes?

PEACHES
Yes.

I wish I were there with you so I could feel you.

PEACHES
Say something else.

I'd kiss you.

She sent me another photo. This one of her bare legs, her thighs cut off at the bottom of the picture. Fuck, she was killing me.

PEACHES
Kisses are nice but that's it?

I let out a soft sound from the back of my throat. Tomorrow couldn't get here soon enough so I could actually show her.

I'd kiss your lips, your throat, the tiny birthmark on your shoulder.

PEACHES
You noticed that?

I skimmed my hand down my stomach, imagining her with me now.

I notice everything.

I'd lick you there then move down to your tits.
Do you want me to lick or bite them?

It was a minute until she responded, and I visualized her plucking at her nipples. Doing the exact same thing I was, touching myself.

PEACHES
Both.

Would you moan for me?

PEACHES
Yes.

I'd move your hand to my cock so you could feel how hard I am for you.

PEACHES
I'm so wet for you.

My breath sped up, my grasp on my phone loosening as I rubbed my thumb over my tip.

Are you touching yourself?

PEACHES
Yes.

Fuck. You're killing me. Tell me what it feels like.

PEACHES
So good.

Touch your clit.

Are you squirming? I want you squirming under my hand.

A few moments later, another picture arrived. This one of her hand on her pussy, her fingers hidden. I hissed, trying not to come, wanting to make it last even if she was on the other side of the country.

> I'd pinch your nipples and suck on your skin until you came all over my hand.

I stroked myself faster as I tried to focus on typing out my next message.

> Then I'd lick your pussy.

> I bet you taste delicious. Like fresh strawberries in the morning.

> So sweet.

> You're so sweet. So hot.

Imagining her wetness on my lips, on my tongue, I panted, giving up the game of texting as I rubbed myself off. I closed my eyes, fantasizing Samantha was next to me, on top of me, below me, until warm spurts hit my stomach. I groaned and picked my phone back up.

PEACHES

> You made me come. You're so good at this.

I needed a moment before I responded, grabbing a tissue to clean myself off.

> Did you make a sound? Or did you stay silent?

PEACHES

> A little sound.

Desperate. There was no other word. I was desperate for this woman.

> I can't wait to make you scream.

PEACHES
> My flight gets in at 7:30 tomorrow night.

> I'll be there.

I didn't want her to second-guess my intentions, so I laid them out there.

> My mom will be at her book club, and my dad has bowling. They'll both be out.

I hated that I was like a kid, sneaking a girl into my house, but I had no other choice.

> Come home with me for a few hours?

PEACHES
> Yes.

CHAPTER SIXTEEN

Sam

As soon as the plane had landed, I checked my phone to find a text from Mike, informing me he was at baggage claim. I'd had the most fun with my girls, eating, drinking, and sunning ourselves into stupors, but after my dirty texts with Mike, I couldn't wait to get home. Couldn't wait to see him in person.

That was why when I spotted him leaning against a pillar with a baseball hat on, I took off at a quick clip.

"Hey," he said, a smile blooming as he reached his arms out for me. I nearly jumped into them.

"Hi."

"How was your weekend?"

"Good." I spoke the word into his shoulder.

"I feel like I lived it with you. Your friend posts a lot."

I smiled against his collarbone before lifting my face to him. "Laney? That's the one I told you about. She said she'd contact you to see how she could help."

He turned his hat backward before curving his hands around my throat, gentle yet possessive as he pivoted my back was against the cement pillar. "Yeah? Well, her stories kept me well-informed of the colors of your bikinis. My favorite is that flowered one with the little ties at your hips." When I raised one teasing eyebrow, he lifted an unrepentant shoulder. "I did take a break from studying that picture to work out and grab lunch with Jimmy."

Then he lowered his mouth to mine, kissing me like I'd been away for three years instead of three days. With his fingers tilting my jaw up, he coaxed my lips open, sliding his tongue against mine. My teenage dream come to life.

I slid my hands from his forearms to his biceps when he backed away, and it took a moment for me to be able to focus on his grin.

"Hey," he said again.

"Hi."

He gave me another quick kiss then righted his hat. While we waited for my suitcase, he asked me to tell him about the girls. I described Gem and Jason's backyard wedding last year, vegan barbecue included, and informed him that Laney had earned a sports scholarship to our university but lost it when she suffered a compound fracture in a softball game and needed surgery, and how Bronte was a middle school teacher, determined to keep a low profile, no matter that she was about to marry an Oscar-nominated actor. When I handed him my phone with a picture of the whole group, including Jason and Chris, his brows drew together slightly as he took it in. "That's everybody, huh?"

"We don't get to see one another a whole lot, so when we do, we're pretty glued together. Jason and Chris are basically best friends now too."

He handed the phone back to me. "Seems like a good group. You're lucky to have them."

I stuffed my cell into my back pocket and fiddled with the ring on my middle finger. "You have a group of friends like that?"

He shook his head, his eyes on the luggage carousel, his jaw set beneath his beard. "By the time I'd come home, the people who used to be my friends had moved away or moved on. I have my family, my brothers. That's enough."

I had to bite the inside of my cheek to keep from telling him he had me too. Because I was leaving soon. There was nothing I could do or offer to make him feel more at home after being away for so long. And before I could formulate any other response, he moved away to grab my suitcase. "Let's go."

Once we were back to our neighborhood, I didn't need to question what was going to happen next, but I did need a shower. Taking my suitcase from his hand, I said, "Give me ten minutes, then I'll be over."

His beard was sandpaper over my cheek when he rasped his words in my ear. "One second more, and I'm coming to get you."

Tingles spread out from my belly, and I didn't waste one more moment. Darting inside my house, I waved to my father on my way upstairs, where I didn't bother to put anything away. I spared just enough time to throw my hair up into a bun and rinse off from the day of travel before tossing on leggings to go right back downstairs.

"Hey, where are you going? How was your trip?"

I backtracked from the front door, leaning my head into the kitchen. Dad sat with his laptop open at the table while he fiddled with papers filled with charts and lines of data.

"The trip was great, and I'm going next door."

"To see Mike? You've been spending a lot of time over there lately," he said, his eyes never drifting from his work. I shrugged anyway. "Okay, well, I'm going to bed soon. I've got to get into the lab early tomorrow to get some work done before the surgery. I'll probably be late most nights too." He glanced up at me then. "Okay?"

Of course now that he was divorced with his kids out of the

SOPHIE ANDREWS

house was when he checked to make sure his long workdays were okay. "Yeah, sure."

He lifted one hand. "Have a good night."

I headed out the back door and crossed through the gate into the Ewings' backyard, finding their back door locked. I lifted the flowerpot from the stoop, the one which hid the key, and opened the door. "Mike?"

"Hey, yeah," he answered from somewhere in the front of the house. He strode into the kitchen. "I was expecting you to come to the front door. How'd you get in?"

"You think I don't know where the key is hidden?"

"I'll have to tell my parents they need to change the locks."

I circled my hands behind his neck. "That means you don't want me coming over to surprise you?"

He squinted, pretending to think on it. "Depends on the surprise."

Then I raised up on my toes and kissed him. This time, it was a little more frantic, a little less welcome-home, and a lot more hurry-up. "Wait, Peaches. Hold on," he said, when I nipped at his bottom lip. "Do you want something to eat or drink or—"

My nails scratched along his scalp as I dragged him back down to me. I'd waited for this long enough.

He let out a delicious grunt and gripped my waist to lift me onto the kitchen table, settling between my open legs. Gliding his hands up my sides, he kissed the spot where my neck and shoulder met. "I want to make it good for you."

"It will be," I said, barely a whisper.

"Everything we've done so far..." His words trailed off into more kisses up my neck.

"Mm-hmm."

Everything we'd done so far had been great, but I could feel something holding him back.

"What is it?"

"I haven't had sex since before..." He backed away to meet my gaze, and it took a few moments for me to understand. "You might need to be a little patient with me."

"Patient," I repeated. It wasn't exactly something I was known for, but I'd been patient this last month. Figuring out how to make it good not only for me but for him, too, seemed like an adventure, not a problem.

With his dark eyes searching every inch of my face and his hands coming to rest on my throat, I had nowhere to go, nowhere to hide. It was as if he could see right inside me.

"I want to make it so good that at the end of the summer, you won't want to leave."

I tried to laugh, but it caught in my throat. Instead, I swallowed down my fear of becoming attached—although that was a lie; I already was. I just had to figure out how to get away —and met him halfway when he leaned down to kiss me.

"You planning on making it good on this table?" I asked between kisses.

He stepped away, tugging on my hand until I hopped off the table. "Gross, Sam. Super unsanitary."

"Hey." I smiled. "I don't know what you're into."

"You." He smoothed his hand down to squeeze my ass. "I'm into you. Now, get downstairs. We've got an hour until my parents come home."

I skipped away from him, laughing. "Exactly what every woman wants to hear."

He grumbled something I couldn't hear under his breath as he followed me down the steps, and I immediately stripped off my T-shirt and leggings. At the bottom of the staircase, he stared, mouth open as I stood with my hands on my hips in only my bra and underwear. I was no longer afraid of what I looked like. I was confident in my curves or, rather, lack thereof. One particular boy in ninth grade, Dillon Miller, said I had the body of a tree trunk, the same size from top to bottom. Well, fuck Dillon Miller.

Because Michael Ewing couldn't keep his eyes or hands off me.

"Come here," he said, reaching for my ribs, his lips at my neck. He'd become an expert at kissing me, and I was breathless by the time he skimmed his fingers over my bra, unsnapping the clasp so the straps fell from my shoulders. He didn't hesitate to bend, sucking one nipple into his mouth as he toyed with the other, and my knees almost buckled.

"You like that?" He breathed over my wet skin and moved his mouth to my other breast until I was practically liquefied in his hands. "I can't hear you."

He stood up, a dare in his eyes, and I shuffled backward to his bed, brushing loose hair from my face. "I'm sorry, I couldn't hear *you*. My blood was rushing in my ears."

With a cocky grin, he stepped in front of me. "Good. You want more?"

I shook my head. "I want to see you." He removed his shirt and allowed me to look my fill. From the full sleeve of tattoos, to the few faint scars on his side, to the ridges and lines of muscle he was beautiful, and I told him so.

He ignored me and sank down to remove his shoes and pants, leaving him in his boxer briefs and prosthesis. We both looked at it and then at each other. If he wanted an answer from me, I didn't have it.

"Whatever's more comfortable for you." I leaned over, leaving little kisses over his shoulder and neck as he sat staring straight ahead for a long moment.

Then all of a sudden, he had my back on the mattress, and all I could see was him over me, his face smiling down at me like I was his favorite thing in the world. "We'll have more chances to experiment. Right now, I need to fuck you the best way I know how."

"Well, I guess that sounds all right." Though my giggles quickly died off as he covered my nipple with his mouth again. Whether it was his insecurities or him simply trying to make it really, *really* good for me, he spent time learning each part of my body. The sensitivity of my breasts, the lines of my rib cage, the ticklishness of my elbow, the curve of my thigh, he spent endless moments adoring each and every part of me.

He slowly lowered himself down between my legs, and I gasped when he licked the flat of his tongue up my center. The way he curled his arms around my thighs to keep me open to him, the scratch of his beard in my most delicate places, the slight pull of his lips as he sucked on me until I was writhing beneath him, it was all so, *so* good. He added one then two fingers, twisting and pulling every ounce of pleasure out of me until my orgasm crashed over me.

I gripped his hair, trying to tug him up to me, but he didn't stop. He kept on going, tucking his shoulders against the bottom of my thighs, making a home between my legs, and I mumbled a string of words that I had trouble deciphering to my own ears.

"I can't hear what you said." He hummed against me, sending shock waves up my spine. "Please keep going? Don't stop?"

I thrashed around, all coherent thought long gone. "Fuck!" I shouted, my skin hot and covered in goose bumps. "Yes, keep going!"

Tongue and fingers and teeth and whatever it was he was doing, I didn't want him to stop.

He didn't.

Minutes passed. Hours. Centuries. I didn't know how long it was until he finally let up, my body ragged and spent.

"I love the sounds you make. Better than I imagined." He settled over me, and I tasted my salty slickness on his lips when he kissed me. "Up on the edge of the bed. On your hands and knees."

I followed his orders, scurrying to the side of the mattress as he grabbed a condom. Then he was behind me, his hands, warm and callused, guiding my hips back to him. He let out a gruff sound and teased two fingers over my opening before sliding into me, and I didn't have any more words as he filled me over and over. Merely sensation and indulgence and everything I'd ever wanted.

"Touch yourself," he panted, his breath coming out in short spurts. "I'm not going without you."

Holding myself up with one hand, I slipped my fingers between my legs, where he thrust into me, slick and hot.

"Come on," he said, like he couldn't stand it anymore. "Come with me."

I circled the pads of two fingers against my clit as he held on to me with a bruising grip, his exhales loud, his thrusts hard and hastening until I was adrift in an ocean of ecstasy.

Nothing had ever felt so perfect as his hands on me, his breath on my neck when he towed me up against him, his gruff voice in my ear, "I know you won't forget this."

He was right. I'd never forget this.

CHAPTER SEVENTEEN

Clomping footsteps on the ceiling knocked my brain awake, and I shifted, lifting my head from where it was tucked against sweet-smelling skin. Forcing my eyes open, I blinked a few times, realizing Samantha was still here, sleeping soundly, her violet hair splayed out on the pillow, the small divots of her spine curved toward me, my arm underneath her.

"Peaches." I shook her hip under the bedsheet.

We hadn't meant to fall asleep, but after we'd had sex, we'd agreed to watch the last *Twilight*. She had thrown on my T-shirt while I completed my nightly routine of removing and cleaning my prosthesis. She watched and asked questions, and I couldn't help but compare her to my ex.

I had thought I was going to marry Bianca. I'd planned on proposing once I'd gotten back from overseas, and I'd still thought I might when she had been there at my bedside at the VA hospital, but then our relationship slowly devolved. Some people liked to tell me "things happen for a reason," presumably because they assumed the platitude would somehow comfort me. It did not. Yet maybe there was a silver lining, in that it taught me things about myself I never would have discovered without going through all that trauma.

I was stronger than I imagined.

I learned what true gratitude meant.

I also learned my worth. That was the hardest lesson to absorb. I was still working on it, though every moment with Samantha showed me Bianca was wrong. I was more than my injury, more than a struggling veteran, more than my bad days, and more than my good days.

I was deserving of the kind of life I wanted for myself and of a love that was not in spite of but because of. An in sickness and in health kind of love. A life that was full and worth more than anything which could be measured.

And last night was one more example of how I was still learning that lesson. Because after Samantha had settled in my arms back in my bed and smiled up at me, laying her hand on my residual limb, we lounged together in easy quiet. Although I wished our time together never had to end, and I knew it would hurt when she left, it was worth it.

Any second with her was worth it.

"Sam, wake up." I checked the time. It was almost eight in the morning. "We have to get up."

She breathed deeply, turning over to face me, and I kissed the corner of her mouth. She was sweet all the time but especially in the morning, tousled and warm. Recalling our conversation from the ice cream shop, I ducked under the covers, kissing a line down her belly until she woke up.

"Mikey?" Her voice was groggy, and I had to laugh at the nickname. I didn't hate it, but that's what everyone called me when I was a kid. I wasn't a kid anymore. I was a man, and she was certainly a grown woman.

"I'm here." I spread my palms over her hips, gently holding her down to kiss the creases of her thighs and warm skin between them.

She moaned, wiggling under my hands. "Good morning."

I licked into her, now knowing how she liked to be teased with the tip of my tongue against her slit until she couldn't stand it anymore, her legs trembling against my ears. "You have to be quiet," I said, reaching one arm up to her breast, rolling her nipple. "Or I'll have to stop."

Her legs immediately dropped to the mattress, though the tension thrumming through her body continued, and I used it to my advantage, stroking with my tongue and playing with her nipple until she came against my mouth, shuddering silently. Moving back up, I let the sheet drop and licked up her throat to her ear. "Good girl."

She wrapped her arms and legs around me as I wound her hair around my finger. "My favorite treat in the morning." I nipped at her jaw. "Sweet and juicy."

She shivered beneath me. "Keep talking like that, and I'll never leave this bed."

"I wouldn't mind."

"Michael, I need you to empty the dishwasher and mow the lawn today!" Mom called. My parents were good about giving me space, never coming downstairs without being invited, but they also expected me to pull my weight, do chores like I did as a teenager. And, of course, always interrupted me at the *worst* of times.

"Got it, Mom!"

"See you after work!"

Samantha snorted a laugh against my chest, and I silenced her with a kiss.

"I don't know," she said when I finally let her up for air. "I guess it's kind of like role-playing, right? Two kids sneaking around behind their parents' backs."

"No. We are absolutely not playing that game."

She grinned like the Cheshire cat, winding her arms around my neck. "But you will play *a* game?"

"When I know we won't be interrupted by pizza rolls, kids getting high, and house chores. Now, come on. Time to get up." I patted her side before rolling off her to put my prosthetic on, but I got sidetracked as she grabbed her clothes from the floor.

With her bra and underwear back on, she dragged her T-shirt over her head and stepped into her navy leggings. Fully dressed, she tilted her head to the side. "What?"

"Nothing."

She approached me slowly, dragging her fingers over my shoulders. "You're staring again."

"I told you. I can't help it."

"It's creepy."

"You don't mind when Edward Cullen does it."

She combed her fingers through my hair. "I thought we agreed that particular detail was creepy." She tugged at the roots. "Don't smile like that. I can't be properly grossed out by your leering."

I grinned wider, pulling her into me between my open legs, and kissed her stomach through the cotton of her shirt. "Thanks."

"You're thanking me? As if I did you some big favor." She almost sounded offended. "I have dreamed of this since I was thirteen." When I lifted one eyebrow, she backtracked. "Well, I didn't exactly know what oral sex was back then, but yeah." She giggled, and the sound lodged in my chest. I didn't want to let her go but forced myself to after a few more strokes of my hands over the backs of her thighs and kisses underneath her shirt.

She stepped away from me, wagging a flirtatious finger. "Don't thank me. Just tell me when the next time will be."

"As soon as possible."

She kissed my cheek then wiggled into her flip-flops and grabbed her cell phone on the way upstairs. I'd barely gotten to the bathroom and turned the water on before my little brother came storming down the steps.

"Did I just see Sam doing the walk of shame?"

I took my toothbrush out of my mouth. "Don't call it that."

"But that's what it is. You fucked her."

"Don't say it like that either."

Jimmy threw his hands up and spun in a tight circle. "What the hell, man? I told you not to—"

"First of all, Sam is an adult. She can make her own decisions. Second of all, don't come here acting like I'm some asshole who wouldn't treat her right. You honestly think I would hurt her?" With a roll of my eyes, I bent over the sink to brush my teeth.

"I don't know. You never... She isn't... It's not..."

I spat into the sink and glared at my brother.

"You know I don't think you're some asshole," Jimmy said, adding quotation marks over the word. "I'm a little surprised, is all."

I finished brushing my teeth then splashed water on my face. "Why are you here anyway?"

"To work out. You forgot?" When I glanced at my brother with one eye closed, water dripping from my nose and eyebrow, he lifted his finger accusatorially. "*You* forgot."

It was true. I'd clean forgot. With Samantha in my bed, I lost track of time, space, my whole being. How was I supposed to remember a workout with my brother when she stole every last bit of my rationality the night before?

Though, I gave it quite willingly. My head and my heart.

And I was fucked.

"Sorry." I brushed past Jimmy to rummage through my drawer for shorts and tugged them over my boxer briefs.

"So, you guys really did...?" He gestured to the unmade bed, the pillow on the floor, the comforter long gone, and the sheet slung around the bottom corner of the mattress.

I didn't answer. I didn't need to.

I began to set up the workout area, and after a few moments, Jimmy followed, setting his water bottle down by the bench. "So, you like her?"

A minute passed, a minute I needed to measure my emotions and words before I paused in adding a plate to the bar. I met Jimmy's eyes. "Yeah, I like her."

He scrubbed his hands down his shorts. "Okay, good." He held up his forearm. "But don't hurt her."

I bumped my forearm against my brother's. "I don't plan on it."

CHAPTER EIGHTEEN

Sam

I paced the length of the kitchen, holding my cell phone out in front of me, typing and deleting **SOS** three times. I wanted to tell the girls, wanted to unload everything about last night. I needed to squee about how tender Mike was with me, and yet how domineering he could be. There was no good reason not to excitedly type it all up, every last detail about how, after we had sex, he'd tugged me down next to him and I didn't fight him. I wasn't a cuddler, but I didn't mind, not with him. He had taken off his prosthetic to get more comfortable, and we had squeezed in close together. I didn't mean to fall asleep, though it didn't take much.

And then this morning. God, I was desperate to tell some-one, anyone—even a stranger on the street—about how perfect it was. And still...

If I spoke the words out loud, that would make them true. I'd have to admit to not only myself, but to someone else, that I didn't know how to do this. I'd done the easy, uncomplicated hookup thing so many times before, I could write a book on detachment. And nevertheless, I was lost with Mike. Lost in a sea of emotion, uselessly paddling against the current.

I had eight weeks until I left for Texas. There was no time to be sentimental. No time to explore what these feelings meant. Hell, I didn't even know how to start facing these feelings. Or if I wanted to.

This was supposed to be fun. Short-term fun.

Grasping for something to ground me in this spiral, I checked the time on the microwave, 8:32. Gem was an hour behind, Laney and Bronte three hours out in California. Even if I did text them, they probably wouldn't get back to me right away, so I did the next best thing. I clipped Eddie's leash on and took him for a walk. When that didn't clear my head, I grabbed my bathing suit and drove over to the local YMCA. I normally swam laps when I couldn't get out for a walk, but I needed a little more time to myself to sort it all out.

With every stroke, I told myself I could do it. I had faced difficult challenges before; having a quasi-relationship with Mike was no different. If I could come back from a crippling eating disorder, I could certainly have a fling with a six-foot slab of muscle. It was only my heart on the line.

Not an important organ.

I simply had to keep my cool, stay in control, and when our time ended, I'd say goodbye and move on. No problem.

Stepping out of the pool, I wrung out my hair, more determined than ever to keep my guard up. But when I got back to the locker room, I found multiple texts from the girls on my phone.

LANEY

Everybody see the Marine posted a thirst trap?

LANEY

Guess he took my advice.

GEM

Your advice?

LANEY

I told him he needed to start posting pics of him working out. Show off the goods, show his possible clients he's good at his job.

LANEY

Plus, you know sex sells.

Gem sent a series of eye emojis.

GEM

I'm looking respectfully.

BRONTE

Screenshot it.

I actually gasped when Gem sent a screenshot of Mike's post and then immediately opened up Instagram to see the real thing. There it was, his very first thirst trap. With Laney and Gem both leaving comments like the turds they were. But there were other comments too. Some of spicy emojis, some saying how brave he was—whether they meant it for his service or his prosthetic leg, I didn't know, but either way, it had me rolling my eyes.

I enlarged the photo, bringing my phone close to my face as if I could somehow sink into the post. He had taken the picture in a full-length mirror. Turned on a slight angle, each shadow and curve of his physique on display, his sleeve of tattoos like the marks of a warrior.

With his head tilted, the tiniest hint of a smile, and a smattering of dark hair on his chest, he looked like a god. I'd never paid much attention in my undergrad antiquities class, but if I had, I'd be able to name him the god of strength and power, sensuality and desire. For now, I supposed I would settle for calling him my own personal hero.

So much for keeping that guard up.

> **BRONTE**
>
> For someone not adept at social media, he excels at the gym selfie.

> I blame all of you for this.

––––––

This neighborhood used any excuse to throw a block party, but the Fourth of July was the biggest one of all. There were more people, more food, and generally more shenanigans. Mr. Tadashi brought sushi from his restaurant and laid it out on the table in the shapes and colors of the American flag. Nancy, the cougar from down the street, made Jell-O shots, and she was doing a pretty good job of getting drunk on them by herself. Octogenarians Mr. and Mrs. Winston had their whole family over, two kids, four grandkids, and three great-grand-children. And, of course, Jimmy was running the activities schedule for the day. He had arrived earlier with a printed-out sign-up sheet for teams and a championship cornhole bracket. Winners got an actual trophy.

"All right, you and I are up," he said with a light back-handed smack to my arm, after two younger women I'd never seen in my life lost their game to Adam and Amelia. For a preschooler, she had a pretty good arm, and the two strangers, whom I assumed were Nancy's daughters, were too busy danc-ing, drinking, and snapping selfies to take down the four-year-old.

"Who do we got?" I asked, setting down my water. I wasn't any better at cornhole than beer pong.

He rubbed my shoulders like he was warming up a major league pitcher. "Albie and his friend Ernie."

"Ernie?"

He grinned and bent down to whisper, "I think his real name is Tim, but he's tall with a unibrow. You know like Bert and Ernie."

Sam bit the inside of her bottom lip to keep from smiling. "I get that Albie is short for Albert, but Bert was the tall, unibrowed one. Ernie was the short one with hair."

With his hands on his hips, Jimmy sighed up at the sky. "I knew I should have partnered with George."

"Hey!" I hip-checked him, and he threw his arm around me, losing his fake exasperation.

"The point is, Samantha, we could definitely take a couple of Muppets."

"Yeah," I agreed, although this was only the first round. Even if we beat Bert and Ernie, I still had to get through the semi- and quarterfinals. "Sure."

"You got this." He pushed a red beanbag in my hand. "Easy touch, huh? Keep it light and loose."

"Light and loose," I repeated before tossing my beanbag way off the mark and nowhere near the board.

"It's okay. It's all right." He hopped on his toes a few times. "You just need to get warmed up."

Opposite us, Albie landed his beanbag on the board before Jimmy took his shot, sinking it. But then Tim whiffed it too, so it wasn't a completely lopsided game.

Jimmy and I squeaked out a win to advance to the semifinals, and the four of us shared a good-sport drink while the next two teams took our spots. Mike and Mr. Ewing and Mr. and Mrs. Lindenbaum faced off as I slowly sipped a margarita.

Mike wore a baseball hat again, and it shadowed his face, but when he tilted his head toward me, the corner of his mouth ticked up in acknowledgment, and I offered him a wave of my pinkie as I raised my glass to my lips. He did the same, lifting his beer bottle to his mouth.

"Right, Sam?"

I blinked away from Mike to Jimmy. "Huh?"

"The year something went wrong with the fireworks and the guy went to the hospital with third-degree burns. What was that? Four, five years ago?"

"Oh, uh, five, I think."

Jimmy went on to tell the story about how the guy came back to continue working on the firework display the next year, building it bigger and bigger each consecutive year. As if he had something to prove.

"It's crazy," Jimmy said, but I couldn't pay attention. Not with Mike's T-shirt clinging to his biceps and back.

We hadn't been able to see each other all week outside of walks and him helping me move boxes up from the basement. It was pretty impossible to be intimate in my childhood bed with my dad in the kitchen and in Mike's basement apartment with his family coming and going all the time, and his mom making dinner for anyone and everyone who dropped by.

I had been waiting to get him alone again, but that was clearly not going to happen at this picnic.

With my mind's eye on Mike's naked body, I was jolted back to reality when Jimmy stood up with a clap. His voice carried far and wide so everyone in attendance could hear him say, "And with that last match, the first round concludes. We'll start the semi-finals in fifteen minutes." Then he held up the printed paper to read aloud, "The two Taylors are up against Bill McCarthy and Dave O'Donnell. The twins up against the Irish mafia, should be a good time!"

Everyone laughed and went back to whatever they were doing, while Jimmy scooted out from behind the table to rearrange the cornhole boards, making sure they were perfect. For as much as he was a clown, he used his powers for good.

"Hey, Peaches," Mike said, taking his seat next to me.

I flicked the bill of his cap a few centimeters up to meet his dark gaze, suspiciously mischievous. "Hi."

"What do you say to a little wager?"

"A wager?"

He nodded, glancing briefly to Albie and Tim, who were busy watching a video on Tim's phone.

I crossed my legs so that my knee brushed Mike's. "What do you have in mind?"

"Whoever's team makes it farther wins?"

"And what's at stake?"

He raised his slashed eyebrow. "Winner's choice."

I stared off in the distance, petting an imaginary beard in thought. "If I win..."

He leaned into me, skimming the tip of his nose over my shoulder, bared by my paisley-print romper. "If you win, what?"

I swallowed, forgetting what I had in mind. Something about Cedar Point. "I'm not sure."

He hummed thoughtfully and sat back up. "Well, if I win, you're coming to bed with me."

I played with the strap on my left shoulder. Under his attention, even the thin spaghetti strap seemed suffocating. "That's not much of a loss for me."

"For what I have in mind..." He lifted one shoulder.

"What?" I squeaked out the question. "What do you mean, what you have in mind?"

He squeezed the back of my neck as he stood up. "Guess you'll have to find out later."

"If we lose," I amended.

He cocked his head to the side, as if the thought had never occurred to him. "If you lose. Shouldn't be too hard."

Then he walked away, crouching down to Amelia, who ran full steam right into him. He lifted her up with one arm and hung her over the back of his shoulder as she shrieked with laughter. Oh god, I had already lost.

But I'd put up a damn good fight.

CHAPTER NINETEEN

Pink and lavender streaked the sky as a crowd gathered around the cornhole platforms for the championship. At stake was a trophy, bragging rights, and time alone in my bed with the woman staring at me while she tossed a beanbag back and forth between her hands.

"We've come to the end," Jimmy said, waving his arms in an arc. "It is now down to the reigning champion of cornhole —" he pointed to himself "—and the man who created him, along with the man who's tormented him," he finished, gesturing to our dad and me.

"Hey." Samantha punched Jimmy's arm. "What about me?"

"And Sammy has come along for the ride," he added quickly and almost incomprehensibly to the laughter of the group, Sam included. Jimmy threw his arm around her shoulders. "Let's hear it for this one, the smartest person I know with the worst throwing arm. But she makes a damn good teammate."

There was a smattering of applause, and Jimmy held his hands out to his waiting audience. "As per usual, the winner's names will be added to the trophy." He hoisted it up to show the crowd. "Lo! Since this tournament began, yours truly has been on the winning team every year. That's four years in a row. Shall we make it a fifth?"

The small crowd applauded, while I, along with Adam behind me, booed. Dad laughed, elbowing us, while Mom had her camera out to capture every moment of the final game.

"Amelia," Jimmy said with a flick of his finger toward Adam's daughter, who held up his cell phone, blaring the *Rocky* theme song as she danced around.

With one last round of laughter, everyone simultaneously backed away a few paces while Jimmy and Samantha took their place across from me and Dad.

Jimmy leaned over, whispering something in her ear, to which she nodded a few times. Then he smacked her on the back and jabbed a finger at me. "You're done," he mouthed.

"We'll see," I said loud and clear, so everyone, including Jimmy's fawning fans, could hear. Then I met Samantha's eyes. I had big plans for her and was confident I would win.

Until she tossed out her first bag, and it inexplicably sailed into the hole. Jimmy hooted in glee. Clearly, while I'd been off eating hot dogs, she'd been getting much better at cornhole.

"Oh, it's like that?" I asked, shaking out my throwing arm.

"It's okay, Mikey, we got this," Dad said and clapped me on the back.

I tossed my beanbag and barely missed the hole.

"Oof, on the outside," Jimmy taunted.

I shifted on my feet. This wasn't going to be an easy win anymore. My brother was anxious to continue his winning streak, and I'd obviously underestimated my girl.

My girl.

What the fuck?

As if she could hear my thoughts, she blew me a kiss before

extending her middle finger. Apparently, my girl could be competitive when she wanted to be.

Ironically, on Jimmy's first toss, the arrogant little shit's beanbag skidded across the platform and landed on the ground with a perfect plop.

"What is that?" I cupped my hand around my ear. "The sound of my name being scratched onto the trophy?"

Jimmy kicked at a patch of grass as our father took his turn, his beanbag also landing outside of the hole on the board. On Samantha's next turn, she flickered her eyes to me before tossing her bag. It hit the board with a resounding smack, and she smiled up at me as she met Jimmy's high five.

The round finished with a cornhole from my brother, tying our scores. And as per Jimmy's rules, the teams switched sides, and I brushed my fingers along Samantha's as we passed each other.

"Tease," she mouthed when she got to her spot. If she only knew. When I won, I'd be teasing her with much more than a simple drag of my index finger over her hand.

The next round progressed much like the first, with a lot of trash-talking and very little movement to tip the scales to a winning team. After switching sides yet again, Samantha hit another cornhole, raising the score to 14-12.

"When we win, you're going to post a thirst trap in a pair of my shorts," she said, loud enough that everyone in a half-mile radius could hear, earning a few snickers from the lingering crowd, although most had lost interest, going back to their food or sparklers.

"You placed a bet on this?" Jimmy asked, his head swiveling between us. "Well, damn. That's why you've suddenly got an arm," he said to her. "Is that all I've needed to do this whole time? Put a wager on Mike for you to start trying?"

Her head popped up from where she'd been screwing the cap back on her water bottle. "You know…" Her eyes darted to me and back to Jimmy, and even though I couldn't fully hear it, I watched her lips form the words. "You know about him and me?"

Jimmy angled his body to face Samantha as they spoke, and I took the opportunity to score another three points. I didn't know what my brother and his best friend—*my* girl—were saying, but I didn't care. I had a game to win and a woman to get naked.

"Hey, James, let's go!" Dad shouted. "We're burning daylight here!"

Jimmy nodded and pivoted away from Samantha, acknowledging that we had to finish this game before the sun set completely, extinguishing our light. Although, I couldn't wait. The closer it got to dark, the sooner I could sneak away and collect my prize.

Hopefully.

On our next tosses, I sank my shot, while Samantha's landed on the wood. I wasn't even paying attention to my brother or father anymore because I couldn't take my eyes off her, playing with one of her earrings and toying with the end of her ponytail. Her head seemed completely out of the game, so as we switched places the next time, I held on to her wrist, leaning down to her ear. "When I win, I'm going to tie you up and smack your ass. How's that for a tease?"

She turned her honey eyes on me, alight with flirtation. "Oh yeah?"

I nodded, letting her go so she could continue to the board, walking backward.

"I don't know. Sounds like a win to me," she said with a cheeky little shoulder raise.

I swiped my palm over my mouth and beard as I took my place opposite her.

"Okay," Jimmy said, bouncing on his toes. "Let's finish this, Sammy."

With her gaze on the ground, the corner of her mouth threatened to tick up into a smile, and she bit into her bottom lip to keep it from blossoming. I didn't hide my grin as I watched her mentally make her decision. It was so obvious. At least to me.

"Yeah, sure," she said and lined up to take her shot, arm jutted out behind her on an angle, so that when she followed through to release, the toss went wild, the beanbag landing a yard from the platform. "Oops."

"*Oops!*" Jimmy threw his arms out. "We had a tie game, and we have to win by two, Sam. What are you doing?"

"All right, all right," Dad said, and I nodded, holding my hand up to my brother. I wasn't above knocking him around.

"Yeah, it's cool."

Sam twisted her face away, evidently no longer able to hide her smile.

Jimmy growled as I took my turn, hitting the board this time, but it didn't matter.

I was going to win. Because Sam was going to throw the game.

––––––

I didn't wait for the fireworks to start before I made my way to Samantha's table, tracing my knuckles across the back of her shoulder for her attention. She startled, wielding her red, white, and blue popsicle like a weapon when she whirled around to me.

"Come on," I whispered, trying not to draw attention from

Amelia, who sat next to her, juice from her own popsicle dripping down her skinny arm.

"Now?"

I nodded. We'd have lots of time with how long this fireworks show would take.

She chanced a glance at Amelia and then at everyone else. No one was paying attention, and she slipped out of her chair, dropping her half-eaten popsicle in the trash on the way as she clasped my outstretched hand.

Down in the basement, I immediately hauled her to me. Her lips and tongue tasted sweet from her popsicle, and I imagined what it might taste like to lick drips of it off her skin. With that thought lodged firmly in my brain, I tried and failed to get her clothes off. "How the hell do you get this thing off?"

She laughed against my mouth, but I didn't find it funny. We had about forty-five minutes, and there were no buttons or zippers on this thing.

"Here." She backed away from me, slipping a tiny strap over one shoulder and then the other. "It's a romper."

"I don't care what it's called. Take it off."

She shook her head at me, a shadow of a smile on her lips as she shimmied the outfit down her torso and over her hips before kicking it off, leaving her in a black strapless bra and underwear. I outlined the barely there line of lighter skin that wrapped up over her collarbones and behind her neck, evidence of her weekend in California. "So, you were planning on putting me in your shorts if you won?"

A shiver racked her body as I moved my hands down her arms to curve around her hips, and she nodded. "Since you're such a big fan of posting thirst traps."

Sliding my index fingers under the thin cotton of her panties, I skimmed my knuckles back and forth over her hip bones. "I wouldn't say big fan."

"Oh." Lifting one shoulder, she puckered her lips into a perfect pout. "Maybe it's me. I'm the big fan."

A burst of laughter from my chest surprised me, and I smoothed my palms over her ass and thighs in languid circles, inching her closer with each pass. "I only posted two, at Laney's directive."

She held on to my waist, curling her fingers into my shirt. "I wasn't sure you'd really follow through."

"One thing about me," I said, leaning in to kiss her throat. "I always follow through." When she shivered again, I kissed the corner of her mouth, but she didn't answer, and I repeated my promise from earlier. "I'm going to tie you up and smack your ass. Okay?"

Though she nodded, I shook my head, needing to hear her voice. Hear her say yes. I backed away three steps, and she swayed toward me as if she needed me to keep her upright. Holding on to her shoulders, I asked again, "Okay?"

"Yeah. Okay."

I let my right hand drift down her arm, dragging the tip of my finger over her bicep and the curve of her breast, along her bare stomach, to her thigh. I smacked it lightly. "Okay?"

With a dare in her eyes, she pressed her chest against me, lacing her hands behind my neck. "Okay."

But when she slanted up to kiss me, I broke her hold to find my fuchsia tie in my closet and some rope from a giant tub in the back, where I stored random tools and home improvement items. I held them up to her. "Which one do you want?"

She tried on innocence. "Winner's choice."

"How about both?" I asked.

She was an angel and a devil, all sweet-looking, yet had that wicked shine in her eyes. "Both?"

"Both."

She bit the corner of her bottom lip, smothering a smile. "Okay."

"Over there." I nodded toward my mini gym. "Hands out."

She offered me her hands silently, and I began to wind my tie around her wrists. As I worked, I could feel her attention on me, and when I pulled the bind tight, I met her stare.

"I didn't expect you to be so…"

Using my hold on the tie, I led her to one of the vertical bars, tying her hands to it. "So what?"

"Efficient," she said on a breathless laugh.

I gave her butt a little squeeze, following with a smack. I might not have had sex with a lot of women, but that didn't mean I didn't know what I was doing.

Standing behind her, I tugged her hips backward until her back was almost flat. When she wiggled her ass, I gave it another smack, harder this time, and she sucked in an audible breath. I soothed my palm over her skin before running my fingers down the back of her leg. "I'm going to tie your ankles to this bench."

She responded by gazing over her shoulder at me, wetting her lips. My blood pulsated through me at the desire in her eyes, at the trust she placed in me. I moved the weight bench so it was in front of her and pushed her underwear down her legs, helping her to step out of them. I stuck them in my back pocket and used the rope to bind her ankles to either end of the bench, keeping her legs straight and spread open.

I worked in silence as the fireworks blasted outside, though they didn't bother me too much. Down here with Samantha, the sound dulled, even though I could still feel them echo in my chest. Then again, maybe that was my heart hammering against my ribs at the vision of this woman giving herself to me.

"If I do anything that you don't like or—"

"I'll tell you," she said then offered me a soft smile. "But I know you won't hurt me."

"Never."

Her grin spread to one that lit up her eyes as she lifted her head as much as she could for a kiss. I bent down, meeting her delicious mouth. "You can be as loud as you want," I told her. "No one will hear."

She moaned against my lips when I skimmed my hand over her shoulder and down her back to undo the clasp of her bra so it fell away from her body. With her completely naked, I dropped kisses up and down the column of her spine, keeping her relaxed and pliant. She arched her back like a cat, letting out a low moan, and I reached between her legs, drawing two fingers down her pussy. And I almost moaned too. "You're so wet already, and we've barely started."

She shifted restlessly, her hips swaying side to side. "I can't help it."

"Maybe I can." I circled her ass with my hand before spanking one side.

She rocked forward slightly and peered over her shoulder at me. "Again."

As if I was planning on denying her. "Yes, ma'am."

I spanked her again then reached over to tweak her nipple.

"Oh fuck," she mumbled, her eyes closed.

"What did you say?" I smacked her backside and twisted her nipple at the same time, eliciting a groan.

"Oh fuck," she said louder.

I bent to place a kiss on her shoulder, murmuring in her ear, "Good girl."

She laughed, tipping her head to the side to meet my eyes. "I'm a modern independent woman. Why do I find that so hot?"

I scraped my teeth on her shoulder blade, right over the

167

phoenix. "Because maybe you're used to being so strong all the time, you want to be taken care of for a little while." Then I smacked her, leaving my palm on the warm and slightly pink skin. "Huh?"

She pressed her hips up and back against me. "Maybe."

"So," I said, dragging my other hand back to her breasts, massaging one and then the other. "Maybe you should be a good girl and let me hear you."

Another tweak, another smack, and she hissed out an affirmative.

I alternated spanks and caresses to her ass while toying with her nipples until she was panting, begging me to fuck her.

When I teased two fingers down her slit again, I found her practically dripping. "Peaches, that name is fitting for you."

"The fireworks are going to be done soon," she reminded me, bringing me back to reality, and I stuck my fingers in my mouth, sucking her taste off them before grabbing a condom from one of my drawers. She watched me over her shoulder as I unbuckled my belt and pushed my jeans and boxer briefs down, her eyes glued to my cock.

"You ready?" I asked, rolling the condom on.

"Yes."

I gave my length one tug before stepping between her legs, lining myself up at her entrance to slide inside her wet heat.

We both groaned, and I gripped her hips to steady myself as I thrust into her. The reflection in the full-length mirror showed her breasts sway with each forward rock, and I was desperate to touch her there, but I didn't want to let go of her, fearing I'd lose my balance. Tightening my grip on her, I blew out a sharp exhale, trying to remain in control, but with the image of her eyes screwed tight, her face tipped up, mouth open, releasing those sounds—her perfect, tantalizing sounds —I felt myself unraveling.

With every thrust, I was losing more control and more of myself to her. I wanted to give her everything. Anything she wanted, I would be. And for now, she said she wanted, "Harder!"

"You feel so good. So fucking good. And this ass," I gritted out in between breaths and squeezed her sweet backside. "Fuck, I'd do anything for it."

Her hair fell out of its ponytail until it completely obscured her face from my view. Outside, the fireworks boomed faster and louder, and I guessed they were coming to the finale. But so were Samantha and I.

Under my hands, tension coiled in her muscles as she threw her head back, letting out a string of incomprehensible words, and I bent over her, the air filled with her scent, my mind adrift in the feel of her as a flash of heat washed over me with my own climax, and I let my weight drop onto her back. She was warm, and I pressed my cheek against her skin before kissing her.

"Your beard scratches," she said, her voice a mixture of amusement and exhaustion. I stood up, dragging a lazy hand down her side. I let go of her with a light pat to her thigh and took care of the condom, putting myself back to rights before undoing the tie around her hands and the rope around her ankles. Taking a seat on the bench, I wrapped my arms around her waist to sit her in my lap, massaging her wrists and fingers.

"Are you sad you missed the fireworks?" she asked, fixing her hair.

"Not a big fan of them anymore." I realized I revealed more than I meant to with those few words, according to her frown. The pops and bangs were still a little triggering for me, but being with her took my mind off them. And before she could offer any concerned words, I curved my hand over of her breast "Besides, you're my fireworks."

She lost the sympathetic glow in her eyes as she narrowed them. "You need to stop."

"What?"

She shook her head again and stood up. "Don't say things like that, okay?"

"What do you mean?"

She bent over to pick up her clothes, and I ignored my instinct to comment on how much I liked the view of her ass in my face. "Don't say stuff like that to me. I'm leaving in less than two months."

"I don't..." My words evaporated from my tongue. I couldn't lie and say I didn't know what she was talking about. This was supposed to be a summer fling, a few weeks of fun, so I couldn't tell her the truth. I couldn't tell her that every day we spent together was more than fun. Each minute we spent kissing solidified my feelings. Each of her smiles made me brand-new. I couldn't tell her she was brighter and bolder than any firework, and that I would give up anything to have a little more time with her.

She put her bra back on and searched for her underwear. I had them stuffed in my pocket, but I didn't want to give them back. If I had to hide my feelings, I might as well keep something for myself. With a quiet curse, she gave up the hunt and slipped her romper back on, towing it up her legs and over her torso, covering all the skin I'd had my hands on minutes ago.

"Well," she said, not meeting my eyes. "I guess I'll talk to you later."

I kept my hands to myself as she kissed my cheek. She clearly wanted out as fast as possible, and I wasn't going to ask her to stay when she so obviously didn't want to. She was the one holding up our end of the bargain. I wasn't.

Less than two months, and she'd be 1,300 miles away.

CHAPTER TWENTY

Sam

The following week, I helped Dad into the house, his crutches catching on the doorframe.

Holding the door open with my hip, I kept one arm on his back and the other out in front of him in case he fell. "Eddie, out of the way!"

"I'm fine. I'm fine." He had repeated that sentiment every time I'd asked how he was doing since the moment he woke up from the surgery.

I nudged Eddie with my foot. "Yeah, but..."

Dad finagled his crutches over the lip of the door and limped his way down the hall toward the kitchen. "I'm hungry."

"Okay. You need to take your pills with food anyway, so what do you want? I can make something or order take-out or—"

"Sammy," he said, sounding a little out of breath—the walk from the car to the house was evidently pushing it—and he plopped down with a grunt in one of the kitchen chairs. Eddie sat next to him, tongue lolling to the side as he put his head on Dad's thigh for a pat. "You've done enough. Go do something for yourself."

I grabbed a dish towel and wrapped it around one of the ice packs in the freezer. "Here. Twenty minutes on, twenty minutes off."

"Samantha," he said again, this time with a little more annoyance. "I know. I don't need you keeping watch over me like I'm a child."

"I'm not wa—"

"I know you think my head would fall off if it weren't attached, and maybe that's true, but I got a knee replacement, not a lobotomy. Please leave me be." He pushed his glasses up his nose. "Go take the dog for a walk or, I don't know. Go do something that isn't waiting for me to fall over."

"I'm not waiting for you to fall over. I just want to make sure you have everything you need."

"I'm fine." He waved me off, shifting a little in his chair as he reached for the tiny succulent on the kitchen table, fiddling with the leaves. "I'm fine."

I didn't think I was hovering, but now that he pointed it out...maybe I was. I had stayed overnight at the hospital, but not because I was worried about my father. He was fine. Grumpy but fine. I stayed because I didn't want to be left alone to my own devices.

In the days leading up to the surgery, I had kept myself busy. I'd made sure to remove all the rugs in the house so they wouldn't impede my dad's mobility post-surgery and turned the living room into a makeshift bedroom. Plus, all the fussing had the added benefit of being able to avoid Mike.

Since our little Fourth of July escapade, I hadn't had the courage to face him. Or my growing feelings for him.

Instead, I played Florence Nightingale. To the aggravation of my father.

"All right. Come on, Eddie!" The dog danced around my legs. "You want a walk, buddy? Let's go to the park."

By the time we strolled down to the end of the block and around the corner, two familiar figures appeared, jogging toward us. Running back to my house was a bad idea, it would look too obvious as an avoidance tactic, but at this point, I wasn't sure I could play it cool either.

"Hey!" Jimmy waved.

I put on a smile as Eddie circled my feet.

"Is your dad home?" Jimmy asked, stopping in front of me, bent over at the waist to catch his breath.

"Yeah. We got in a few minutes ago." Then I forced myself to face Mike, shirt off and tucked into the back of his shorts, his chest covered in sweat. It was criminal to look that good while working out. "Hi," I said, noting the different prosthetic leg. It was black and curved, unlike the one he normally wore. "How're you?"

"We were out taking some action shots for my new website." He handed his phone over to me to flip through a few photos.

"They're pretty blurry."

"Hey." Jimmy stood up straight, running his hands through his hair. "Even the best photographer would have trouble getting a good shot of his ugly mug."

I handed Mike his phone back. "Laney's getting you all fixed up?"

"She's trying." He hooked his hands onto his hips, and I kept my eyes from drifting down to the muscle there. "So, how've you been?"

"Good. We're trying to wrap up all the loose ends for the house," I said, about as awkward as I felt when we'd first spoken at the Memorial Day picnic. The conversation was so stilted it was as if we were strangers. As if he hadn't had me tied up naked to his workout bench last week.

Jimmy wiped his brow with the hem of his T-shirt. "My mom said her friend is going to be the real estate agent."

"She's coming in two weeks to look at the house and take pictures."

He sucked air through his teeth. "That's so close. Are you ready?"

"For the most part." I untangled my feet from the trap Eddie had created with his leash. "All the big stuff is done. It's the basement that needs sorting through now."

Jimmy huffed. "That's the worst part. It's like the Batcave down there. Who knows what's hiding out behind one of the walls of boxes."

I rubbed at my forehead, picturing it all. "I know, but most of it's going in the trash. Old DVDs and stuff. I think some of my mom's clothing is still hidden down there somewhere."

"Well, if you want help, let me know," Jimmy said and elbowed Mike. "You ready?"

He nodded then glanced at me. When I offered him a shy smile, he started off after his brother but turned around after a few paces. "Hey, about the other night. I'm sorry if it got weird. I didn't—"

"It's not weird."

He tipped his head to the side. "You're playing with your earring."

I dropped my hand. "What?"

"It's a tic you have. You play with your earring. You're saying it's not weird, but it's weird."

"I—" No use lying when he could see right through me. "*I'm* sorry. I guess I'm not used to seeing the guys…"

He lifted that one eyebrow, patiently waiting for me to continue, but now that I started to explain, I wasn't sure I wanted him to know. This was supposed to be an emotionless thing. There was no reason to open up my box of secrets.

"What?"

"Nothing. I gotta go." Eddie was starting to get himself twisted up again, and I shook the leash to get his attention. "Come on."

"Don't do that." Mike curled his fingers around my wrist. "You've always told me what's on your mind. Don't stop now."

I forced out a laugh. "There's nothing on my mind, all right? If you want to hear about Eli, the guy I was having sex with back in Michigan, I'll tell you. Although I assumed you didn't want to hear how I'd text him to come over and bring pizza, and then he'd leave right after." When he frowned, I tossed my hand out. "I didn't think so."

"You think I'm like this Eli guy?" His question was spiked like thorns on a rose. The problem was, Mike was nothing like him.

I had no problem saying goodnight, see ya later to Eli.

With Mike, though, I had trouble. Which was exactly why I needed some space. We weren't dating, and this wasn't my fairy tale. These were a few weeks with the guy I had a crush on as a kid. That was it.

Eddie yanked on the leash, and I followed him, still looking back at Mike. "No, you're not like him. You're not like any guy I've ever been with."

Then I pivoted and trotted away before I said anything else I might regret.

CHAPTER TWENTY-ONE

Mike

I didn't like how I'd left my conversation with Sam yesterday, so when my mother shoved two bags full of Tupperware and groceries into my hands to take next door, I willingly obliged. I rang the doorbell and waited while I listened to Sam yell out that she'd get the door.

She opened it with a flourish, her hair down with pieces flying around from the force of the swinging door. "Hey, what are you doing?"

"Who is it?" Phil Kohler grumbled, ambling down the hall on his crutches.

"Dad! Sit down! I told you I'd answer it."

"I can do it."

She blew out an aggravated breath and stared up at me as if I could help. But I knew stubborn when I saw it.

"Looking good, Phil. My mom thought you guys might want some food."

"Well, that's very nice of her. Come on in," he said, and Samantha moved to the side so I could enter their home. I followed behind Mr. Kohler, who tottered at a snail's pace with his crutches, and behind me, Sam sighed. I guessed she probably had a tough time keeping her dad off his feet.

I peeked into their living room, where pillows and sheets were laid out on the sofa, with a laptop, cell phone, and dirty dishes piled on top of the coffee table. "Been sleeping on the couch?"

"Yeah, it's been hell on my back, but Sammy doesn't want me going up the stairs yet." Phil slumped down on one of the chairs in the kitchen and leaned over to prop his foot on another, but Samantha was there, helping him. "Pain in the ass," he mumbled, unable to keep his frown from inverting to a smile.

"And where would you be without me, huh? I don't see Gavin around here to help."

"That's why he's my favorite child."

Samantha mumbled something under her breath that sounded like it was about her brother's balls dropping as she unloaded the bags.

Phil tipped his chin toward the counter. "Is that pulled pork I see?"

She held up the glass dish. "Yep. You want some?" At his nod, she placed the dish on the kitchen table along with the buns and pasta salad my mom had packed up. "You want me to—"

"Get out, Sammy," Phil said, gesturing to the back door with his fork. "Mike, please tell her to leave me alone."

She propped her hands on her hips, her head tilted in a challenge, and I wasn't about to get in the middle of this fight. "You want to go for ice cream or something?"

"Yes, good idea." Phil dug into the food. "Go get ice cream."

She relented with a low, "Fine. I'm driving."

Samantha's car was a little Toyota, and even though I wasn't excessively tall, I needed to adjust the seat. "Good god, this is tiny."

"Yeah, but it gets the job done. I'd like something bigger for

177

all the moving I've had to do recently, but I basically packed up my clothes and computer in Michigan and sold everything off. When I get to Texas, I'll have to buy more furniture."

"You didn't keep anything?"

She shook her head, fiddling with the vents, blasting the air conditioning. "My apartment there is mostly furnished, and anything I don't have, I'll get secondhand. Why bother dragging my life down there or buying new if I'm not staying, you know?"

She spoke as if I had any idea what she was talking about. I didn't. "You're not staying there?"

"The internship is a year."

"And then what?"

"I don't know." Slowing at a red light, she faced me. "Depending on where I want to be licensed to work will determine what I'm going to do."

I digested that information, but it was difficult to keep down without grimacing. Not that I allowed myself to dream about a future with her, but if she wasn't coming back here, there was no hope to even cling to. "And you don't want to come back to Ohio?"

"I'm honestly not sure. I want to keep my options open. In order to get my license, I'll need to do postdoc hours, and not every state is the same. I plan on doing more hours so I can cover more bases. Then when I decide where I want to go, all I need to do is pass the test."

"Oh. Is that all?" She was so flippant about all the work she was going to do, didn't she realize how impressive it was? She was so smart and so driven, but she may as well have been describing her grocery list. She should be proud. I was damn proud of her.

"What about you? Your website looks good. I see none of Jimmy's photos made the cut."

"Yeah. I've been talking through some ideas with Laney." I wrapped my hand around her knee. "She's been really great. Gem, too."

"Gem?" she squeaked.

"We've been having some lively debates over DM."

She snorted a laugh, probably because Gem was an antagonistic little shit. Reminded me of Jimmy, except with a more caustic wit.

"But I like her. I told her I wanted to improve my flexibility, so she gave me some stretches to try. What? What's that face for?"

"I don't have many friends, and you're stealing them all."

I tightened my fingers around her thigh as she pulled into the parking lot. "Not all of them. I haven't talked to Bronte yet."

"But that right there," she said with an amused shake of her head. "You know enough about her that you're basically friends. Soon, you'll be included in our text thread."

Even though it as a joke, both of our smiles faded. I didn't know if it was for the same reason, but I assumed so. Yet another reminder that she was leaving at the end of August.

"What do you need me to do?" she asked. "Write you a Yelp review? Maybe take some non-blurry photos?"

"The only photos I want you to take are naked ones of yourself."

She tossed me a cheeky eyebrow raise then stepped out of the car, her T-shirt so large it almost covered up her microscopic shorts. "Well, come on." She spun on her heel, all tension between us seemingly forgotten. "You're buying."

Once we had our ice cream, we claimed a bench outside.

"Oh my god. It's so hot," Samantha moaned.

I agreed, taking a big bite of my vanilla peanut butter. "Whose idea was this anyway?"

She cut her eyes to me. I couldn't have been any more transparent with my invitation to get her out of the house, and now we were sitting here, roasting outside of an ice cream shop while small children shrieked around us.

"Your dad was annoyed, and you seemed...frazzled."

"I don't get frazzled," she said, tilting her head to lick her chocolate and peach mash-up.

"No? Let me guess, you don't sweat either. You glisten."

"Exactly."

I trailed the knuckle of my index finger down her temple. "Well, you're glistening a lot."

She knocked my hand away. "You could be a gentleman and not point it out."

"You know I'm not much of a gentleman," I said, earning a heated stare so long drips of peach ice cream splattered on the ground between her feet.

If this was my chance to get back to...wherever we were, I wasn't even sure anymore. All I knew is that I wanted her naked and breathing heavy underneath me, her sweet mouth on mine. I tugged on her wrist, licking the line of ice cream off the side of her hand, and she moaned, inching closer to me, nearly in my lap.

"You better hurry up and eat," I told her with another lick at the corner of her palm, and she narrowed her gaze on me.

"I really don't appreciate you turning me into some kind of horny cat in public."

I barked out a laugh and let go of her to finish my own ice cream. We both raced the sun to try to beat it from creating a puddle of flavored milk at our feet.

"You gonna tell me what's up with you being a helicopter parent with your dad?" I asked, before biting into my cone.

"I don't know." She wiped more melted ice cream off her arm, she was losing the battle. "I guess I sort of feel bad for him. It's not like we were ever super close, but now that Gavin's going to school and he's selling the house, it feels like... I guess it feels like he doesn't have anyone. Mom has Lina, but he's been alone for all these years, and he had to get this surgery and no one was around to help."

"Except for you."

"Right. That's why when he told me, I knew I had to come home."

I finished my cone, brushed my hands off, then gave her my extra napkins. "Sorry about the circumstances, but I'm not sorry you are here."

She slanted her eyes to me in warning. She's ordered me to stop saying things like that to her, but she had to know, even if I didn't outright use my words. I was practically a dog at her heels. She had me by the balls.

Another line of chocolate dripped down her shin. "Ugh," she grumbled. "I'm all sticky. You want any of this, or should I throw it away?"

"Toss it."

She threw her mess of a cone away, along with the dozens of napkins it took to clean herself up. But before she could start toward her car, I wrapped my hand around her forearm. "You still mad at me?"

"I was never mad."

"Upset," I amended, pulling her fingers toward my mouth. "You were upset."

"I was..." She trailed off when I sucked her index finger into my mouth, her pupils huge and pleading as her mouth parted so sweetly. Her pulse beat wildly under my fingers around her wrist.

"Was what?" I asked, all innocent-like. "Frazzled?"

"Wh-what are you doing?"

I didn't know if she was asking in more of a broad sense—

What was I doing? Showing her how she deserved to be worshipped from the tips of her fingers to the tips of her toes because she was an incredible woman—but I answered in the immediate sense.

"Trying to help," I murmured. "You said it yourself. You're all sticky." Then I sucked on her middle finger, my teeth scraping along the tip. "Sweet as always. Like peaches."

She reached her other hand up to my neck, leaning in to kiss me. Until some little tornado on two legs crashed into the back of her, sending her flying into me. I didn't stand a chance of staying upright.

We both collapsed to the ground, and I muttered a low, "Shit."

The little boy was momentarily stunned as he stared at his wreckage before yelling, "Sorry!" over his shoulder and taking off in the opposite direction.

"I hate kids," Samantha mumbled, pushing off the pavement, and I chuckled. "Are you okay?" she asked.

"Yeah. Fine." I clasped her proffered hand and stood with a grunt, checking out the scrape on my elbow.

"Does it hurt?"

I swiped my palm over it then down my pants. "It's nothing."

"You're bleeding."

I waved her off and headed to her car. "It's nothing."

"Mike." She grabbed my bicep, forcing me to turn to her so she could take a look. It really was nothing, but her worry sent pangs of yearning through my chest. The more she gave me these little moments of honesty, the harder it was for me to keep my heart from leaping out of my throat.

When she finally let go of me, I dragged my index finger across her jaw. "You worried about me?" I tweaked her nose. "That's adorable."

She did a terrible job of playing it off. "Don't get blood in my car."

I tipped my head to the side, steering us back into neutral territory of flirting. "You want to kiss it and make it better?"

"Maybe."

"Maybe we should hurry back, then."

In unspoken agreement, we both hopped in the car, and flew back to Samantha's house. It was a good thing, too, because her father was trying to climb the stairs.

"Dad! What are you doing?"

He faced us with a heavy sigh. "I want to shower."

"You shouldn't be going upstairs. Especially by yourself."

He opened his mouth to argue, but she barreled on. "And shower? Dad, you can't stand in there on your own. Take a bath, if anything. Although, how you think you're getting up there is—"

"I'll help you."

She whipped her head to me, but I shrugged, unrepentant.

"I know how hard it is after surgery. You got a folding chair?" When she nodded, I said, "I'll help your dad up while you get the chair. We can stick it in the shower, so he can sit. Sound good to you, Phil?"

"Sounds great."

Sam relented as her father grinned widely at me, patting me on the back like they were old buddies.

By the time I got him upstairs and situated on the closed toilet lid with the water on, she reappeared with the chair and positioned it under the spray.

"I can't wait," Mr. Kohler said, staring into the shower like a man eyeing a feast after a famine.

"Do you need help getting out of your clothes?" Samantha asked, but he shooed her away.

"I don't need my daughter looking after me while I shower."

She held her hands up and stepped out of the bathroom. I followed but left the door ajar. "I'll stay out here and check on him in a few minutes. Make sure he's all right."

She launched herself at me. "You're going to get so laid tonight."

I kissed her neck. "Looking forward to it."

After I helped her father out of the shower and into fresh clothes, he took some pain medication and was out. Probably exhausted from overly exerting himself.

So, I held Samantha's hand, escorting her out their back door and across our adjoining yards to my back door. When it creaked open, my mom called out, "Michael, is that you? What were you doing so—" She stopped mid-stride into the kitchen when she spotted us. "Oh, hi, Sam." Her eyes drifted down to where our fingers were linked. "I didn't realize you'd be coming over."

She sputtered a response. "It's not... I, uh..."

"Mr. Kohler needed some help getting showered and changed," I explained. "We're gonna watch a movie."

"Okay. Sounds good," Mom said with an alarmingly bright smile. Like she was real happy about us holding hands in front of her. "Your father and I are heading up to bed soon." Then she winked.

Fucking hell, my mother's enthusiasm just screwed me over because Samantha turned to stone next to me.

"Hey, you okay?" I asked when we got to the basement.

She kept her gaze on the floor, her cheeks flaming red. "Your mom knows."

I decided playing dumb might be the best way to smooth it over. "Knows what?"

But, of course, it wasn't.

"Knows about *this*." She growled, fisting her hands by her sides. "*This* isn't how it's supposed to work."

"I'm sorry." I reached for her hand, but she evaded me.

"Oh, for Christ's sake, stop apologizing. You could make this a little easier on me, you know?"

"Make it easier?" I scrubbed my hand down my face. I thought summer flings were supposed to be easy, but this relationship may have been the hardest of my life. "What are you talking about?"

"I'm talking about you, about your mom, about Jimmy..." She paced in a small circle. "It wasn't supposed to be real. Your family knowing makes it feel like this is a real relationship, and it's not."

Taking shrapnel may have hurt less than those words and when I blanched, she deflated, obviously remorseful. Yet she didn't apologize. She may not have meant to hurt me, but if that's how she felt, that was her truth.

We agreed to the summer.

That was it.

I was the one hoping for more when I knew, from the beginning, it wasn't possible.

"I have to go." Then she ran out of the basement and the house. And maybe out of my life for good.

CHAPTER TWENTY-TWO

Sam

It had been one week since I had last seen Mike, and I didn't know whether to be proud of my self-restraint or let it all go and run next door to beg him to forgive me. I knew I had wounded him. It was written all over his face. So when he hadn't respond to my text the next day, I assumed what we had was over. The summer was cut short.

I couldn't pretend this was some longtime crush come to fruition or a casual fling. My feelings for him were real, and I lashed out, unsure of what to do with them. Even though what I had with Mike was more real than anything I'd ever experienced before, I had no idea how to proceed.

So, maybe what happened was for the best. We couldn't be together, and there was no point in continuing this...heartache when I was leaving in a few weeks. It would only hurt more at the end of the summer to say goodbye. It was better to break it off early than wait until the last minute.

Like a Band-Aid, rip it off.

Yes, this was for the best.

Steam rose from the pan, and I turned down the heat on the stove before opening the window to get my dad's attention on the back porch. "Dinner's almost ready."

He acknowledged me with a nod then hoisted himself up from the table, where he'd been reading a book. He was doing well, going to physical therapy, and following all the guidelines at home, doing some simple exercises while watching television.

And for once, he actually rested. He didn't go outside to tinker with his garden or look over data on his laptop. He sat and did nothing for a while every day. Most of the time, Gavin and I joined him, sometimes each in our own world with a cell phone or iPad, or other times, we watched television together. We talked about the classes Gavin had signed up for at school and the work I would be doing in Texas, and it was really nice, being together.

Too bad this chapter was about to come to a close.

A professional on his crutches now, Dad made his way into the kitchen and took a seat at the table. I set down two plates of summer vegetable stir-fry and rice.

"Smells delicious. Thank you." He blew over a forkful of vegetables to cool it. "Where's your brother tonight?"

"Out with Ava."

He swallowed down a bite of food. "What are you up to tonight?"

I picked at the squash and onions. "Not much. Finishing up going through the last of the boxes and maybe read a little."

We ate in silence for a while until he asked, "You haven't been out with Mike lately."

My father was a brilliant man but often had his head buried in the sand, so his question left me with my mouth hanging open. He didn't notice as he scarfed down dinner. "But if you want to finish up the boxes, I can help."

"Oh yeah, okay," I said, catching his eye before he went quiet again.

The real estate agent was scheduled to come next week to

get the house on the market, and after these last few things were gone through, we would finally be done. The house would be ready to sell.

After Dad and I finished up eating, he made himself comfy in the living room, and I carried the remaining boxes and containers in. With Janis Joplin playing quietly on my phone, we sorted through the junk and keepsakes, old photos, and framed college degrees. Dad held up what looked like a papier-mâché animal of some sort, but the face had long ago been mangled. The only way we knew who created it was Gavin's messy name scribbled on the back.

"Not much of an artist," Dad said with a laugh as he set it down.

I flipped through a little dusty photo album. "He improved as he got older."

"Yeah, but he's too much like me. Too analytical. You're the artist like your mom."

I raised my head to him. "You think so?"

With his hands and eyes on what he was doing, he answered, "Absolutely. You're curious and imaginative, independent and compassionate."

All these years, I had always thought I was like my dad, academic and a bit like the Tin Man, all head and no heart. Though, seeing myself through my father's eyes, maybe I was like my mother. And as much as I'd like to deny it, I hid my emotions so I didn't get overwhelmed by them because I felt things so deeply.

"Look at this." Dad showed me a plastic coffee mug with a photo in it of the Kohler clan. Mom held baby Gavin next to Dad, who had his arm around me. We were all smiling. "I wonder what this was for?"

He turned it upside down, presumably looking for a date or name, but found none and shrugged, placing it next to him instead of in the junk pile. I went back to the photo album, full of Polaroids of my parents when they were younger. I studied them with a growing smile. Of Mom in overalls and a spiky pixie cut eating pizza, of Dad in an oversized T-shirt and shorts at the beach, waving at whoever took the picture.

"How did you and Mom meet?"

"Me and your mother?" Dad lifted his eyes to a spot on the wall, lost in thought. "A party, but I don't remember where or when. She and I had friends in common, and... What I remember was that she had sunflowers on her dress, so I told her about a study that planted sunflowers around certain crops to attract predacious insects to control the pest population."

I laughed. "Such a nerd."

He flashed me a rare smile. "She loved it." With an audible breath, he said more quietly, "For a little while, at least."

I continued to flip through the album, finding more pictures of my parents together.

"I'm sorry, Samantha. I don't know if I ever told you that."

I met my dad's gaze, his eyes red-rimmed.

"I know how hard the divorce was on you, and I'm sorry that I never..." He blinked a few times. "It was too late by the time I realized I needed to get out of my own way, and I'm sorry. You deserved better than that."

I appreciated the apology and nodded my acceptance, my own eyes stinging.

"I never stopped loving your mom, but I didn't know how to show her. And I fear that I was a bad example for you."

"That's not—"

He held up his hand to silence me. "When you love someone, you show them. Like right now—" He arched his hand around the floor. "You didn't have to come home for the summer to be with me, but you did without being asked. Because *you* show up when you love someone. And you deserve that in return. When you decide you want to love someone, make sure they show it every day. That's what you deserve."

I touched my cheek, surprised to find a tear there, and wiped it away. "Thanks, Dad."

He fixed his glasses on his nose with a sniff and focused on the items in front of him, while I put the photo album to the side, in my own keep pile. I was sure neither one of my parents would want it, but this was my history. The silly pictures of my parents young and in love, it was how I came to be in existence, and I wanted to keep them. I also kept the family photo of us at an amusement park. Gavin was a toddler clinging to my hand, while our parents stood behind us.

Then because I was good at showing it but needed practice saying it, I sat on the couch, next to my father, and threw my arm around his shoulders. "I love you, Dad."

"I love you too, sweetheart."

CHAPTER TWENTY-THREE

"This is ridiculous." I slouched back in my chair. "It's been hours."

"We have to figure it out. It takes time." Adam leaned closer to the laptop screen, his fingers smoothing over the touchpad as he fiddled with the audio.

Behind us, Jimmy bounced on an exercise ball. "Using a YouTube video to tell us how to make a YouTube video, how existential."

Both of my brothers had come over to help me film and edit what I hoped to be the first content for my YouTube channel. It was Laney's brainchild. We'd been texting quite often lately, and after I'd mentioned Emily's idea about helping her nephew, she suggested I start a channel. She explained how I could eventually make money through it, and it sounded like a good idea. The problem was, now I had to produce the videos. Not knowing where to start, I asked my brothers for help.

So far, it'd been a lot of work for a five-minute introduction. Jimmy filmed multiple takes of me introducing myself and talking a little bit about my injury, but he would say something like, "Do it again and less frowny this time."

Since Adam was the computer whiz, he was the one who

volunteered to figure out how to edit the video, saying, "How hard could it be?" But I knew that eventually I'd have to learn to do this all on my own, and I already dreaded it.

"If this takes off, we get a cut, right?" Jimmy asked.

I ignored him, absently checking my cell phone. It'd been a week and a half since Samantha ran out of the house like her pants were on fire, and though she'd texted twice, I didn't know what to say, if anything at all.

She'd made her position perfectly clear. She didn't want what we had to be "real."

It didn't matter what I felt or what I *knew* she felt. She didn't want it anymore.

"Okay, I think we're good," Adam said and played on the video one more time.

Jimmy pointed at the screen. "Spectacular cinematography. Look at that light on your face."

I didn't think it looked spectacular in any way, especially in the lighting.

"Great job, Jim. Thanks for your help," Jimmy said in a stage whisper, feeding me lines.

"Great job, Jim," I repeated, monotone. "Thanks for your help."

"What do we think? Ready to go live?" Adam peered over at me for the go-ahead, and I waved my hand.

"Yeah, let's do it."

He hit the button before standing up, stretching his back. "Congratulations, you are now a YouTuber."

I grunted.

"What's with you, man?" Jimmy flicked a resistance band at me. "You've been in a bad mood all week."

"It's nothing."

"But there is something," Adam said, like the know-it-all he was.

I rubbed at the back of my neck, stupidly leaving my cell phone undefended, and Jimmy snatched it up.

"Peaches? Who is... oh my god, it's Sam, isn't it? I don't know if I should be excited or a little grossed out. Do I want to know why you call her Peaches?"

He scrolled for a moment before tossing it back in my lap with a gagging sound, and Adam spun around, interested now. "Samantha Kohler? You have something going on with Sammy?"

With my elbows on my knees, I mumbled my response into my hands.

"Didn't catch that one," Jimmy said.

I sat up, eyeing my younger brother's shit-eating grin. "I said I don't know."

"You don't know?" His lip curled. He was pissed at me. "A few weeks ago, you knew. What? Did you get into a fight?"

"No."

"Then what happened?"

At his raised voice, I narrowed my eyes until he gave up his tough guy act. He could only pull that if I actually did something wrong, which I hadn't. Unless, of course, hoping for something out of my reach was wrong.

"I didn't hurt her. I know that's what you're assuming. It got weird. She... I don't know. It was just for the summer anyway, no strings attached."

At that, Jimmy nodded as if it made sense. But I didn't want it to make sense. I wanted it to be different. I wanted a chance to be with her.

"That's what you want? No strings attached." Adam asked, cleaning off his glasses with the hem of his shirt.

"It doesn't matter what I want. She's going to Texas at the end of August."

Adam put his glasses back on, and for once in his life,

Jimmy kept his mouth shut when I would've really liked some kind of insight into his childhood best friend.

"We haven't talked in a few days," I muttered, and he sucked air through his teeth.

"Sorry. I didn't know."

"Why would you?" I tipped my head back to stare at a crack in the corner of the ceiling. "No one was supposed to know, according to her."

"Easier to say goodbye that way," Adam said after a few moments, and Jimmy and I both gaped at him. "What? I'm the one married here, so I think I have more experience with relationships than you two morons."

We folded our arms, ready for our lesson.

"It's not that hard to understand. If she's leaving at the end of the summer, why would she want to tell people about it? Why would she want to make it harder for herself to leave? Anyone with even semi-decent observational skills can see Sammy's a runner."

I leaned forward. "A runner?"

"Yeah, she'll run away before she can get hurt. Lauren was the same way."

"So, what did you do?" Jimmy asked.

He shrugged. "Kept showing up. Told her I'd wait for her—or run with her if she wanted me to."

"Aww, Adam." Jimmy punched his shoulder. "Didn't know you were such a sentimentalist." Then he gestured to me. "So, what should he do?"

My older brother extended his legs and crossed them at the ankles. "I don't know. You said she's going to Texas. *Is* there anything you can do?"

There was nothing I could do. Sam and I were headed in two different directions.

"Fuck." I dropped my head in my hands.

"Sorry, man," Jimmy said quietly. "I didn't realize you had feelings for her."

"How do you know I have feelings for her?"

"Because you're talking about her," Adam answered. "You only talk about the really important things."

Jimmy nodded in agreement, and I slouched back in my chair with a groan. My brothers were right. I hated when that happened.

CHAPTER TWENTY-FOUR

Sam

Trisha, the real estate agent, had come by, very happy with the condition of the house, and snapped pictures of the interior and exterior before discussing price points, but I hadn't paid much attention as I was busy texting the girls. Bronte's wedding was in a matter of days, and her happiness was palpable. Really, all of them were excited, except for me. I couldn't quite match their enthusiasm, especially when Trisha came back to the house this morning, For Sale sign in tow.

"We're all set." She shook hands with Dad and then me, like I had anything to do with it. "You are officially on the market."

"Thanks for all your help," he said, leaning on a cane. He'd given up on the crutches as soon as his therapist gave him the go-ahead.

Trisha smiled, straddling the line between professional and flirtation. "It is my pleasure, and I'm sure you'll be hearing from me soon. We'll get this house sold in no time."

Dad escorted her a few steps to her car, saying their good-byes, before he circled around to face me in the yard.

"Dad, were you flirting with the Realtor?"

"I...flirting, no. I don't even know how to do that."

"That. You guys smiling at each other like that and the quiet voices you used to say goodbye. She put her hand on your arm."

"Oh." His brow rose. "Well then, yes. I guess we were flirting." He let out a quiet, pensive hum and started off to the front door. "I think we should celebrate. Where'd you put that bottle of wine you found in the basement?"

"In the cabinet above the stove," I said, meaning to follow him, but my mother's little gray sedan pulled up in the driveway. She'd taken Gavin shopping for everything he'd need for school. The back seat was filled with bags.

"Hey," she said, getting out from behind the wheel. "It's really happening, huh?"

Dad reversed course and headed over to her. "Hey, Carol. Didn't expect to see you."

"When Sam told me the Realtor was coming over today, I thought I'd say my goodbyes." She tipped her chin in the direction of the house as Gavin came around the hood of the car to stand with them. She looped her arm around his shoulders then waved me over to hold my hand. "Feels...big, you know?"

Dad nodded, and my eyes stung with tears.

"We were going to go in to have a glass of wine," he said to Mom. "Would you like to join us?"

My parents weren't often in the same room together, so it shocked me when my mother smiled. "Sure. Why not?"

"Can I have some?" Gavin asked, trying on a guileless puppy-dog face, and I let out a dubious huff. They'd never in a million years.

Yet, in another surprising turn of events, my parents looked at each other, exchanging some silent conversation, before Dad shrugged.

"Yeah. A little."

I sputtered a watery laugh as my parents and brother

walked into the house through the garage door, while I stayed back, staring at the For Sale sign, the bright-red background and white letters impossible to miss. The house I grew up in would no longer be the place I called home. My brother was off to college in a few weeks, and I would be living the farthest away from my family that'd I'd ever been. Although I had never been afraid to leave the nest and chase my dreams, this all did feel very...big.

The For Sale sign made everything different.

With a deep breath, I pushed my hair back from my face and made my way into the house, settling in the kitchen, where my parents and brother were already seated, an open bottle of red wine between them.

Gavin swallowed a sip and cringed, and we all laughed as I slipped into the last open chair at the round table that had been there since I was a kid. Then I poured myself a healthy glass, laughed some more at Gavin, held my mom's hand, and listened to my parents reminisce. Maybe it was the wine, or maybe it was that this was a kind of ending, but for over two hours, we were a happy family once again, around our little table for the last time.

By the time Mom backed out of the driveway with a few honks of her horn, I was feeling threadbare enough to text Mike.

> Can we talk?

I should have known he would text back immediately. He was too good not to.

MIKE
> Do you want to go for a walk?

> Meet you out front.

I tucked my phone away and called Eddie.

"Come on, you big lug," I said, leading him out the front door.

"You talking to me?"

I lifted my attention from the dog to Mike, where he stood a few feet away. My chest ached, seeing him there with his baseball cap on, his head tilted slightly at an angle, his gaze taking in every inch of me as if to make sure I was all right.

"Hi," I said, having trouble keeping my bottom lip from quivering. I must have drunk more than I thought.

"You all right?"

I didn't get to answer because Eddie ran out ahead, jerking me forward so that Mike had to steady me when I fell off the step.

"You good?" he asked with his hand gripping my upper arm. I nodded, but as he started to move away, I shook my head, voice catching. "Please."

He stepped close enough that the heat from his body and the smell of his soap comforted me. "Peaches," he said, so low even that made me want to cry. "What's wrong?"

I shook my head again, not sure of the answer. What was wrong? Nothing. Everything.

A moment passed in which he studied me, his eyes bouncing between my own. Whatever he found in them had his face dropping in concern, then he took my hand in his, locking his fingers with mine, gently caressing the back of my hand with his thumb.

The sun had begun to set, and long shadows mirroring the trees lined the street. Eddie happily danced back and forth, his tongue lolling out to the side. But I couldn't find my words yet, and Mike didn't ask me to until we arrived at the park. Once Eddie was tied up to the pole, Mike pushed me on the swing, high enough to clear out my lungs and head.

Clear enough for my father's words from last week to enter my memory. *When you decide you want to love someone, make sure they show it every day.*

"Are you okay?" he asked once I brushed my feet back on the ground, slowly coming to a stop. He sat on the swing next to mine. "Is it your house?"

"It's the house, my family, it's everything."

He placed his hands above mine on the chains and turned us to face each other. "What's everything?"

"It's all changing. It's not that I thought I had some great childhood or anything, but it's sad to know it's over. It's really over. And my best friends... Gem has a baby. Bronte's getting married..." I didn't realize I'd started to cry until he dragged his thumb under my eye. "I feel like I've had my head down, I've worked so hard for so long, and now I'm looking around, and suddenly, everything is different."

He gently brushed the pad of his thumb over my cheek and across my upper lip. "I understand that feeling. It's over-whelming."

I stuttered a breath, more tears spilling from my eyes, and he leaned over, kissing them away.

"I hate when you cry," he said, a little more than a hair-breadth away, skimming his nose along mine.

And that made me cry more. He was so gentle, so patient, and he had no reason to be. Not after the way I had treated him.

"I'm sorry for what I said to you. I was scared."

He curved his hands around my cheeks and jaw, holding me as if I were the most precious thing on earth, easily broken. Then he kissed me sweetly and leaned his forehead against mine. "I know."

For endless minutes, he showed me how much he cared for me. In his tender kisses and touches, in the way he didn't push me to give more than I was ready for. No different from how'd he been all summer. Giving me exactly what I needed, even if I believed I deserved something else, something less than.

What a fool I'd been.

"Mike," I said, leaning out of his embrace.

"Hm?"

"Bronte's wedding is next week."

"Okay."

"Would you want to come with me?"

He dropped his hands to my legs, holding on to the sides of my knees. "To some private island where she's marrying a celebrity?"

"Yeah."

"Am I allowed?"

I laughed, and it felt like the first laugh in a long time. "Yeah."

"I'm not a very good dancer."

"Me either."

"I'm more of a swayer."

I laced my fingers with his. "Sway with me, then."

Then he quirked his lips to the side as he stared at me, a little bewildered. "What do I need to do? That's pretty last minute."

"All you need is a passport. Chris rented out all these suites at the resort." At his eyebrow raise, I shrugged. "He's rich. What can I say? My best friend can do stuff like that now."

"What about a plane ticket?"

I grabbed my cell phone and pulled up the **Four Chicks and Two Dicks** text thread.

> Mike is coming to the wedding.

BRONTE

> !!!!!

I held my phone so he could see it as I typed.

BRONTE

I'm so happy!

Laney sent a series of champagne bottle emojis.

He's worried it's too late.

Beside me, he said, "I don't want to be a wedding crasher," and I typed that up too.

Then everyone else sent a variety of GIFs, emojis, and texts.

PLANE GUY

Not crashing! Everyone's invited!

GEM

Everyone?

PLANE GUY

Well, not EVERYONE. But you know…

BOY SCOUT

How big is this island anyway?

PLANE GUY

Not sure. 2000 acres or so

GEM

Please don't tell us how many people could fit comfortably on the island.

BOY SCOUT

I wasn't going to. I'm just interested in how much usable space there is. If it's a private island, I'm sure a lot of the land is undeveloped.

GEM

Can you turn the 1 and 0s off?

BOY SCOUT

1110001010101000111001010101

Gem responded with an eye roll emoji.

PLANE GUY

Mom and Dad are fighting again.

LANEY

That's not fighting. That's their foreplay.

Mike sniffed a laugh as he rested his chin on my shoulder. "Why do you have the girls' names listed but not the guys'? Who's 'Boy Scout'?"

"That's Jason, Gem's husband."

"And 'Plane Guy' is...?"

"Chris. He and Bronte met on a plane."

"Right. So why don't you use..."

I laughed at his confusion, like a math problem that didn't make sense.

He slanted his head back to meet my gaze. "What do you call me?"

"'The Marine,' obviously."

"Do the girls call me that too?"

I loved that he called Gem, Bronte, and Laney "the girls" like they were his friends too. "Yeah, they do. When we first start talking to a guy or something, we almost never use their real names. We talk about them by their descriptors, like 'What's going on with Plane Guy?'"

He nodded, although he clearly didn't get it. Then I kissed his cheek. "We're going to have so much fun."

CHAPTER TWENTY-FIVE
Mike

Samantha wasn't kidding when she said Chris would take care of everything. She explained that he didn't speak to his family anymore, so it was really important to him to have Bronte's family and friends there. He immediately got a plane ticket for me and even upgraded us to first class. When I asked her about paying him back, she shrugged. "I've tried. He won't take anything. You'll understand when you meet him."

Not that I currently had any money to pay the guy back with anyway, so I endeavored to tamp down my pride and enjoy the ride. After a couple of connections through San Juan and then Tortola, Samantha and I finally passed through customs and stepped right onto a private water taxi that navigated us to Peter Island.

As we approached the private island, she wrapped her arms around my waist. "I'm glad you're here with me. I would've been doing all of this by myself. The seventh wheel."

I brushed back pieces of her hair that had been kicked up in the wind and kissed the top of her head, noting the shadow of insecurity in her voice. She was always so confident; it was a privilege to be able to witness the parts of herself she hid from the rest of the world. "Thanks for bringing me. Five days on a private island. Who'd say no?"

The closer the boat got to the lush greenery of the island, the more she buzzed with energy, and by the time the captain docked, she practically flew up the gangplank, running toward the welcome center.

I reached for our bags, but a bellhop stopped me, so I trailed Samantha inside, where we were introduced to the concierge, who led us down to our beachfront suite. A bottle of champagne and a fruit platter awaited us, courtesy of the future Mr. and Mrs. Cunningham.

Samantha helped herself, popping a piece of mango into her mouth while I uncorked the champagne. As I poured us each a glass, she opened the French doors to reveal a small patio off the bedroom, leading to a large grassy area with palm trees and hammocks, and the sandy beach beyond that. With champagne in hand, we explored the suite, from the huge Jacuzzi tub to the king-sized bed to the two-person shower.

"That's handy," she said, nodding to the bench in the shower. As if I needed a demonstration, she stepped inside, perched herself on the wooden seat and crossed her legs. "Quite comfy."

"Yeah?"

She raised one eyebrow, sipping her champagne, and all my blood headed south.

"You want to try it out right now?" I asked after I found my voice again.

"Not yet. I want to see if anyone else is here." She took me hand as she sauntered back out of the shower and guided me outside, singing a loud, slightly off-key version of the *Golden Girls* theme song.

But maybe that was their call because suddenly, a head of long blond hair poked out of a window.

"Sammy!"

"Laney!"

Samantha sprinted toward Laney and jumped into her waiting arms before they tumbled to the grass in a fit of giggles. I jogged over to make sure they were okay, and when Laney spotted me, she gasped. "It's the Marine. In the flesh!"

She scrambled to her feet and hugged me. She was almost as tall as I was. "It's nice to finally meet you," she squealed and let me go to sling her arm around Samantha. "Can you believe this place?"

"Christopher's really outdone himself," someone said from behind me.

Samantha and Laney spotted them, another round of shrieks set off.

They were like a tornado, the three women hopping and hugging and sharing a bottle of champagne which somehow appeared.

"Hey."

I pivoted to the voice to find a tall and tanned blond guy making his way toward me.

"You must be Mike," he said. "I'm Jason."

"Yeah. Hey. Nice to meet you."

Jason rocked back on his heels, hands into his pockets. "You came with Sam, right?" At my nod, he tipped his chin out at where the girls now stood, heads bent together as they talked. "I came with the one trying to give Sam a piggyback ride."

"Gem?"

"Yeah. Welcome to the jungle." He tossed me a smile. "It's like trial by fire with these ladies." Then we strolled out to meet them, and Laney and Samantha both greeted Jason with a hug.

After Samantha formally introduced me to the group, Gem regarded me with a critical eye. "The Marine."

"The vegan," I said in return.

Jason slipped his arm around his wife's waist. "Be nice."

She pressed her hand to her chest, mouth agape. "Me? I've been very nice. Haven't I, Michael?"

I stared down at Gem, who gave me the distinct impression that she could command an army of her own. "Yeah, very sweet."

Jason snorted, and she shook her head, letting out a tiny grumble. "If you're going to lie about me, you need to use a more convincing adjective than sweet, my friend."

Laney shook her head. "No, it's true. You're sweet."

"On the inside," Samantha said.

"But sour on the outside," Jason added. "Like a Sour Patch Kid."

That elicited a chuckle from everyone, including Gem, who pinched her husband's side, and just like that, I was inducted into the group.

We congregated on our patio since it was in the middle of the suites, eating the fruit and drinking champagne. Bobby, Laney's boyfriend, showed up after he'd finished a business phone call in their room. He was an Australian chef turned semi-famous restaurateur. While the girls caught up, I chatted with the guys about whatever random things we could find in common: sports or the weather or the girls. Every once in a while, a cackle would bubble up from where the girls sat on the bed. Jason would smile at them, Bobby pretty much ignored them, and I observed it all. Including the way Samatha's voice went so soft I couldn't hear it anymore as she spoke to Gem and Laney. When Gem rubbed Samantha's back, I knew she was explaining to them what she'd confessed in the park, that she was having a hard time with all the changes.

I understood how difficult it was to undergo a transition, and I worried about her because of her past history. I didn't want her feeling out of control, so when she'd asked me to come with her, I hesitated for only a moment. Though I had been uncertain of how this trip would go, she needed an anchor right now, and I could be that for her.

But what shocked me most was when she got up from the bed to sit on my lap. In front of everyone. Like a declaration.

Laney grinned.

Gem's brow hiked up.

And right as I was about to curl my arm around her waist, leaning into whatever this feeling was, the door to the suite burst open.

"I heard there was a party happening here."

A chorus of cheers rang out, and there were only two people who could produce that response, the bride and groom.

"We were signing the marriage licenses and getting my family settled," Bronte explained, her dark-as-night hair pulled back into a ponytail and swinging as she hugged her friends. "Sorry we're late."

"Yes, you're terrible hosts," Gem said, and Chris ruffled her hair before introducing himself to me.

He was shorter than I thought he'd be, but grinning from ear to ear. "Thanks for coming."

"Thanks for making room for me."

He waved me off. "Anything for Samantha." He leaned in closer to me. "Those girls there are like my sisters. I'd do anything for them."

And like Jason, Chris got that dopey look on his face while he stared at Bronte while she told a story about their flight down here yesterday. I wondered if that was what I looked like when Sam smiled over at me.

But I was sure I did.

I just needed to see what it looked like on someone else to know the face I'd been staring at in the mirror all these weeks was one with hearts in my eyes.

"Oi, ladies and gentlemen." Bobby clapped a few times. "Should we take this reunion outside? I could use another bottle of champagne too, eh?"

Everyone agreed and settled in pairs. Jason and Gem flopped down in the grass, Bobby and Laney in a hammock, Chris and Bronte on chairs they'd pulled out, and Sam next to me in the shade of a palm tree.

Fruit and champagne turned into a dinner of burgers and fries as the conversation flowed from topic to topic. I could barely keep track, but it didn't matter. Not with the way Samantha kept her hand on my thigh or the occasional seductive glance over her shoulder. If it weren't for the rain that started to fall, we might have stayed out all night under the stars, but instead, each couple ran inside to their respective bungalows.

Samantha laughed, shaking off her arms from the sudden downpour, her shirt clinging to her like its life depended on it. "I guess that's what they get for booking this trip in the summer in the Caribbean."

"I don't mind," I rasped, towing her up against me.

She crawled her fingers up my chest, to the base of my neck. "What do you think of everybody?"

"It was nice to finally meet the people you talk about all the time."

She leaned up onto her toes to kiss me. Her tongue tasted like rum and Coke and pineapple, and if I could, I'd drink her up. I settled, instead, for stripping her down.

"You want to check out that shower now?" she asked as I peeled off her shirt.

I kissed her shoulder and unhooked her bra to skim my

hands over her breasts, her nipples catching between my fingers. She wrapped her arms around my waist, and I glided my hands along her rib cage to her back, bending her backward as I licked up from her breastbone to her throat, provoking a sigh when I sucked on the soft skin below her ear.

"In case I haven't told you enough," she rasped, "I'm really glad you're here."

I kissed my agreement into her skin then tapped her ass as I stood her up straight. "Go on. In the bathroom."

She let her hand drift over my side, ghosting over my swiftly hardening cock as she turned away from me. Inside the bathroom, the walls of the shower were clear, displaying the two heads on either end and the bench in the middle along the wall. I stripped off my shorts and underwear before stepping inside it to have a seat to remove my prosthesis, although it was hard to concentrate with the way Sam had spun around, bending to take off her own shorts, her sweet backside round and naked.

As if she didn't know what she was doing to me, she raised a shoulder. "What?"

I merely lifted my eyebrow and held out my prosthetic. With a sugary smile, she carefully set it down on the tiled floor outside the door. But before she could turn on the water, I grabbed her waist, hauling her back to me, and nipped her shoulder. "You think you're so cute, huh?"

"I don't know. Do you?" She wiggled out of my grasp. "You like a hot shower?"

My gaze roamed over her. From the wisps of her purple hair to the subtle slope of her stomach and hips. "Mm-hmm."

"Me too." She turned on the water and regulated the temperature then opened the gel soap. She acted as if I wasn't there watching her lather her skin up, the heat and steam amplifying the sweet, tropical-fruit scent, and I glided my hands over her body, unable to keep them off her even as drops of water fell onto my face. I barely stopped to blink, my gaze never leaving the curve of her thighs, the color of the phoenix on her back, the lines of her arms as she washed her hair.

Once she finished, she held up the bottle of shampoo to me. "Your turn."

She squirted some into her hand again and worked up a lather in my hair, her fingernails scratching along my scalp, sending a jolt of pleasure straight to my dick.

"Head down," she murmured, washing out the shampoo, her fingers working their magic until all the tiny hairs all over my body stood on end, even under the hot water. "Head back," she said, wiping water away from my face so I could see the pout of her lips. "Feel good?"

I answered by grabbing hold of her waist to yank her to me, licking and sucking on the rivulets of water flowing down her stomach. When I latched on to one of her nipples, she moaned, the sound reverberating around us. I was obsessed with how sensitive her breasts were, and I alternated toying and nipping at each one until she had to put her hand on the wall next to my head to steady herself.

"Turn around," I said, helping her onto my lap, spreading her legs wide, settling them over my thighs. With the streams of water falling on top of her, I eased my hand to her center, spreading her open with my fingers, and she dropped her head back on my shoulder. I kissed her ear, whispering how this was my favorite thing, touching her, feeling her desire for me, knowing how bad she wanted it, how I wanted to hear her. Louder. Longer. Give it up.

My chest rose and fell in time with hers as I kept one hand on her breast and the other between her legs, and with her ass pressing back against my cock, writhing over me, I couldn't help but be as worked up as she was, our slippery skin making everything too easy, too good. As soon as she climaxed, her moans filling the shower stall, she slipped off to the floor of the shower to put her mouth on me. Then I was the one panting and moaning. This beautiful woman was everything I ever wanted.

And later, after we had dried off and fell into bed, with my arm around her as she slept, I had to take a calming breath, a minute to slow down. I didn't know what would happen after this trip, but for the next few days, I had her on an island in the sun.

CHAPTER TWENTY-SIX

Sam

The rain didn't stop. It kept coming down. All through the morning, which Mike and I spent in bed, and continuing during the "welcome lunch" that included Bronte's parents, siblings, and brood of nieces and nephews. Some of Chris's friends were there too, a handful of people he worked with, but everyone together barely numbered two dozen people. It was intimate and fun—and completely waterlogged.

Laney lifted her margarita in a toast to the sky. "I bought three new bikinis."

"Put 'em on, babe," Bobby said. "Whether it's the ocean or the rain, you'll still get wet, right?"

Laney eyed Gem, who got up from her chair, ready for anything. But before either Laney or Gem could race out into the rain, Jason caught his wife around the waist. "Not in the thunderstorm."

She blew a raspberry at him. "You ruin all my fun."

"You'll have no fun if you're struck by lightning." He kissed her temple, placing her cocktail in her hand.

"I see what you're doing. Trying to get me liquored up so I won't say no when you bring up a baby again."

I thumped my own glass down on the table. "Huh?"

Bronte suddenly perked up from where she had her head on Chris's shoulder. "What did you say?"

Gem slugged down some of her drink, already half in the bag as Jason gazed down at her like a lion sunning himself. "You heard me. He wants another kid. I came here to fu—"

At the happy shriek of Bronte's niece a few feet away, Gem lowered her voice and inclined her head toward the table. "This Boy Scout thought he could convince me to have another kid with multiple orgasms last night."

Chris clapped his hand on the arm of his chair in laughter. "Did it work?"

Jason grinned down at Gem, who rolled her eyes. "I guess we'll find out next month."

I plopped my chin in my hands. "But you had Willow, like, yesterday."

"That's what I said!" Gem jerked her thumb at Jason. "And what'd you say? That you wanted enough for a basketball team?"

"That's right. Five little starters."

"Good god, why?" Bobby grimaced, earning an elbow from Laney.

Jason took a sip of his ice water before setting it down extra carefully. "Because I love my wife, and my daughter is so perfect I can't wait to make more."

Bobby ran his hand down Laney's head, pulling her toward him. "Me and this joey got a lot more exploring to do. Eh, babe?"

Laney pressed her lips into a tight smile, her eyes down on the table. "Not too much more."

He pinched his thumb and index finger together. "A bit. Before we settle down."

"I think we're pretty settled," she said, trying and failing at a lighthearted laugh that was so high-pitched no one could believe that it was real, but Bobby merely shrugged, his gaze out on the rain.

I wiggled in my seat, uncomfortable with the friction building at the table, and a big hand landed on my back. I peeked over to Mike and his silent question but couldn't answer now. I couldn't tell him how I felt bad for my friend, who had been up and down with her boyfriend lately, but also that I'd begun to consider what settling down meant for myself.

This summer had me considering lots of things I never had before, and the muscles in my back coiled at the mere thought of leaving Mike in a few weeks—days, really.

When I offered him a small smile, he skimmed his palm down my spine, leaning forward to kiss my cheek.

"Well, I can't wait to have babies with Bunny." Chris pulled Bronte into his side as he tipped his chin to where Jason and Gem sat. "Give you two a run for your money."

"Bunny," I repeated in the mock scornful way I always did whenever Chris called Bronte that. Except underneath the table, I kicked at Bronte's foot, meaningfully shifting my eyes toward Laney, calling attention to how our friend had her arms crossed, her body angled away from Bobby.

Bronte nodded in understanding then slid her arm from around Chris. "How about we leave these boys for a bit and have some girl time?

"Yes. Let's get day drunk," Gem hooted.

"You boys up for some poker?" Chris asked, to which all the guys agreed with shrugs.

"All right, then." I patted Mike's shoulder. "Watch out for that one. He uses his acting technique to bluff his way through the game."

Chris leaned back in his chair, chuckling good-naturedly.

"You're mad because you have absolutely no poker face. Terrible liar."

I waited for my friends to come to my defense, but no one disagreed. Not even Mike. He only wrapped his fingers around my thigh as I stood up next to him with a dramatic flourish. "Sorry, Peaches, but your face gives everything away."

"Peaches!" Laney crowed.

Bronte lifted her orange cocktail from the table. "We're putting that at the top of our agenda to discuss."

Mike looked in question to the men at the table, and I tried to pretend I was equally as confused, but the two gossipy bastards opposite me laughed.

"Sam makes fun of Bronte and me because I call her pet names," Chris said.

"She hates pet names," Jason added then extended his hand out to Mike. "Except from you, apparently."

Mike swiped his palm over his mouth, hiding a growing smile. "Does that mean we have an agenda for discussion too? Are these posted somewhere? Girls' and guys' discussion guides?"

That earned some laughs from everyone, and Laney pointed at him while saying to me, "I really like that one."

"What about me?" Bobby asked.

"Maybe I'll like you later."

"Don't drink too much so I can remind you why you like me in your bed," Bobby said, chuckling, although no one else did.

Gem curled her lip, surely some snarky comment on the tip of her tongue, but Jason stood with a barely audible, "Don't, Gemma," and kissed her on the mouth before sending her off with a pat on her back. "Have fun, ladies."

"So, poker?" Chris unfolded himself from his chair, clearing the tension with a resounding clap. "Let me go find some cards," he said, his voice fading as we walked toward Bronte's suite.

Once there, we ordered more drinks, settled on the bed, and started in on our agenda.

"Okay, so can I just say Bobby is very handsome and charismatic and *that accent*... But, like... What's with the jokes?" Gem huffed. "Unless he's talking about food, he's not funny."

Laney held up her drink as if it were a stop sign. "I know. It's like he has to be the center of attention all the time. We're working on it, but I don't want to get into that right now. Besides, that's not on the agenda." She whipped her head to me. "Let's get right down to it, Peaches. What do you have to say for yourself?"

Bronte sat cross-legged, her eyes bright and a little drunk. "Yeah, you conveniently left out basically every detail at my bachelorette."

"There aren't any details, really."

"He called you 'Peaches,'" Gem said. "Peaches! Is it 'cause of your ass? I bet it is. How do you get a bubble butt like that?"

Laney checked out her own butt in the mirror. "I know, right? Mine is flat and wide. No matter how many squats I do, it's al—"

Bronte snapped her fingers. "Hey, we're getting off topic. We're talking about Sam and Mike. We can circle back to butt workouts after."

"Sorry, Miss Hollinger," Gem mumbled, and Laney bowed to me.

"There's nothing to tell. Like I said." I tossed back the rest of my fruity alcoholic slushie and stuck the umbrella behind my ear. "You know I really like peach-flavored stuff." I indicated my now empty glass as evidence. "He started calling me that one day, and I guess... I don't know. It stuck."

"It stuck. That's for sure," Bronte said around a sip of her drink.

"Peaches is adorable," Laney added.

Gem flipped onto her back, lining her legs up against the wall. "The fact that you brought him here at all says everything we need to know."

I picked up my next drink. "All you need to know for what?"

"Don't play innocent with me, Samantha. We are one and the same when it comes to this," Gem said and then back-tracked. "Or, we used to be one and the same. And I know no one listens to any advice I ever give, but—" she eyed me, her head upside down "—I wasted a lot of time ignoring how I felt about Jason. You're going to be real mad at yourself if you waste any more time with that man out there."

"We don't have any time. That's the problem."

"Because you're going to Texas?" Laney guessed, and when I nodded, Bronte waved at herself.

"Look at what happened to Chris and me. We were across the country, and we figured it out."

"Yeah, but wasn't it terrible?"

Bronte popped the cherry from her drink into her mouth. "Yes, and it was also worth it. So, maybe you should start thinking *yes, and* instead of *no, but*."

Gem righted herself. "Whoa."

"That was really deep," Laney whispered solemnly.

I considered Bronte's words carefully. *Yes*, I was moving to Texas at the end of the month, *and* could I also be with Mike? "How, though?"

Because my friends could always read my mind, Bronte said, "You can figure out a way."

Laney shifted so her feet hung off the bed. "You're only in Austin for a year. You could do long-distance."

"Or you could ask him to move with you," Gem said, like that wasn't the scariest option in the world. "What's the worst that could happen? He'd say no?"

"We barely know each other."

"Technically, haven't you known each other since you were kids?" Laney asked.

"*Biblically*, she means." Gem smacked my leg. "Right?"

"I mean we've known each other as adults in this particular relationship for a few weeks. That's not the basis for asking someone to move their whole life to another state."

"Why not?" Bronte asked, her straw between her lips.

"*You* are asking me that? You, who would write a literal agenda for this chat if we allowed you to because you like order and predictability so much, are asking me why not invite a man who is supposed to be my summer fling to uproot his life and move in with me?"

"Correct," Bronte answered before slurping her drink, rattling the ice at the bottom, while Laney and Gem broke up into a fit of giggles.

I was not drunk enough for this conversation and slugged back more of my drink. "Again, I point to Exhibit A, to you and Chris. You didn't want to move to LA with him."

"Well, actually—"

"Don't you 'well, actually' me. Did you or did you not want to move to LA with the man you are marrying?"

"We live there in the summers. Like people who move to Florida in the winter."

"Snowbirds," Gem muttered, folding a piece of paper with the resort's logo on it.

"It's a compromise," Bronte said. "You and Mike could do that too. Find a solution that makes you both happy."

I propped my feet on the bed. "I hate when you're so logical."

"I know," Laney whined. "So annoying when your friends help you solve a problem. Just the worst."

"The absolute worst," Gem agreed, revealing the paper crane she had made. "And now for our next act, we'll play a game. Fuck, marry, kill. The bride is first. Chris Pine, Chris Hemsworth, Chris Cunningham. Go."

We all oohed and aahed and laughed and drank for a few hours, first playing games and then talking about memories from college. When the boys finally arrived, breaking up our fun, I was still smiling as I leaned into Mike, holding on to his arm.

He kept me walking in a straight line. "You had a good time tonight."

"We always have a good time. Did you?"

"You were right. Chris wiped the floor with all of us."

"He's a cheat," I sniffed, and with my ear against his side, I felt rather than heard his laugh. "I told you. I don't trust him."

"He's a good guy."

I peered up at him through loose pieces of my hair, and he brushed them away. "He is a very good guy. So are you."

"Yeah? I get the seal of approval from the girls?"

"Yep. Although I can't tell you what they said. On pain of death."

He opened the door to our room, leading me inside and straight to the bathroom, where he handed me a water and a couple Tylenol. "I don't doubt it. I wouldn't put it past Gem to murder anyone."

I swallowed down the pills then grabbed my toothpaste and toothbrush. "She wouldn't do the actual murder. She'd be the distraction. Laney would do the murdering. Bronte would be the cover story."

"You guys have it all figured out already?"

I nodded, my mouth filled with foam.

"What about you? What would you do in this crime scenario?"

I spat into the sink. "Get rid of the body."

He leaned on the counter, a hint of a smile curling his top lip. "How'd you figure that out? Draw straws or what?"

"Nope." I finished up with my teeth. "Even though Gem's good for a verbal beating, she wouldn't have it in her to really take anybody out, but she has no problem getting and keeping attention." I swished some water around in my mouth then squirted face wash into my hands. "Bronte is the only one who could keep our story straight, and she's so sweet, no one would believe she's lying." I proceeded to wash my face and dry it before meeting Mike's charmed grin. "That leaves Laney and me for the dirty work, and since she looks the way she does, we figure she would be able to take the man by surprise. She could shove the knife into his side while he's distracted by her beauty."

"Why not you?" He curved his hand over my shoulder. "You have been quite a distraction to me all summer."

"You're saying you think I'd be able to take you out."

He spun me around and gently pushed me to the bed, where he stripped off my sundress. I hadn't worn a bra underneath, and his eyes dropped below my face for barely a second before he picked up one of his T-shirts to put on me. Then he yanked the covers back on the bed and when he had the sheets tucked all around me, he sat down next to me.

"You've already taken me out," he said, gliding his knuckles down my cheek and across my jaw. "You killed me that first day at the picnic. When you hit me with those eyes of yours as you rambled nervously. And you dig the knife in a little deeper every time you take my hand and tell me a secret. Because even though you wear your emotions on your sleeve, you don't speak them out loud very often."

Even in my rum-soaked brain, his words were loud and clear, and while I desperately wanted to reply, confess everything I'd been feeling, I couldn't. It all got stuck somewhere between my heart and mouth, settling like pebbles in my throat, and I coughed.

"Hold on," he said and got up from the bed to return with water.

I took it gratefully, yet I still couldn't talk. At least not about everything inside me. "How come you manage to be so quiet and still say the most beautiful things?"

He kissed my cheek then stood up again. "I never thought about it before my brother pointed it out the other day." He lifted his arms at his sides in a *what can you do?* motion. "He said I only talk about the things that are most important to me. I didn't realize that was true until recently."

Then he offered me a quick smile. "Go to sleep. I don't want you too hungover tomorrow. The rain stopped, and I want to go swimming with you."

———

I had woken up with a slight headache, cured by some hair of the dog and morning kisses from Mike underneath the covers. Laney texted that Chris and Bronte were busy doing pre-wedding things, so she and Bobby were already on the beach. Mike and I made our way to the water's edge and I gaped at Bobby who was swimming laps, actual laps. In the ocean.

Laney rearranged her lounger. "He's at home out there. Like a shark."

"I haven't swum in..." Mike's words trailed off, his eyes somewhere off in the distance, and I grabbed the SPF.

"In a while?" I guessed, squirting some into my hand to spread along his back.

"I already put some on," he told me.

I grinned, knowing full well he did. While I'd dug through my suitcase for my bathing suit, he'd sprayed some on all over before putting on his special waterproof prosthesis. "Don't want you getting burned."

He swung his hand back behind him to grip my hip with a squeeze. "Terrible liar."

"How's the business going, Mike?" Laney asked.

To answer, he lifted his hand flat in the air, wavering it side to side, and I took my time rubbing the lotion into his skin, tracing his shoulder blades, the thick muscles at his shoulders and on either side of his spine.

"Even with the channel?" When he didn't answer, Laney tilted her head up to him. "Have you been posting regularly like I told you?"

He stayed quiet, and I hissed out an "uh-oh" as Laney shot up, removing her sunglasses and oversized sun hat to frown at Mike.

"We haven't known each other long, but if there is one thing I'm good at, it's my job."

I dropped the SPF into my beach bag. "That's true."

"I'm more than happy to help," she went on, "but I can't do the work for you."

Mike grunted.

"What does that mean?" she asked him, then poked her head around his shoulder to ask me, "What does that sound mean?"

"He's thinking."

"Well, you want to think out loud for my benefit, Marine?"

He huffed. "I don't know what to say, what videos to make. It took hours to make that five-minute introduction."

"Yeah, it was your first one. You'll get better at it once you get the hang of it." Laney plopped her sunglasses and hat back on then laid out on her chair. "I didn't think you'd give up so easily."

"I'm not giving up. I'm saying it's not my thing, talking to a camera."

"It doesn't have to be your thing, and you don't have to take any of my advice. You could keep on doing what you're doing. No one's forcing you. Then again, you can find some of that testicular fortitude they're always going on about in those military commercials for new recruits and put the work in."

"I thought Gem was the ballbuster," Mike muttered, staring down at Laney, yet she didn't wither under his gaze like some other people might. She beamed up at him instead.

"Depends on the day. Now, can you move over? You're blocking my sun."

He turned to me, but I only slid my sunglasses on and smiled.

"You girls are savage. Jason was right. You're a bunch of she-wolves."

I bumped the side of Laney's fist when she held it aloft, and Mike failed to hide his smile as he gave us a dismayed shake of his head before walking out into the ocean with me.

"I thought you'd back me up with her," he said once we were in the water.

"Tough love. That's what they're there for. The only one who will go slightly easier on you is—"

"Bronte," he finished, pulling me to him. "I'm learning the ropes quick."

"Yeah?" I wrapped my arms around his neck, legs around his waist. "Like what?"

"I'm not sure if I'm allowed to tell you. On pain of death."

"Hey." I cinched my legs tighter as if that would do anything. It didn't. He merely skated his hands to my backside, his fingers playing with the edges of my bikini. "You keeping secrets from me?"

He met my eyes and smiled into a kiss, the water lapping at our throats as he sank us both lower into the warm water. "You didn't tell me your gossip."

"Because there wasn't any. We talked about how I'm the Tin Man and then got drunk." I didn't think I had to elaborate anymore. It wasn't as if I hid who I was from Mike. I'd been honest with him from the beginning. The problem was now I didn't know what to do or say about the feelings I couldn't hide since apparently I had no poker face.

Although, he didn't push it, so I didn't either. Save the *feelings* for a later date. Maybe after more cocktails.

"I learned," he started, letting go of me to float on his back, "that Jason calls his daughter 'chicken' and that he really does want another kid."

I swept my arms out over the top of the water. It was so calm and blue, it almost looked fake. "That's not a secret."

"He doesn't seem to like Bobby much."

"I don't know if I particularly like Bobby at the moment," I said, watching the man in question swim toward the surf.

"He said he's feeling pressured to propose."

The bastard! "Pressured," I whisper-shouted. "That can't be true. He was the one who brought it up after an argument they had a couple weeks ago." When Mike tipped his head up, his wet hair clung to his forehead, and I swiped it back. "What else?"

"Chris talked about Bronte's family a lot. Said he doesn't speak to his own."

"That's a sad story. Did he tell it to you?"

"Not really, just that they basically disowned him."

I nodded. "What else?"

He laughed. "We played poker with pretzels and drank

beer. It wasn't anything deep, but it gave me a better understanding of you guys. Of how close you are."

I paddled behind him, wrapping my arms around his shoulders, pressing my chest against his back. "You get one of us, you get the rest of us."

He hooked my legs on either side of his hips then slowly sliced through the water with his arms. "Good thing I'm pretty strong. I can carry the lot of you."

I kissed his shoulder and rested my chin in the crook of his neck, enjoying the gentle ride but utterly unable to respond to his offer. He wanted me. For real. Not for the summer or for a fling, but for real. He would accept everything that came with me, all of my emotional and physical baggage, including but not limited to the form of three other women. It was a lot to carry, and I didn't know how to ask that of him.

"I thought you were the swimmer," he said, cutting through my mental breakdown. "But here I am, carrying your lazy mermaid ass around."

I threw back my head and giggled in relief at being able to avoid the topic for now. "If I'm a mermaid, what are you?"

"Pirate."

"Come to pillage and plunder my treasure?" I ground my hips against him, and he stopped swimming, guiding me around to his front.

We were closer to the beach, and I was able to stand now, my toes finding the sand. With one hand against my lower back and the other woven into my tangled, wet hair, he kissed his words into my mouth. "I want more than your treasure. I want everything."

CHAPTER TWENTY-SEVEN

Samantha and I spent a few hours soaking up the sun with her friends. Although, now, I thought I could call them my friends too. I was beginning to understand their inside jokes and nuanced glances they sent one another. And before we knew it, it was time to get ready for the wedding.

I had packed my navy suit but decided to forgo the jacket. Even with a sunset ceremony, it was still too hot for that many layers. It didn't take me long to shower and dress, but Samantha stayed in the bathroom for a while, though when she came back out in a long, flowing dress that reminded me of ocean waves with tiny straps tied behind her neck, my breath caught in my chest. With her lavender hair pulled back from her face and those enormous eyelashes she'd worn in LA, she really did look like a mermaid.

She held her hands out at her sides in question.

"You are stunning," I told her, and color rose in her cheeks. I smoothed my palms down her shoulders and arms. "Like something out of my wildest dreams."

Taking her lips with my own, I tasted them with a faint touch of my tongue, and she curled her fingers into my hair, tugging at the roots, inviting me to kiss her harder and deeper.

Plunder and pillage. After trying to get her alone for so many weeks, I was able to touch and kiss her whenever I wanted, and I still couldn't get enough. I feared I never would.

"I guess you don't want to be late to your best friend's wedding, do you?" I asked, easing away from her.

"No," she said after a while, like maybe she was considering it, and I smiled, shaking out my arms as if that would help cool my blood. I made sure my tie was straight before holding out my hand.

"Then let's go."

The ceremony was set up on a small overlook, with the few chairs in rows facing a decorated arbor, highlighting the turquoise water beyond it. The sky was painted in pinks and purples, and I didn't hesitate to wrap my arm around Sam when she asked Gem to take a picture of us.

"Our first picture together," she said, showing me the screen of her phone, and I didn't miss the way her throat worked on a swallow.

She was cracking.

She'd been cracking.

I didn't think it would be long until she gave up on this being for the summer, yet I wasn't going to push her. I knew she needed to come around in her own time. Until then, I'd continue to do what I had been, showing her how it could be between is. How it would be between us, if only she could let go of whatever held her back.

Because I loved her.

I *loved* her.

A single guitar player strummed soft chords, and Sam absently linked her hand with mine as she talked animatedly with Laney about something I couldn't pay attention to since I was so busy trying not to confess my epiphany. How I'd loved her from maybe the first moment at the picnic when she stumbled over her words. And then fell in love with her again on the soccer field when she was so vulnerable with me, and every time she wasn't afraid to talk about my injury, and especially when she flashed me her smile. The wide, carefree grin that curved her cheeks so much she kind of looked like a chipmunk. I loved that too.

Loved it so much I hadn't been paying attention when Chris strolled down the aisle or when the officiant asked everyone to stand. Samantha had to tug me up, a bemused laugh escaping that she'd caught me daydreaming. I was positive she wouldn't be laughing if she could see inside my brain, to know she was the reason I forgot all time and space.

The guitarist switched tunes as Bronte appeared on her father's arm in all white, a long, thin veil billowing behind her as she walked toward Chris, whose face had gone red.

Gem stretched her arm in front of me to tap Samantha's arm. "For once in her life, she's not crying."

"I know," she said, and Laney, on the other side of Samantha, bent her head down too.

"But look at him, he can't control himself."

"Neither can you," Samantha murmured. "Who has the tissues?"

Jason, at the end of the row, stuck out his long arm, offering tissues to the ladies, mumbling something about how Gem had been a crier since the baby.

Then we were all asked to be seated, and there was no more whispering to be had. Only Chris and Bronte, in front of everyone, exchanging vows and rings and kisses. And it was official.

"I am happy to introduce Mr. and Mrs. Cunningham," the officiant bellowed, and Chris held on to his wife's face with such tender care that a pang of jealousy lodged between my ribs in that moment. That Chris got to declare his love in front of everyone.

"Get a room," someone shouted. I guessed it was Bronte's brother, but I couldn't be sure, and Chris finally broke the kiss with the dopiest, happiest smile anyone had ever seen.

They didn't walk back down the aisle, but instead, the newlyweds greeted each of their guests for hugs and hand-shakes. A photographer snapped pictures with everyone, and by the time the sun had almost completely set, the party began.

With such a small group, the resort set up two long tables on either side of a wooden floor in the grassy space between our suites. Lanterns and candles lit up the whole area, and small bits of food were served on never-ending plates. There was no official "agenda," but multiple people gave short speeches. Bronte's father could hardly get through his because he was crying so much. There was another from her sister, one from Chris's friend and business partner, Wes, and then finally Chris, who raised his glass of champagne in the air toward the small crowd, saying, "Thank you all for coming here to this tropical paradise to celebrate our wedding. If I haven't told you before, you all being here means the world to us. I thank you from the bottom of my heart. And to Bronte, my wife," he said as if he still couldn't believe it. "You're my saving grace. I love you, baby."

The guests quietly clapped as they kissed, and music played from hidden speakers. Chris and Bronte led the danc-ing, but Samantha and I hung back. After she finished her glass of champagne, she climbed on my lap.

I traced shapes with my fingertip between her shoulder blades. "I'm surprised the three of you didn't get up and do some song or dance for Bronte,"

"Nah, we're not like that. Besides, Gem can't carry a tune to save her life, and I told you I'm not a good dancer."

We watched as a dance circle formed around Chris and Bronte during a Prince song.

"Nice wedding, though."

She nodded. "Yeah. Beats a big wedding with bland food and having to sit with people you don't know."

"Is this the kind of wedding you want?" The question slipped out before I could think better of it, but now that it was out, I couldn't retract it. So, I dug in. "Something small like this? Or on a beach?"

"I don't know if I'll get married," she said, her gaze still on the other guests, though the hand she had on my neck had stopped petting me.

"You don't know?"

"No." After a while, she slanted her eyes to me. "I've seen what divorce can do to people. I've felt it."

This was the conversation we needed to have, and I rearranged my hold on her so she was turned more fully to face me. "Not everyone gets divorced."

"No, not everyone does, and not everyone is cut out for marriage."

I felt her tense under my fingers. "You think you're not cut out for it?"

I refused to let her go when she tried to peel away from me, and I could see her jaw working in the lantern light for a few moments before speaking. "I don't know if I am or not, and I'm not much looking forward to finding out by getting divorced."

"But why do you automatically assume that's going to happen? You have to work at marriage, like people work at everything else."

"Like you would?" Her brow rose as she puffed out a sound

of annoyance. "You were just telling Laney this morning that working on your business isn't your thing."

Her accusation had me slumping back against my chair.

"I didn't mean that. I'm sorry, Mike. I didn't—"

"No, you're right," I said, because it was true. I hadn't been working as hard as I could on growing my business, but we were talking about two different things. And I didn't want her to think I would give up so easily. "But that doesn't mean I wouldn't work at my marriage."

She played with my loosened tie. "I had a conversation with my dad a few weeks ago, while..." She wrinkled her nose and sniffed. "While you and I weren't talking. He basically said he was sorry for not doing more when he was married to my mom. He took a lot of responsibility for everything that happened. Said he should have tried harder."

I opened my mouth but froze when she lifted her watery eyes to me.

"Even if he worked harder, my mom still would have fallen in love with Lina. Some people aren't meant to be married."

I didn't know if Samantha was saying *she* wasn't meant to be married at all or not married to *me*. Either way, I didn't like those answers. "Marriage doesn't make a relationship any easier or harder. If you are committed to someone, it takes the same amount of energy and love. I thought I would marry Bianca and didn't, but it still hurt when we broke up."

"Exactly." She blinked, and a fat tear rolled down her cheek.

I towed her to my chest. "Sweetheart, I can't promise that I will never hurt you, but I can promise that I would never give up on you." I kissed her temple, her ear, any part of her face that wasn't buried against my neck. "I wouldn't give up on us."

"What did I tell you about saying those kinds of things to me?"

I stroked my hands down her back over and over until she sat up, the corners of her mouth threatening a smile, and a flutter of hope danced into my heart. "I can't help it. I need to tell you, and I need you to hear me."

She bit into the corner of her bottom lip as she stood, taking me by the hand. "I hear you." Then she led me out onto the dance floor, where the others danced to some fast tempo song, but Samantha strung her arms around my neck. "Sway with me?"

I answered by pulling her against me, lacing my fingers at the small of her back. She'd taken her heels off long ago, and she let her head drop to my chest. We swayed for a long time until Gem ambled over, a wine bottle in hand.

"I'm going to have to steal her for a bit," she told me, snatching Samantha away.

She gave me a quick kiss on the cheek then held out her other hand to Bronte, who had her arm looped in Laney's. The four women paraded down to the beach, the moon illuminating their shadowy figures.

I leaned against a tree, arms crossed, keeping an eye on them as they passed the wine bottle back and forth. According to all the flashes, it looked like Laney was taking some photos of them all bunched together.

"Oh, good."

I glanced to my left where Chris wandered up, his shirt untucked and sleeves rolled up to his elbows.

"You already got eyes on the girls. I saw Bronte sneak off but not where she went."

"I wanted to make sure no one walked off into the water."

"Gemma would be the one to do that," Jason said, appearing on my right, his hands shoved into his pockets. "Hard to keep that one in line sometimes."

"But you love to be the one to do it, huh?" Chris chuckled,

and Jason lifted a shoulder with a half smile as a burst of giggles rose up from the girls.

We were quiet for a minute until Chris blew out a breath as if an idea had just occurred to him. "When Bronte's dad had a heart attack, she was so stressed she was cleaning and organizing the dish towels in her parents' kitchen. I thought it was the oddest, most wonderful thing I'd ever seen." He took a sip of his drink, his eyes out to the women. "We weren't even together then, but I knew I loved her."

His words were an invitation, and Jason accepted it. "The first time I walked into Gemma's apartment, it was a mess. Clothes everywhere, art supplies all over the floor. Her turtle and goldfish lived in her kitchen, and she had compost in the corner. I'd never met anyone so ridiculous in my life."

"And you loved her for it," Chris said, never taking his eyes off his wife, who was dancing, circling underneath Laney's arm.

"And I loved her for it," Jason agreed, full-on grinning as Gem was doing some kind of yoga or gymnastics.

I tipped my head, squinting, trying to find Samantha. She appeared to be doing the backstroke. On dry land.

After a moment, I felt eyes on me and noticed my two new friends patiently waiting for my turn. "I guess it was..." I thought back to all my time with Samantha, not really able to pinpoint an exact day or time I'd fallen for her. It had been a little more every time we were together. "We go for a lot of walks with her family dog, and the first day, she called him Eddie. I thought it was a funny name for a dog, but then she said his full name. Edward Anthony Masen. It's from *Twilight*."

"Oh yeah. Okay," Chris said with a nod.

"You know it?"

"Famous actor, remember?" Jason jerked his thumb toward Chris, who flipped him the bird.

I continued, "Sam's totally unapologetic about everything. She is completely herself. She likes what she likes and doesn't care if other people do too. She asks for what she wants, no matter what people think of her. And she named her dog Eddie."

"We are three lucky bastards," Jason sighed, and that had me searching for the missing other half.

"Where's Bobby?"

"I saw him chatting with the chef," Chris said into his drink. "Something about putting him on some show, who knows. You know that guy is thirty-eight?"

I couldn't believe it. "Thirty-eight?"

"He acts like he's eighteen sometimes," Jason muttered.

"He seems like—" Chris flung his hand out toward the ocean. "Oh shit, Jay."

"Yep. Got her, got her." Jason sprinted to the sand. Gem was headed straight for the water.

Chris and I let out a chuckle and started off too at a much more leisurely pace since the other three were in the middle of hysterics, falling over in giggles as Jason swung Gem up into his arms.

The things we'd do for the women we loved.

CHAPTER TWENTY-EIGHT

Sam

I woke up to warm skin against mine and hot kisses along my shoulder. I blinked my eyes open to the sun cutting across the bedroom, highlighting the cream sheets knotted around our legs.

"Good morning." Mike dragged his hand up my torso, settling between my naked breasts.

After the boys had broken up the party, the reception had all but petered out, and everyone had staggered back to their suites in a haze of romance, food comas, champagne eyes, or all of the above.

I'd come home, stripped naked, and immediately attempted to seduce Mike, but he held me off, promising to make it up to me in the morning. He'd said I needed water and sleep, and he wasn't wrong. After the last few days with my girls, I could use some extra vitamins and maybe a short hibernation. But not until I got what was owed.

I shifted to my back, smiling at the sight of Mike's bare chest and hair sticking up behind his ear. "Morning."

The warm, hard length of him pressed against my thigh. "Did you sleep well?"

"I always sleep well next to you." I stretched my arms up,

and he bent his head, sucking a nipple into his mouth, my yawn easing into a moan.

As he placed his hands on either side of me, moving down to suck on my lower breast, nibble at my rib cage, memories from the reception filtered into my mind. The way he'd held me after I'd confessed how afraid I was of being hurt. How he'd promised he wouldn't give up on me or us.

When my parents divorced, I'd felt so out of control that it led me down a very dark path. I never wanted to be that deeply damaged ever again, and I knew in my bones that if I truly allowed it, I could be. And Mike could be the one to do it because I loved him.

I loved him, and that gave him the power to hurt me.

Though if I was going to start thinking like Bronte told me to... *Yes*, I loved him, *and* it could be something wonderful.

I could love him loudly and openly and without reservation or time limits. We could figure out how to make it work. All I had to do was say the words. Yet as he picked up his head, his eyes shining with passion and appreciation and something that I thought looked an awful lot like love, my words lodged in my throat, right where he kissed me.

The only thing I could get out was, "Need you."

He breathed heavily against my ear. "I know. I know."

"Please, I need you."

He nipped at my jaw then gently rolled me to my side. Behind me, I heard the familiar sound of a condom wrapper ripping open before his hands returned to me. He curled one arm under my neck, the other over my hip and between my legs.

He stroked me languidly, sucking at my shoulder, but it wasn't enough. "More."

He was pressed up against my back, the hair on his chest

tickling my skin, the muscles along his torso hard, and I ground against his erection. "Please."

He flattened two fingers against my clit, teasing at my ache, and I arched against him. "Harder."

"I know what you need," he rasped.

I hooked my arm around his neck, holding him to me. "I know, but..."

"If you know, then let me give it to you."

I nodded and turned toward his arm curled around me, kissing his bicep. I may have needed practice saying the words, but I could show him how much I loved him, and how I trusted him to love me back.

"Samantha," he murmured, dipping his fingers inside of me, "I..."

"I know," I breathed, my voice barely audible. My skin flushed. My pulse thrummed all over. "I know."

When his fingers left me, I whimpered, and he kissed my jaw. I swear I could feel his heartbeat against my back—it was beating as fast as my own—and he guided himself into me before lifting my thigh up.

Every morning, we'd done this, had slow, lazy sex, but never quite like this, speaking with only our breaths and kisses. We'd played and laughed, experimented and explored, but this was different. As if this wasn't just fun. This was important. It was special.

As he rolled his hips to deepen his thrust, I laid my hand on top of his, interlocking our fingers. "It feels..."

"I know," he said, all lips and teeth, and he crushed me to him so there was no space between us, except for the one thing yet to be spoken aloud. And when we both fell over the edge together, I wrapped his arm around my middle, pressing his palm to my chest so he could feel what I did. Love.

It was everyone's last full day on the island. Chris and Bronte were going to stay for their honeymoon, but as all their guests sat down to their last meal together, it was decidedly more subdued. The brood of children Bronte's siblings brought along looked and sounded exhausted. The adults weren't much better. A lot of sunburned shoulders and hushed, hungover voices.

I held Mike's hand as we made our way to the restaurant for brunch, walking on sunshine and unicorn glitter, despite the sleep exhaustion.

"You look chipper this morning," Laney noted, sipping on a mimosa.

"Blindingly so." Gem held her head in her hands as Jason rubbed her back.

"She puked up her intestines last night," he explained, nudging the water glass closer to her.

Brunch was spread out among the tables, shrimp cocktail, fresh pastries, mini quiches, flatbreads, salads, and little skewers with salmon, potatoes, and dill. I filled my plate as Mike looped his arm around the back of my chair, pushing the fruit plate toward Gem. "Eat the citrus. They're high in vitamin B, good for hangovers."

I was tempted to boop him on the nose for being so cute and smart, and I knew it was irrational, but being in love really did feel like I was in a cartoon. This time, there were no road-runners and anvils, only a heart beating out of my chest and an urge to keep my mouth permanently attached to Mike's.

Interrupting my daydream, Gem dropped her hand to the plate for a slice of grapefruit. Putting it in her mouth, she mumbled, "I hate grapefruit."

"Maybe you shouldn't have—"

She swung her head over to Jason so fast, her sunglasses almost flew off. "That's how you want this day to go? My best friend got married last night."

"And you got so drunk you wanted to take a midnight swim in the ocean. I saved your life."

"And don't think I won't cut you open with this—" she grabbed the utensil closest to her without looking "—this spoon and shove grapefruit down your throat, Boy Scout."

"The question is not would you, it's *could* you, isn't it?" Laney asked.

Jason curled his hand around Gem's face, not at all offended by his wife's threat. "I think it depends on what the spoon is made of."

"Quality of the metalwork," Mike added with a nod, and I bounced in my seat, giddy at how well he got along with my friends.

Bobby reached for the curved salad tongs. "I'd reckon these could do some damage."

Gem slid her sunglasses back into place and munched on an orange, while the rest of us continued our discussion of spoons as a murder weapon.

After making the rounds with the rest of their guests, Bronte and Chris strolled over to our table, hand in hand and glowing.

"I see everyone enjoyed themselves last night." Chris grinned down at Gem.

She gave him the finger in return.

"Mike, I was talking with Fitz earlier," he said, his thumb poised over his shoulder, pointing at where Bronte's brother sat with his family. "You met him, right?"

He swallowed his bite of quiche. "Yeah, briefly."

"He's looking to get back into the gym. I said he should talk to you."

Mike nodded his thanks.

"I told him how... You know what?" Chris glanced between me and Mike. "You want to talk to him now?"

"Yeah," Bronte agreed. "They're leaving in a bit, so you might as well."

I smiled encouragingly before he got up to follow Chris. Bronte stole his seat.

"You look extraordinarily happy this morning," she said to me.

"And you look very married this morning."

Bronte rested her chin on her hand, her rings sparkling. "Thank you."

Bobby's cell phone buzzed on the table, and he checked the screen before pushing back from the table with a, "Hey, mate. No, no, I'm not busy..."

Laney tossed back the rest of her mimosa, her eyes on his retreating form, then thumped the glass down with a little more force than necessary. "What time are everyone's flights?"

Jason polished off his coffee. "Ours is this afternoon."

"Gotta get back to the baby," Gem explained.

"Mike and I leave first thing tomorrow morning," I said, and Laney blotted at her mouth with a cloth napkin.

"We're flying to New York City. Bobby has a meeting with some investors, but it's just a layover for me."

I wanted to ask her about that, but before I could, Jason checked his watch then stood up. "We should go pack, Gemma."

"No," she whined. "I can't. I'm too tired."

He tugged at her elbow. "Come on."

"My legs don't work."

He sighed and scooped her up, eliciting an unexpected squawk from her. He held her like a rag doll. "Sometimes I think you're like this on purpose."

Gem swatted at him, her head upside down. "I *know* you're like this on purpose."

"We'll be back to say goodbye," he said to us then spun around.

Gem groaned. "Not so fast."

Whatever he mumbled to her had her laughing as he carried her away.

I snorted. "They're not going to pack."

"Definitely not," Bronte agreed.

I shielded my eyes from the sun with my hand when Laney also stood up. "And where are you going?"

"I got my period this morning," she said, and Bronte and I both commiserated in her agony before she departed the table with a wave, leaving me with the bride.

"So, tell me honestly. You like being married?"

"Well, it's only been about twelve hours, but so far, so good. Why?" She smiled. "You changing your mind on the institution?"

I lifted a shoulder. "Mike and I were talking last night."

My friend didn't say anything, merely brushed her bangs out of her eyes and raised her brow.

I was difficult to admit my feelings to myself, let alone someone else, but like Gem had said weeks ago, admitting them are the first step. "I told him I didn't know if I wanted to get married, but he made some convincing arguments."

"Convincing arguments like he loves you?"

"No." My cheeks burned. "He didn't tell me that."

"But you love him, though?" She guessed in that intuitive way she had.

I swallowed down the lump in my throat and met her steady gaze, my silence answer enough.

Bronte clutched her hands to her chest. "I'm so happy for you."

I tried to play it off. "Happy for me? Nothing's happened yet."

"So, wait. You didn't tell him either?"

I shook my head.

"Samantha."

"What? Don't say my name like that."

She tsked me, sitting back against the chair. "Tell him. What are you waiting for?"

"I can't just blurt it out."

"Why not?"

I huffed, waving my hand down the length of her body. "Marriage is changing you."

She aimed her attention to the ocean, quiet for a few moments before she said, "Screw your courage to the sticking place."

Bronte was infamous for quoting lines from books, and unfortunately for me, none of them were ever from *Twilight*. "Who said that?"

"Lady Macbeth."

"Oh, that's what I get? A lady trying to get her husband to kill the king."

Chris cut off Bronte's explanation when he called for her. "Bunny, Wes is leaving."

"Don't get cold feet now. You're halfway there. All that's left is to tell him."

I guffawed. "All that's left, she says."

Bronte tossed her hand up behind her head as she trotted away. "Better than 'out damned spot.'"

CHAPTER TWENTY-NINE

I zipped up my suitcase. The alarm had gone off bright and early at six this morning, and after so many days of sleeping in, Samantha and I struggled to wake up. I showered and dressed first, giving her a few more minutes to sleep in, but now that she was in the shower and I had more time to fully wake up, I required coffee.

"Hey, Peaches," I said, leaning into the bathroom. "I'm going to run down to see if we can get some coffee to go."

She was mid-shampoo, her hair all lathered up, her entire silhouette exposed to me through the glass, and I soaked up the round curve of her ass, her hips and belly, the slope of her breasts. I memorized her all over again, and if someone asked, I could draw her with my eyes closed if I had to.

"You want me to see if they have cold brew?" I asked, meeting her gaze.

"Yes, please."

"Vanilla?"

She dropped her hands under the spray of water, smiling at me. "You're good to me."

"That's the point." I rapped my knuckles on the doorframe. "Be back in a bit."

After asking the concierge where I could find coffee to go, I was directed to one of the restaurants.

"How can I help you?" an older gentleman behind the bar asked.

"I'd like two coffees to go, please. Do you happen to have any flavored syrups?"

He motioned to a few bottles lined up behind him.

"Vanilla. She likes a lot of it in her coffee. And could you put it over ice?"

"No problem." He got to work as a now-familiar chuckle sounded from the other end of the bar.

I lifted my eyes to Bobby, where he sat with a coffee mug in one hand and his cell phone in the other. "These women and their sweet coffee. What's the point? They might as well chug a fruity energy drink and call it a day."

I didn't necessarily disagree, but I wasn't exactly friendly enough with the guy to share inside jokes. "You're up early."

"I'm not much of a sleeper."

The man behind the counter slid me my coffee, plain black, along with some sugar and cream if I wanted it. I dumped a little of both in before placing the lid on. "How'd you enjoy the trip?"

"Pretty good, yeah. I have meetings to get to in New York. I think Laney's pissed I'm not coming right home with her."

I tried to connect the dots of what I knew about both of them. "Is it hard, working together and being in a relationship?"

He leaned back in his chair, stretching his back as he scrubbed his hands through his hair. "It's not bad. She's solid." Then he crossed his arms, pursing his lips, and although I didn't know Bobby well, it seemed like he had something on his mind, so I took a seat, waiting for Samantha's coffee. "I love Laney, I do, but this trip wasn't, uh, as easy as I thought it was going to be. Lots of talk about marriage."

When I was given the cold brew, I offered my credit card in return to pay.

"She's not giving me an ultimatum, but she takes everything I say so literally. I mention marrying her one time a few months ago, and now she brings it up all the time. But, hey, come on," he said, holding out his arms as if he were speaking to a crowd. His audience was me and the man behind the bar.

"I've got things I want to do," Bobby said.

I sipped my coffee. "Sounds like Sam."

"Yeah? She's smart, that one."

I nodded in agreement.

"What do you think? You ready to pop the question?"

I didn't answer. It wasn't really a matter of if I was ready. It was more about if it was right, and if Samantha wanted it.

"No." Bobby chuckled. "You're like me, huh? In transition. Still working on your personal training, right? I get it. I mean, how can I settle down when I'm still working on expansion? I can't stop everything when I've got plans."

He kept right on talking as my mind whirled. This Australian talked a mile a minute, and not all of it sounded right to my ears.

"I know Laney's been helping you out. She told me it's been tough for you to attract clients." He sucked air in through his front teeth. "I know how that is. But you gotta keep pushing. You've got loads of work to do, and I know you wouldn't put that aside for Sam. Like I won't put mine aside for Laney," he said, putting his own words and actions on me. Words and actions which hadn't even occurred to me. "Sam's going to Texas, right? And, what? She expects you to drop everything and move there with her?"

I didn't know how to answer. Because first of all, that hadn't come up, and second, I didn't have a lot of anything to drop. I'd barely had to reschedule any clients to come on this last-minute trip. I'd barely had enough clients to scratch by on the equivalent of minimum wage. If it weren't for my parents offering me room and board, I wouldn't be able to afford rent on my own.

Bobby blew a puff of air from the corner of his mouth. "No way. You can't do that," he said, referring to me apparently moving to Texas. "Austin is so much more expensive than... Where do you live?"

"Akron, Ohio."

He threw his hands in the air. "Right. Wherever that is. Austin is so much more expensive than that. And Sam expects you to be able to afford moving?" He shook his head in dismay on my behalf. "You know these girls want us to provide for them, as they should, but then they get mad at us for making a living."

He was speaking in generalities now, and I wanted to defend Samantha, defend myself, but I was so far down my own mental spiral that I couldn't climb out. If I was going to be with Samantha, how could I provide for her? *What* would I provide for her? Right now, it was a whole lot of nothing.

"Look at me," Bobby said, holding his arms out, and I dropped my chin toward my chest. My brain screamed at me to go, stress already working its way through my bloodstream. I didn't need coffee at this point. My anxiety had me wide awake. But Bobby kept right on going. "I'm not strapped for cash, and I've been around the block a few times, yeah? But you, you've got a long way to go. Don't let your girl slow you down." Then he got *that* expression on his face, his gaze dropping momentarily to my leg. "I can't imagine what it's been like for you. Don't fall to the pressure. You keep doing what you're doing, you'll get there. Whether it takes you one year or fifteen years, does it matter? No. You keep working at growing your business and worry about all the relationship and marriage shite later, right?"

He slapped my back like we were buddies. We were not, and I had had about enough of his inane chatter. "I've got to go."

"Hey," Bobby called out. "Listen to me, mate. You'd be better off with money in your bank account. You'd be surprised how warm it can keep you at night."

I wasn't aware of the path I took back to the suite, my thoughts too riddled with numbers. The few numbers behind the dollar sign in my bank account, the number of times I introduced myself to new members of the gym who turned me down for training sessions, the number of times I stopped and started working on my YouTube channel, the number of classes I had taken to get my certifications, the number of doctor and hospital visits, the number of surgeries.

I couldn't avoid what those numbers added up to, the fact that I still had a very long way to go. Whatever it was Samantha was looking for, I couldn't give. I couldn't support her like she needed when I couldn't even support myself.

And that fact hit me like an explosion. I'd been playing at love all summer like it was a game. But I knew better. Life wasn't a game. Love was serious, and I wasn't ready for it.

When I agreed to a summer with Samantha, I put my own desires ahead of what I knew was true. Maybe I had been trying to avoid my own problems, but I couldn't run from them anymore. I couldn't kiss and touch Sam without thinking what it would mean for us and a future I couldn't promise her.

She deserved so much more than what I had.

Opening the door to our suite, I found Sam on the floor in

little shorts and one of her band T-shirts, her hair pulled back, with my Marines cap on her head. She packed a curling iron into a pocket of her suitcase then held her hand up for her coffee. "Thank you. You're the best."

As she sipped her drink, I slouched on the bed behind her, my palms suddenly clammy.

"Ooh, this is delicious. I'll be ready in a minute."

I nodded, unable to find words. I had, in my wildest dreams, imagined us together. Although I had never thought of how or when or where, I'd pictured lazy days cuddled on a couch, holding hands during a walk, brief kisses while we danced around each other in the kitchen. Dumb daily shit that didn't mean anything, yet somehow meant everything.

Now, I couldn't picture anything. I didn't want to.

Bobby's words rang in my ears. *You keep doing what you're doing, you'll get there. Whether it takes you one year or fifteen years...*

Samantha was leaving in a matter of days, and there was no way I could change my circumstances that fast. And I certainly wasn't going to ask her to wait for me until I figured my life out. She had goals and a timeline. She was headed for great things. Meanwhile, I was headed back to my parents' basement.

She stood up and laid her hand on my shoulder, gently shaking me. "Hey, you okay?"

"Yeah." I forced a smile. "Tired, is all."

"Me too." Her honey-brown eyes were soft and glowing under the bill of my cap. Then she tipped it up and leaned in, kissing her words against my mouth. "I don't want to go home."

I let out a harsh breath. "Me either."

I didn't want to face what I knew I had to do. The thing I'd been dreading all summer. The day I'd have to say goodbye.

A few hours later, I nudged Sam awake once we landed at the Akron-Canton Airport. I hadn't been able to sleep on either of our flights, but once we were seated, she'd promptly closed her eyes, her head falling against my shoulder. And she stayed in that position, occasionally inhaling deeply or shifting her legs or hands, nuzzling her cheek against me. Each tiny movement that got her more comfortable drove my unease up another notch.

When Bianca had broken up with me, I'd been miserable for a few weeks, on top of my lingering depression over my injuries and long recovery after my amputation. But this, this impending end to what I had with the woman who let out little, sweet breaths of air against my neck, was so much more painful already. I'd had enough physical pain to last a lifetime and couldn't imagine anything worse.

But now, I knew. I'd already lost my heart.

Samantha held it in her hands when she woke up, stretching her arms above her head. She held it in her smile when she gazed over at me, sleepy and beautiful. She held it in her own heart, the same heart she showed me in our bed when we made love in the morning glow of our room with sunlight slanting across her skin and a breeze filling the air around me with her scent.

I didn't know if I would ever recover from this loss.

"I can't wait to get home," she said, her words muffled in a yawn as she followed me down the jet bridge, linking her hand with mine. "I feel like I could sleep for a full week."

"You partied hard."

She leaned into me. "Did you have fun?"

"I always have fun with you."

"But did you really?"

"Yeah." I dipped my head down, and she was staring up at

me, still from under my cap. I tipped it back with my knuckle. "I did. Why?"

She faced forward, stepping away from me to avoid a toddler running between the two of us. The kid's mom was jogging after him, and Samantha shook her head with a laugh before taking my hand again. "You seem... I don't know. You're quiet."

I avoided her implied question and instead said, "I'm always quiet."

"Not with me."

Something clawed at my chest and throat, and I inhaled a deep breath to clear it away. It didn't budge, even when I tapped my hand against my chest like I had a cough.

"I didn't know if you were upset with me or something," she added quietly, so quietly I almost couldn't hear it as we trudged to baggage claim. Fellow passengers chatted all around us, but I could only focus on Samantha, her hand in mine, her eyes searching my face for any emotion. But I was a blank slate. I didn't want to give anything away.

"No, I'm not upset with you. I'm sorry," I said. "I'm fine. Just thinking about things."

"I've been thinking too."

I feared the answer yet still asked the question. "About what?"

"You and me." She didn't blink or fidget. She was absolutely sure when she spoke her next words. "I have been trying to avoid it, avoid my feelings, but after this weekend, I don't want to anymore. I love you, Mike."

Time stopped. The white noise silenced. My breath caught.

This beautiful, brilliant woman had laid herself bare. She loved me. *Loved* me.

And all I could do in return was swallow down the rock in my throat, adding to the growing mountain in my gut, and I could see the light extinguish from her eyes the longer I waited. With every second, I felt the place where my heart resided next to hers start to crumble. Soon, there would be nothing left of me. Or of her.

Her eyes toggled between mine. Her desperation called to me. She needed a lifeline. I knew how difficult it was for her to verbalize those words.

And yet...

I leaned down, stroking my fingers along her cheek and jaw, down her throat, to her pulse. It raced. It was too fast. She was nervous.

Her teeth bit into her bottom lip as recognition dawned in her eyes.

Then she stepped away from me, her hand dropping from mine, the tips of our middle fingers the last to touch, and I wanted to grab hold of her again. Wanted to make her feel better. Give her what she wanted.

But that wasn't fair. To either of us.

I couldn't act like everything was fine when it wasn't. I couldn't continue what I'd been doing all summer, playing and flirting and pretending like what we had between us wasn't the most important thing in my life. I did love her, but I couldn't say those words back to her when I didn't know how we could be together.

I refused to be a weight around her ankle, holding her back. I wouldn't force her to support me and herself as she completed her work and education, while I stumbled along behind her. If I told her I loved her, like I so desperately wanted to, she would give me everything she had. Because that was what Samantha did. She gave everything she had for those she loved. She'd give up her time, energy, and money for me, even if I didn't ask her to. Even if I didn't want her to, she still would. She was a fixer and a problem solver, but I was not hers to fix.

"Sam, I—"

She cut me off with a stiff shake of her head and grabbed her suitcase when it circled around on the belt. She briefly met my stare before sliding her sunglasses over her eyes. "Don't."

So I didn't.

CHAPTER THIRTY

Sam

I kept it together. During the walk to Mike's car as he tried to apologize. Then all through the ride home, when he glanced over at me every so often as if I'd suddenly start talking. I'd said my piece, without equivocation or second thought, and he'd said nothing—in fact, he had looked terrified—so I'd turned around and took a deep breath, holding it in to save face until I got home. After he parked his car, contemplating me expectantly, I calmly stepped out of the passenger seat and walked inside my house before the first tear fell.

That was when I let it go.

"So stupid," I cried, wiping my eyes as I shut the front door before resting my back against it. I never should have opened my mouth. Never should have been honest.

What I should have done was listened to my gut, kept my feelings away from Mike, and never even invited him on the trip to begin with.

Being there with my friends, seeing how happy they were, it was contagious. I couldn't help but be happy too. For the first time in my life, I wanted to let go, take a walk into the unknown, thinking Mike would be there to guide me.

He wasn't. He'd left me hanging, literally. He'd dropped my

hand. He hadn't fought for me, or even offered any other words in return. I'd said I love you, and he'd blinked his eyes wide like I'd just threatened to take his life.

When it was really the other way around. I'd taken a leap, and he wasn't there to catch me. The pain that eased through me felt like he'd thrown my heart into a food processor, and all I could do was stand there while he blended it up.

"Hey, Sammy, what are you doing in there?"

At my father's cheerful voice, I made sure my face was dry, before realizing I still wore Mike's hat. Merely holding it in my hands was like another round in the blender, this time on chop, and I bit the inside of my lip to keep it from quivering.

"Come on in here. We've got good news!"

I cleared my throat. "We?"

"Trisha's here," Dad said, and I momentarily pushed aside my heartbreak to feed my curiosity.

At the kitchen table, Trisha and Dad had two glasses of iced tea in front of them, their elbows nearly touching.

"What's going on?" I asked, and Dad stood up. "Where is your cane?"

He lifted his arms, showing off how he stepped forward without hobbling. "I don't need it anymore."

"That's the good news?"

"And we sold the house."

Behind him, Trisha, grinned, extending jazz hands. "Congratulations!"

"Already?" I reached out to put my hand on the wall, digesting all this.

"It's a beautiful home," Trisha said. "There were three offers."

"I couldn't have done it without you, Sammy." Dad wrapped his arm around me, kissing the top of my head.

And I suddenly had trouble breathing with the sharp pain in my chest. "Does Gavin know? Mom?"

"Yeah, of course. Gav's at Ava's, but he texted your mom earlier to tell her. I don't know—what's wrong? Are you crying?"

"I'm fine. I'm fine," I said, brushing my father's hand away. "It's a little sad. But I'm happy for you, though, Dad."

"You should be happy for you too," he said. "We're getting a great price on it, and I thought I could give you and Gav some money. You're going to need it, a little nest egg for yourself."

"That's…" I hiccupped in a ragged breath. "That's really nice. Thank you."

"Are you sure you're okay?"

"I'm fine. Jet-lagged, that's all. And maybe a little PMS-y."

Trisha smiled kindly at me. "Understandable. Phil, come on and sit. Let your daughter relax." Then she winked at me like we had some kind of understanding. "Right?"

This was the second time we'd met, and I didn't know her from the cashier at the grocery store, but obviously, something was going on between her and my dad. The *please like me* step-parent vibes were undeniable.

But I didn't want to deal with that shit right now. I dragged my suitcase upstairs and hopped in the shower with the water as hot as I could stand it. I stood under the spray until my skin reddened and the steam was so thick it was hard to breathe, before getting out to wrap a towel around my body. I could feel myself starting to unravel, to lose control, and the anxiety that I'd learned to control long ago was creeping out from my stomach, clawing up my neck, settling into my brain, muddling my thoughts with negativity, tempting me to skip dinner.

But as I swiped my hand over the fogged-up mirror, revealing the reflection of my blotchy face, I knew how to solve this. I couldn't and wouldn't give in to my worst instincts.

After dragging a brush through my hair, I slipped into my comfiest clothes and emptied my suitcase into the laundry basket. Over dinner, I mentally prepared a list of what I needed to do. Collect all my things, which weren't many, and make sure I could move in to my apartment two weeks early, then figure out a drive plan.

With the house officially sold, my father doing well, my brother off to school soon, and my mother getting ready to begin a new school year, there was no reason for me to wait around until the end of the month. I would leave for Austin as soon as possible. Maybe even tomorrow if I could swing it.

There was nothing to keep me home any longer.

I could start the next chapter of my life, pretend this summer never happened. I could forget how I'd lost myself in someone else and bury the pain of my silly unrequited love. I would go on as I had always planned, alone but safe in the knowledge that no one could hurt me unless I allowed them to.

It was my own fault that I allowed Mike to hurt me. And in order to fix it, I'd simply pack up and move on. Slap on a Band-Aid and call it a day.

CHAPTER THIRTY-ONE

Mike

Samantha hadn't responded to any of my texts. It'd been three days since we'd arrived home, when she had slipped out of my car without so much as a goodbye. So, it was more than a little shocking when my little brother casually strolled downstairs.

"What are you doing?"

"Trying to sign up for a class on virtual coaching. It's on discount if I sign up before tomorrow."

"I figured you'd be helping Sam with packing up her car."

I jerked up from my bed, where I'd been working on my laptop. "Huh?"

"She texted me and told me she was leaving today." Jimmy held up his phone screen as evidence. "I came to say goodbye."

I shook my head to clear my racing thoughts. "She what?"

"I came to say goodbye. She's packing up her car right now. I thought you'd be out there with her. Why aren't you?"

Without thinking or answering, I stepped into my prosthesis and pushed past my brother upstairs. I opened the front screen door with so much force, it hit the doorframe, but I didn't care or stop. "Sam!"

She briefly paused, in the middle of loading a laundry basket full of what looked like folded clothes and bottles of laundry detergent and other random cleaning supplies into her trunk.

"What are you doing?" I asked, jogging over to her. Even though I had to let her go because it was for the best, that didn't mean I was prepared for it to end so abruptly. "I thought you weren't leaving for another two weeks."

"Yeah, well..." When she struggled to fit the basket inside, she shifted another bag over to make more room, letting out a soft grunt. "Thought I'd get a head start."

"But you don't have to be there until September first."

She moved around me to grab a big black bag from the sidewalk and put that in her trunk too before slamming it closed. When she tried to walk away, I snagged her wrist, needing to explain. "Can we talk?"

She didn't meet my gaze. "About what?"

"About us."

"About us?" She tugged out of my grasp, dropping her attention to the road, where she rubbed the toe of her sneaker on what looked to be dried gum. "Why? There isn't anything else to say. We agreed to the summer, and now the summer's over."

"Pea—"

She flashed her eyes to me then, hot and full of anguish. "Don't call me that."

I took one step back. "I'm sorry."

Her shoulder brushed against my arm as she stepped around me toward her house. Even that small graze of her skin on mine was torture. "Sam, please, wait."

She didn't stop, and out of the corner of my eye, I saw Jimmy standing in our front doorway. I ignored his folded arms and scowl to speed ahead of Samantha, holding my arms out. "You can't run away like this."

"Run away?" She forced out a laugh, but it was strangled,

and she wasn't smiling. "I'm not running away. I'm going to Texas, like I'm supposed to."

"But...that's not... You can't..." I dragged my hands through my hair before throwing them out to my sides. "You're angry with me."

"I'm not," she said placidly, and I had a flashback of when she had acted just as coolly and unperturbed after she thought I'd turned down her offer to this fucking stupid idea of being together for the summer.

I held up my palm to her. "You know I know you're lying, right?"

"Are we done here? I need to finish loading up my car."

"No, we're not done."

She flattened her mouth into a straight line, letting out a tiny, annoyed sound, yet I soldiered on. "I'm sorry," I said, pleading. "I'm so sorry that I've hurt you."

She tried to argue, but I curled my palm around her forearm. She could act as aloof as she wanted, but I knew that wasn't how she felt. She could never hide the truth from me.

"I know what it took for you to..." I swallowed, my throat like sandpaper. "I know that you won't believe me, but you mean more to me than I can say."

"Yeah?" She met my eyes with a sarcastic lilt to her lips. "There are words for that. Three of them, actually."

I coasted my fingers up to her shoulder, a shoulder I had kissed only days ago. "I know, and you took me by surprise when you said them."

"Did I, though?" She cocked her head to the side, and I took advantage of the angle, settling my hand along her neck. She closed her eyes, and I could feel her relaxing under my touch. I stepped even closer, bringing my other hand to her face, my thumb stroking her cheek until she opened her eyes. "It couldn't have been a surprise. All summer, I've been telling you not to be sweet to me. But you kept going. You talked to me as if you loved me. You treated me like—" she licked her lips, and I wanted to kiss away her self-doubt because I did love her "—you wanted me to fall in love with you."

She wasn't wrong, and I hated myself for it.

"I told you I don't do casual," I said.

"And I don't do serious."

Giving in to a terrible idea, I pressed my lips to her forehead.

And it truly was a terrible idea because she bunched my T-shirt in her fists.

"I'm sorry, Samantha," I said, whispering the words against her temple, although my apology didn't matter. The damage had already been done, but I at least wanted her to understand my reasoning. "You deserve someone who can give you what you want."

She wrenched back, her brows knitting over glassy eyes. "What I want? What is that?"

"Someone who can be your partner." I let my eyes drift past her, back to Bobby's conversation, and to this last week while I worked to figure out how to make more money. "Someone who can provide for you."

She sniffled, bringing my attention back to her face. She looked pissed now. "And you don't want to do that?"

"It doesn't matter what I want." When she shook her head, I dropped my hands to hers, bringing them together against my chest. "I don't want to hold you back. You have things you need to do, and so do I. We said we'd have fun for the summer, and we did. I think it would be best if we left it at that."

"Really?"

I nodded unsteadily. If I weren't holding on to her hands, I might've lost my balance.

"You say I'm a bad liar?" She huffed out a shaky breath. "So are you. You don't want to leave it at that. You're just afraid. After everything..."

I thought she might cry, but she didn't give in to tears. Instead, she ripped away from me. When I listed toward her, she held up her hand, keeping me from touching her again.

"After I was the one to tell you the truth, now you're going to lie to me?" She set her fists at her sides, her face pulled into beautiful determination. "You're letting Bianca and your past dictate your life. I told you I love you, but you're so deep into your insecurities that you don't believe me or don't want to or won't admit to yourself that you can be happy. Whatever it is, it's bullshit."

When I tried to argue, she pointed her finger at my chest, stopping me. I didn't know what I would've said anyway.

"I'm not the one running away. You are. I'm doing what I was supposed to from the beginning. I'm only sorry that the first person I let myself fall in love with wasn't the man I thought he was." She stepped away, sending me one more withering glare. "And you have no idea what I want. If you did, you'd know I don't care about anything else but you. I only want you."

Then she stalked back to her house, where her brother and father were in the garage, fiddling with Gavin's car. She hugged them both, shouting her love over her shoulder as she jogged by me as if I didn't exist.

Glancing out of the passenger side window, she waved at Jimmy, still standing at the front door, then started her car and drove off.

"What the fuck was that?" Jimmy nearly shouted as I shouldered my way past him on to my way downstairs. "I told you not to hurt her."

"Stay out of it."

"Stay out of it? That's all you have to say? After I watched you break one of my best friends' hearts?"

At the bottom of the steps, I swung around on him, frustration and anger coursing through me, so much so that I felt the need to hit something. Instead of my brother, I knocked my fist into the wall and hissed in pain.

"I don't know what happened between you two, but I've never seen you happier than you were this summer, and you're a fucking idiot if you let it end like this."

I clenched my left hand over the throbbing knuckles of my right hand and sat on the edge of my bed. "It's not that simple."

"Nothing is ever simple. That doesn't mean you throw it away." Jimmy grabbed the chair from the desk and towed it over to sit down in front of me. "What's with you, man? Ever since you moved home, it's like..." He circled his hand in the air, searching for his words. "It's like you're looking for excuses."

"Excuses?" I repeated with a jerk of my head. "You don't know what you're talking about."

"I do know. You used to be different. You'd never back down from anything, and now you barely even try."

"Fuck you," I growled, moving to stand, but Jimmy shoved me back down.

"You say I don't understand, then explain it to me." When I didn't speak, he sat back, crossing his arms over his chest and his legs at the ankles. "I've got all day."

I attempted to wait him out. One minute and then two passed, and my stubborn little brother appeared as if he had no cares in the world, and I finally gave in with a rough exhale. "You don't know what it's like to have your life turned upside down. Everything you thought it'd be, isn't. Everything you thought you'd have is gone."

"You're right. I have no idea what that's like, but why are

you trying to make it seem like you're somehow worse off than before?" He held up his fingers as he listed his points. "You got dumped, but Bianca was no big loss. You got a new leg, so you aren't in pain anymore. And you're out of the military. Things seem pretty swell to me."

I clenched my teeth. "Swell?"

"Yeah, well...at least until a few minutes ago." My brother flicked his hand out. "I can't understand what's so bad now. I didn't think you actually enjoyed being a Marine."

No, I didn't particularly enjoy it, but I at least had a purpose. "I was good at it."

"And?" Jimmy raised his shoulders. "Who gives a flying fuck? You had a job that made you move around all the time, kept you away from your family, and got you shot at. *Shot at.*" He let out an unsteady breath that sounded suspiciously like he might cry, and he shook his head, leaning his elbows on his knees. "Forgive me for being happy to have you home and not in a box in the ground."

"I should be happy about being blown up?"

"Yeah." He scrubbed at his eyes with the palms of his hands then met my gaze. "I don't know if it's misplaced honor or what, but just because other people are suffering worse than you, doesn't mean you need to feel bad about it."

I bent forward too, mimicking my brother's position, trying to hide how close to the truth he'd gotten.

He went on. "When you got out of the hospital and went back to California, I was really worried about you. I knew how messed up you were, and quite frankly, I never liked Bianca. I think she was one of those women who was only interested in the idea of you because she got to put one of those bumper stickers on her car like, *Don't mess with me. My boyfriend is a Marine.*"

I jammed the heels of my hands against my eyes as I puffed out an aggravated laugh. Because he was exactly right.

"Then when you moved back here after she broke up with you, I thought you were turning a corner, you know? You got the prosthesis, you decided to get certified to train. I was like, man, Mike's back. But I was wrong."

I dropped my hands yet still couldn't look my little brother in the eyes.

"You're lucky to be alive, but it's like you feel bad you made it out."

I had to swallow three times to clear the dust from my throat, but I couldn't do anything about the sting of tears in my eyes.

"Maybe you need to go back to counseling. I don't know. All I know is that the guy who used to be my brother wouldn't feel so bad for himself. Wouldn't back down from a challenge."

After a minute, I lifted my head to find Jimmy staring intently at me, and I repeated my reasoning to him. "I can't be the guy she deserves."

"That's you feeling bad for yourself again."

"I'm not—"

"Sam needs someone to love her and be there for her. You don't want to do that?"

I narrowed my eyes. "Being in a relationship is more than *wanting* it."

"Tell me, oh wise one, what else is there?"

"Relationships can't be one-sided. I can't ask her to wait around for me to figure my shit out. I'm living in my parents' basement, for Christ's sake." My voice had steadily risen higher, so I was almost yelling, "You think she really wants someone like that?"

"Apparently." Jimmy threw his arm out toward the steps.

"She was out there crying over you, so I'd say so, you fucking potato. Stop making excuses. Sam is not Bianca."

That took the wind out of my angry sails, and I dropped my head. "I know she's not."

Samantha was like no other woman I'd ever been with. She was honest and sweet, smart and funny. It normally took me a while to warm up to people, but not with her. Maybe because we'd known each other since we were kids, or maybe because she had a way of making everyone around her comfortable. Either way, I never felt I had anything to prove to her, like I did other people. Or myself.

"Do you love Sam?" Jimmy asked.

There was no question. "Yes."

"Do you want to be with her?"

Again. "Yes."

"Then I don't understand the problem. Contrary to what you might think, you don't have to be everyone's hero all the time. Seems to be a waste of time feeling bad about what you don't have instead of what you do." With that, Jimmy stood up and hit my shoulder. "And you do know Albie works in finance, right? If you're so worried about spending the rest of your days here with Mom and Dad, why don't you go talk to him?"

"Albie? Our neighbor?" When he nodded, I tipped my head to the side. "I didn't know that."

"Yeah." He tossed his hand up over his shoulder as he marched back upstairs. "Next time I see you, I want to hear your plan of attack. Or whatever it is you jarheads say to each other."

CHAPTER THIRTY-TWO

Sam

I had stopped at a motel in Tennessee for a night. Since I loved roller coasters, barbecue, and Dolly Parton, I'd been tempted to check out Dollywood, but my heart wasn't in it. I didn't feel like having fun.

I had thought getting out of Akron, away from Mike, would make it easier to breathe, but the farther I got, the more I remembered. The whole drive, over twenty hours total, I replayed my time with him. Every kiss, touch, and moment he looked me in the eyes, remembering how they crinkled in the corners when he smiled, I couldn't turn it off. It was a movie playing on loop in my mind.

And when I finally arrived at my apartment, I shuffled inside and promptly slid down to the floor. This summer was not at all what I expected. I was kidding myself when I thought I'd be able to move on from him like I did every other relationship in my life.

Mike was right when he'd said I ran away, but that wasn't the case this time. In the past, I had kept myself closed off, choosing to leave before I could get hurt because it was easier that way. Yet telling Mike I loved him wasn't easy. It was one of the most difficult things I'd ever done. Packing up and moving down here, that was hard too.

For the first time in my academic career—hell, my entire life—I had second-guessed my decision and had actually wanted to stay in Ohio with Mike. So, I'd set aside my fear and told him the truth, in hopes that we could make a real go of it, no matter what it looked like. It wouldn't be easy, but I was willing to work through it because I loved him, and he loved me.

Although he didn't need to say it out loud, and I did my best to ignore it, I had felt it for a while. In the way he held my hands, in those quiet moments when he said nothing at all, and in every simple promise he made and kept, I knew he loved me. That was why I had the strength to tell him.

But he was a fucking liar. He was the one always going on about honesty, yet he refused to be honest with me, didn't even give me his real reason for letting me go. And it hurt. Plain and simple.

In my more cognizant moments, I attempted to minimize the pain by reminding myself I should have been proud for putting myself out there, but even my emotional psychology and positive self-talk didn't help. It wouldn't.

I sent out the **SOS** message to the girls, and when they all appeared on FaceTime, including Bronte, still on the island, I covered my eyes with my hand.

"Where are you?" Gem asked.

"Texas."

Bronte pushed her sunglasses up on her head. "I thought you weren't leaving for another couple of weeks."

"I told Mike I loved him," I said and rushed out the rest before they could interrupt. "And he said we should go our separate ways."

They were all quiet as I cried.

"I'm sorry," Bronte said after a while. "I pushed you."

I dabbed at my eyes. "It's not your fault."

Laney shook her head. "I don't understand. You guys were like..." She linked her fingers together. "There's no way he doesn't love you."

I sniffled. "He said he didn't want to hold me back."

Gem dropped her chin in her hands. "Dumbass."

"Gem," Bronte chided quietly.

"What?" She gestured to her screen. "He is! You don't let someone like Sam walk away after she tells you she loves you."

"Maybe he thinks he's doing the right thing," Bronte said. "Chris and I walked away from each other, thinking it was the best decision."

"But it wasn't," Gem said.

"No," Bronte agreed, then lifted one shoulder. "Maybe he needs some time to realize it."

"Or maybe it wasn't meant to be." I dropped my head back against the wall. "Not every story has a happy ending."

"But you should have one." Laney frowned, her face close to the screen. "Would it make you happy if I kill him?"

That got a laugh out of me. "Please."

"Okay." Laney nodded resolutely, banging an imaginary gavel. "Everyone knows their job. Sam, you won't be involved, for obvious reasons. We'll meet back up at oh-five-hundred."

"Oh-five-hundred." Gem wrinkled her nose. "What's that?"

Laney rolled her eyes. "Military time."

"It's five in the morning," Bronte clarified. "And isn't that how people in Europe tell time too? Zero to twenty-four-hundred."

"But why in hundreds? If anything, it should be something with sixty since there are sixty minutes in an hour. What does one hundred have to do with anything?" Gem turned, calling out, "Jason! Why do people say oh-five-hundred and not oh-whatever the multiplication of sixty is?"

Laney snorted a laugh. "Why would he know?"

"He's super smart and knows a lot of weird shit. Jason!"

When the man in question finally appeared, Gem asked him again, to which he responded, "I don't know. Google it," earning a grumble from Gem and a laugh from the rest.

I smiled. From murder to the proper way to tell time, I could always count on my friends to ease my mind.

CHAPTER THIRTY-THREE

Sam

The North Campus neighborhood was a fifteen-minute walk from the University of Texas, with lots of trees and people on bikes. There was always something going on in Austin, concerts to attend, new food to try, but in the month I had lived there, I hadn't done much besides work and explore the parks and walking trails. Though with the temperature constantly at surface-of-the-sun highs, even my walks didn't last long. I'd mostly spent my nights in my small but comfy condo on a safe and quiet street with a great barbecue joint a block away, watching *Golden Girls*, trying to ignore the root of my reluctance to make Austin my new home.

Everything was wonderful with my friends, and they'd sent me coloring books and flowers with their best wishes in my new city. And my family life had taken an unexpected turn. Since Dad had gone Facebook official with Trisha, she'd apparently pushed him to become more friendly with Mom, which led them to decide it would be better for all parties involved if communication was improved across the board. That was how we all ended up in a family chat. It was filled with reminders from Mom about birthdays of extended family members and a science fact of the day from Dad. Gavin was required to show proof of life every Monday morning, and he even asked me to help him with some Psych 101 homework. It was probably the best my family had ever been.

With everything going so well, I should have been happy. I should have been living it up, and yet I couldn't rid myself of the lingering pain in my chest. In the exact spot where my heart used to reside.

Although Mike had texted me twice, I hadn't spoken to him since I'd left Ohio. He had messaged me a few days after I'd arrived in Texas, checking in, and then last week, he'd sent me a video link to his YouTube channel. I hadn't bothered to watch the video and didn't respond to either message, afraid I'd collapse under the weight of my sorrow, more than I already had.

I hoped a night out with a bucketload of liquor would help to lift me up a bit. That was why when Farid had invited me out to a downtown bar, I'd accepted. He was also finishing his PhD, and we'd often eat lunchtime burritos together. A few days ago, I'd given him a brief synopsis of my summer, that there was a boy and it didn't work out, and in return, Farid had told me he'd recently broken up with a guy too. Then he'd swiftly declared we needed to drink and dance to get over them.

"If you can't fuck 'em, fuck 'em," he'd said, and I agreed wholeheartedly. Fuck 'em.

As I stepped out of the shower, my phone buzzed with a text from Farid, informing me that he'd be at my place in half an hour. I sent back a couple of emojis then blow-dried my newly dyed hair. One of the first things I'd done after moving was to find a good hair stylist to get rid of the purple. It reminded me too much of Mike and how he'd roll the strands between his fingers. Unfortunately, I also couldn't go with any other combination of "mermaid colors" or anything close to peach. With few options left, I'd chosen a black to platinum ombre. I'd never had my hair this dark before, but it suited my mood, and I hoped the ghost of summer past would quit haunting me soon.

After slipping into jeans and a plum-colored crop top, I was in search of shoes when a knock sounded on my door. Farid was perpetually late, so, of course, the one time he was early, I wasn't near ready, and I laughed as I opened the door.

"My makeup isn't even—" My smile dropped. "What are you doing here?"

Mike gazed at me, his dark eyes flaring as they coasted over my face, and his brows narrowed ever so slightly, like he was studying data on a chart and he wasn't quite sure what to make of it.

"What are you doing here?" I asked again, resting my hand against the doorframe, suddenly not quite able to find my equilibrium.

"Are you okay?"

I closed my eyes and shook my head, frustration rapidly overtaking my confusion. After unceremoniously dumping me, he was going to show up here after a month and ask if I was okay? The audacity.

"You look a little pale," he said, and I snapped my eyes open, hating myself for reflexively taking a step toward him. I'd grown used to his constant concern and discerning attention over the summer, but I didn't think I'd still be susceptible to it.

"I'm fine," I bit out, hanging on to my anger by my fingernails.

He lifted his hand from where it had been hidden behind his back and held out a bouquet of flowers. A huge spray of roses, carnations, daisies, and lilies, all in varying shades of orange, peach, and cream. "I saw these, and they reminded me of you."

273

"Mike, what are you doing?"

When I didn't accept the flowers, he dropped them to his side. "You never replied to my texts."

"Yeah. Why would I? Our summer is over, and you said it would be better for both of us if we went our separate ways."

He licked his lips and ran his free hand over his closely shaved beard, then set it against his sternum, his T-shirt all wrinkled. I didn't recall ever seeing him in anything with wrinkles. The guy was a walking commercial for an ironing board.

"Did you watch the video I sent you?"

Finally finding my footing, I crossed my arms in answer, my patience quickly dwindling.

"It got a lot of views," he told me. "I wanted you to see it."

"You came here to tell me that you want me to watch your video?"

"And to tell you I'm sorry."

I didn't know what to say, unsure if I even wanted an apology. However, I found my arms loosening, my spine going lax. He reached out his hand as if to curl it around my bicep but stopped midway, his fingers suspended in the air between us.

"I practiced what I was going to say the whole way here, and now that I'm standing in front of you, I'm..." His throat bobbed as he swallowed, and he flickered his gaze from my eyes to my hand. He was looking for permission to touch me.

As my brain wavered back and forth over if I wanted to give it to him or not, my body unwittingly responded by stepping outside into the open-air hall, letting the door close behind me. We were barely two inches apart as he stared down at me.

"With you in front of me, it's hard to speak," he said, and I dropped my head so he wouldn't see how my eyes watered. "Samantha," he whispered. "I'm so sorry."

I blinked a few times, clearing my vision, before meeting his gaze again. "I don't know what you want me to say."

"You said enough. I just want you to listen. Okay?" He deliberately raised his fingers between us again, offering me an opportunity to stop him. I didn't, and he rolled a few pieces of hair between his thumb and index finger, studying them as if they were fine strands of gold. After a few moments, he tucked them behind my ear and took a deep breath, fisting his fingers, as if he was holding on to the feeling of me.

I couldn't quite grasp the fleeting hope that streaked through my chest...like maybe I wanted him to.

"I sent you that video because it's the first one in this new series I'm planning. I'm going to do short workout tutorials every week based on questions from people with limb differences. When I started posting photos on Instagram, showing myself lifting with my prosthetic, people left comments and questions. Some of them wanted help. Laney sent me—"

I lurched back. "Laney?" She hadn't mentioned anything about continuing to help Mike. "You're still talking to Laney?"

"Yeah. She sent me some resources so I could learn how to film and edit my own videos. And Gem—"

"Gem? What the hell?" My friends were traitors. While they were supposedly plotting Mike's murder, they were really still chatting with him the whole time.

"As soon as you left, I knew I made a mistake. I never should have let you go." He cringed as if in pain. "But I couldn't come to you and apologize and tell you how much I love you without doing the work to fix it."

There it was again. That streak, and I blinked. Then blinked again, but he plowed right on.

"After you left, Jimmy sat me down and tore into me."

I tried to follow along, even stepped closer to him, unconsciously linking my fingers with his, but it was hard to hear around the rushing in my ears. He had said he loved me. I was 90% sure I hadn't imagined it.

"He basically said I have a hero complex."

"Hero complex," I repeated, an involuntary smile crawling across my face. "I don't think it's a complex."

His gaze dipped to our joined hands. "I've always been the strong one, the guy in charge, but I lost a sense of myself when I was injured. I thought I had moved past it, but I didn't realize how much resentment I was still holding on to until you came around. My life looks a lot different than I thought it would, and I was convinced that I couldn't be the guy you needed."

"I don't understand." I grabbed hold of the hem of his shirt. "Why do you keep saying that? The guy I need. What do you think I need?"

He let out a gruff sound and raised his eyes to mine. They were red-rimmed. "I want to take care of you. I want to protect you. After Bianca—"

I heaved a sigh. "Of course it's Bianca. That wench."

He stifled a grin, and when he finally tamped it down, he drew our hands up to his chest, towing me even closer. My leg snuck between both of his, and I could feel the heat radiating off him, even in the humid evening air.

"I didn't want to lose you, but I let my insecurities get the best of me. When I say I want to be the man you need, I mean a man who can love you with his whole heart." He turned my palm flat against his chest. His solid, hard chest, with the rapidly beating heart beneath it. Like my own.

The gaping hole that had been open when I'd left Mike in my rearview mirror was suddenly filled up again. Almost too much. I couldn't contain it, and when I inhaled, the air stuttered through my lungs until my eyes stung with tears.

Happy tears this time.

"That's what you need," he went on. "Someone who's not afraid to let go and not be in charge. Sometimes I'll be strong for you, and sometimes you'll be strong for me. I needed time to remember who I was, figure out how to be confident in myself again."

"And what do my friends have to do with this?"

He quirked his mouth to the side, stroking his knuckles over my cheek, wiping at the wet tracks there. "It's too bad none of them have political ambitions because they get shit done. Gem threatened me with bodily harm if I screwed this up, but she did agree to help me out with a couple of my videos. We're going to partner up to do some yoga for amputees stuff. And Bronte sent me equipment from Chris, a tripod and a GoPro to film. Laney's got me hooked up on social media." He lifted one shoulder. "She said she's going to make me an influencer."

I leaned into him, resting my forehead against his shoulder, inhaling the familiar scent of his soap. "How's that going so far?"

"A lot of shirtless selfies," he said against my hair, and I breathed out a laugh. "I got in contact with some gyms here."

I tipped my head up in interest. "Yeah?"

"Yeah. It would take me a while to build up a list of in-person clients, but I'm going to start virtual training and coaching too."

"You've thought a lot about this. Done a lot of homework."

He playfully glowered at me. "It's amazing what can be accomplished when you ask for help. I even have an accountant now."

"Like a full-blown adult." I dragged my thumb over the slash in his eyebrow. "Now I'm the one who feels inadequate."

He bent down, skimming the top of his nose along mine, his breath on my cheek. "Never. You're perfect the way you are."

"So are you," I said, tilting up to meet his mouth, but as he brushed against my top lip, Farid's voice echoed off the walls around them.

"What do we have here?"

Mike broke away, holding his arm out as he stepped in front of me. The natural protector. And big dummy that he ever thought he couldn't provide me with anything. He'd only ever given me security and love, *exactly* what I needed.

"Am I interrupting something?" Farid asked, cocking his head to the side. "I said half an hour. I'm not that late."

Mike let out an audible breath. "Are you—" He pivoted to me, the light in his eyes dowsed. "Do you have a date?"

Behind him, Farid tossed his hands out. "Yeah, don't we have a date?"

I cast my friend a death glare to silence him as I held on to Mike's shoulders. "This is bad timing."

"You're right. I shouldn't have come here. I didn't realize you'd..." He pointed toward Farid with the flowers. "Sorry."

"No. No. Farid is my friend." I waved for him to step over. "Farid, this is Mike."

Farid, a good three or four inches shorter than Mike, scrutinized him up and down before slanting his eyes to me. "This the guy from the summer?" When I nodded, he pouted. "What happened to if you can't fuck 'em, fuck 'em?"

Mike frowned. "Fuck 'em?"

"Does this mean we're not going dancing?" Farid asked, and Mike seemed to shrink in size.

"You were going dancing? But you only sway."

"Only sway?" Farid repeated, brushing his dark hair back from his face, craning his head side to side. "Why am I even here right now? I feel like I've been duped."

"Farid is going through a breakup too," I explained to Mike, and at his pained expression, I backtracked. "With his boyfriend." Then I said to Farid, "Mike surprised me. He came to apologize."

Farid gestured to how I held on to Mike. I couldn't get close enough. If I could, I'd jump into his pocket like a baby kangaroo. "And I guess you accepted it."

Mike angled his head down to me. "No, she hasn't, actually."

"Because we were interrupted." I eyed Farid, and he gestured between us.

"By all means, continue. I'll be inside drinking your wine."

"I don't have any," I said, staring up at Mike.

"My god," Farid grumbled as he made his way into my apartment.

"So, you and Farid..." Mike started.

"Are friends," I finished.

"And you were planning on going out?"

I snaked my arms around his neck. "Yes."

"But then I showed up."

"And now I can't get drunk and dance and make out with strangers."

He combed his fingers through my hair. "Sorry."

"I'm not."

He kissed my forehead. "You forgive me?"

"Depends. Are you moving in with me?"

He nodded toward a duffel bag a few feet away. "I have all my bags packed."

"That's it? That's all you brought?"

With his arms banded around my back, he lifted me up, my feet dangling a few inches from the ground. "All I need is you." Then he kissed me, and with him holding me against his chest, I could feel his heart beating against mine. Like they were mirror images of each other. "But," he said, nipping at my lower lip, "there are some other boxes in my car."

"You can get them tomorrow. We're going to sway tonight."

He ducked his face into my neck. "I missed you."

"I missed you too," I murmured, tugging on the roots of his hair until he set me down. "And I love you."

He inhaled sharply and curved his palm around my cheek in the way that made me feel like the most precious thing on earth. "I don't know if I'll ever get used to hearing that."

"Well, I guess I do need some practice saying it."

"I love you," he said, pressing his forehead to mine. "I love you, and I know you love me without ever having to say it. Your love language is acts of service."

I dragged my fingers over his beard. "You learn that one from Bronte?"

"Yeah," he rasped, his fingers tight against my lower back when he said, "but I've known what's in your heart for a long time."

I whispered my "I love you" into his mouth before stroking my tongue against his, pulling at his lips, promising a future together with my kisses, and when we finally broke apart, he smiled—his biggest one yet—before placing the flowers into my hands. "For you, Peaches."

"You know," I said, floating on air, "turns out I love this whole serious relationship thing." Then I swung my door open, calling out, "Farid, meet my boyfriend."

He was on the couch in the living room, eating pretzels. "You guys are going to make me the third wheel, aren't you?"

And Mike laughed, a carefree sound that I would carry with me forever.

Epilogue
MIKE

I hauled Sam onto the couch and moved the laptop so we were both on-screen.

"There she is," Bronte said, waving.

Samantha held up the bottle of champagne in explanation. "Couldn't forget this." She peered at the screen as she unwrapped the foil from around the bottle. "Where's Bobby?"

Laney waved her hand. "A big shindig at the restaurant."

Since Samantha and I had gotten back together, I'd officially been inducted into the group chat, **Four Chicks and Three Dicks.** When I asked Sam why Bobby wasn't included, she shrugged and said he wasn't interested. He'd evidently told Laney, "They're your friends, not mine." Not that I minded.

The Aussie had unknowingly stoked a fire, which resulted in me breaking Samantha's heart. And even though I didn't blame Bobby, I still thought the guy was a bit of a dick. And not the good kind.

Although, I had grown closer to Jason and Chris over the last three months. We had our own guys-only text thread and weekly online video game nights.

Two years ago, I never would have imagined my life like

this, but I wouldn't want it any other way. Moving to Texas to be with Samantha was the best decision I'd ever made. I still wasn't making a huge amount of money, but it was enough to stash some away for the future and take my girl out for Wednesday night dinners. Those were the nights she cut out of the office early, when we got to explore our new city together, just the two of us. Because the weekends were for sleeping in late after lazy and long nights in bed together. Then Farid usually came over, because, yes, he was our third wheel, but he was a good guy. And a damn determined client. Since he'd started training with me, he'd put on a few pounds of muscle and began dating again.

"So, how are you two lovebirds doing down in Austin?" Laney asked before anyone could question her more about Bobby.

"Great," Samantha and I answered at the same time.

"Finishing each other's sentences and everything," Chris said, his arm draped over Bronte. They both wore matching pajamas.

"Seems like yesterday Sammy was going on about how she loved sleeping alone," Gem said wistfully.

When Samantha couldn't uncork the champagne bottle, she passed it to me. I wrapped the bottom of my T-shirt around the cork and turned until it released with a soft pop. "Wasn't it yesterday *you* texted everyone that you couldn't wait to go to California to get away from Jay and sleep alone in a bed?"

Gem moved closer to the screen, wrinkling her nose. "Michael, I really don't appreciate you using my own words against me."

Jason yanked Gem backward, his arm stretching across the front of her shoulders.

"Do you see?" she said to no one in particular. "He's a human octopus, tentacles everywhere, all the time."

He kissed her neck, mumbling something about doing good work with those tentacles.

"Yes, you seem so distraught," Samantha deadpanned as she held up two coffee mugs for me to pour the champagne into.

"What are you going to do by yourself, Jay?" Bronte asked.

"I don't know," he said, settling Gem down against him. "Eat a lot of animal products, probably." When she elbowed him, he glanced down at her with a grin before facing the screen again. "Willow's starting swim lessons. She's got her first one while Gem's away."

Bronte cooed. "Aww, are you sad you're going to miss it?"

"A little," Gem said, and Laney lifted her glass of red wine.

"That's all right. We're going to have lots of fun. But it's a bummer Sam and Bronte can't come."

The girls all nodded. Laney's birthday was coming up, and since Gem was attending a yoga conference in San Francisco, they'd all tried to work out a weekend together, though Bronte had some kind of commitment at her school, and Samantha couldn't take off.

"When are we all going to be in the same room again?" Bronte asked, and Chris held up his hand.

"Was that a question for the entire group or just the girls?"

"Group at large."

Samantha leaned back against me, curling her hand around my thigh. "Maybe over the summer? I doubt I'll be going anywhere until I'm finished with my hours."

I had been hoping to whisk her away somewhere once she graduated. A weekend at the ocean, maybe, a swim with my mermaid, but I kept that suggestion to myself.

"We should go to Vegas," Laney said as Jason offered, "A cabin in the woods."

Samantha ticked her index finger in the air. "It's, like, eight hundred degrees in Las Vegas in the summer. You know I don't do well in heat."

I muffled a chuckle against her shoulder. As much as we both really loved Austin, she was a cold weather woman, and while we hadn't discussed it yet, I didn't think she would want to stay in the South.

Laney wagged her head side to side. "Well, there are these things called pools. The casinos are air-conditioned. And if you two decide you want to make it official, we can get Elvis to perform the ceremony."

Beside me, Samantha tensed almost imperceptibly. She still hadn't completely thawed on the idea of marriage, but I was nothing if not patient. I would wait forever, be by her side for all time, whether there was a white dress and rings or not. I dropped my arm around her shoulders, changing the subject. "There're too many people in Vegas."

Chris pointed at his screen, nodding in silent agreement.

"Before we decide where, we should decide when," Samantha said.

Bronte sat up. "I have an idea."

"She's got that twinkle in her eye," Gem said.

Laney sipped on her wine. "That *let's make a resolution* twinkle."

"I have a resolution not to make resolutions," Samantha said, and Bronte waved her hands.

"Hear me out. It's not a resolution..." She raised her hands as if weighing the idea on a scale. "Well, maybe it is. We're all together right now—" She cut herself off, realizing that we were an odd number. Technically, we weren't all together since Bobby was missing, but Laney circled her hand for Bronte to continue. "What if we plan to always celebrate New Year's together in person? Instead of each of us having to check calendars and plan vacation days, let's make it a thing. From, I don't know... Let's say December 27th to January 1st, every year, we will all be together." She arched her finger in a circle toward the screen, repeating, "All of us."

Jason nodded as Gem said, "As long as I don't have to plan anything."

Chris huffed. "You think I'd let anyone take the joy away from my wife of arranging a group vacation? Never."

I teased my fingertips over Samantha's arm. "What do you think?"

"Yes," she said. "Of course."

Laney's eyes focused somewhere off-screen. "Next year, yeah. I'll be there."

Samantha burrowed her shoulder farther into my side, her muted worry for her friend palpable in her need for her own reassurance.

On-screen, Bronte clapped. "Done and done. And right on time." She lifted her phone to show off the time. In Pennsylvania, it was about to be midnight. "Happy New Year!"

She and Chris lifted glasses of champagne, and we all followed suit, toasting to our screens. Although Sam and I were an hour behind, along with Gem and Jason in Illinois, we kissed anyway.

Chris rubbed his palms together. "Pals, it's been nice, but I mean to begin the year with a good-luck kiss with my bunny."

"We *just* kissed," Bronte pointed out.

"He means NC-17," Laney said with a wink at the screen, "my innocent one."

Chris guffawed. "Innocent? She may look it, but last week, she—"

Bronte covered his mouth with her hand. "Okay, let's leave that discussion right there. Thank you."

Samantha snorted a laugh into her champagne, and after Chris had signed off with an eager wave, everyone else did too. Gem said she wanted to check on Willow, and Laney had to eventually "make an appearance" at Bobby's restaurant, and after shutting the laptop screen, I turned to Samantha.

I pushed her hair behind her ear, my fingertip lingering there. "Did you want to go out?"

"I was thinking we could play a game."

I curled my hand around her neck, urging her toward me. "What did you have in mind, Peaches?"

She let out a low moan when I opened my mouth over her pulse in her throat, lightly sucking at her soft skin. "We have almost that whole bottle of champagne."

"Yeah." I worked my way up to her jaw.

"I know you don't like to drink it."

I nipped at her. "Mm-hmm."

"But I do, and you haven't let me tie you up yet."

I shifted back enough to meet her eyes.

"I want to be the one in charge this time," she said, then stood up, taking the bottle in one hand and my fingers in the other, towing me down the hall to our bedroom, a flirtatious smile curling her perfect, wide lips.

Little did she know, she was always in charge, and I would follow her anywhere. Forever.

Acknowledgments

Indie publishing is a wild ride. Thank you, reader, for coming along with me.

I wouldn't be able to put out these books if not for the encouragement of my friends, especially Ellis Leigh and Brighton Walsh, and the help of my editors, Libby and Lisa. I'd especially like to thank my street team for helping me spread the work about my books. I'm forever grateful.

If you'd like more information about me, you can find it at: https://sophieandrewsauthor.com.

About the Author

Sophie Andrews is a contemporary romance author who writes steamy books that will leave you smiling. As a millennial, she's obsessed with boybands, late 90s rom-coms, and will always be team Pacey. When she's not writing, she's most likely trying to wrangle her children or drinking red wine. Or both at the same time.

Also by Sophie Andrews

Tangled Series

Tangled Up

Tangled Want

Tanged Hearts

Tangled Beginning

Tangled Expectations

Tangled Chances

Tangled Ambition

Printed in Great Britain
by Amazon